A HERO'S RETURN

By
Marshall Thompson

Order this book online at www.trafford.com
or email orders@trafford.com

Most Trafford titles are also available at major online book retailers.

Printed in the United States of America.

ISBN: 978-1-4251-2643-8 (sc)
ISBN: 978-1-4251-2644-5 (e)

Trafford rev. 06/09/2011

www.trafford.com

North America & international
toll-free: 1 888 232 4444 (USA & Canada)
phone: 250 383 6864 • fax: 812 355 4082

Hunnish Expansion from the
5th to the 7th Centuries.
The Left-hand army remained over China
while the Right-hand extended further
West in conquests.
The technology of war reached new
heights with the perfecting of the
composite recurvd bows
combined with mobile attacks.
Atlas General LARUSSE & LIBRAIRIE
1959 Ref. AG- 4128 w/permission
WEST ROMAN EMPIRE 4 -6 TH C.E. CENTURIES
ROME
EAST ROMAN EMPIRE 4 - 6 TH C.E. CENTURES
ROMAN EMPIRE
ALEXANDRIA
DESERT
WEST HUNS 400C.E.
BUDA-PEST
CRIMEA
CONSTANTINOPLE
ANTIOCH
KIEV ON PORTAGES
VOLGA RIVER
GETCHET CITY
HORSE ROAD ON STEPPE LANDS
OPEN 6 MONTHS
IRTISH RIVER OPEN 6 MONTHS
OB RIVER
URAL MOUNTAINS
TURK HOMELANDS
CHIPCHAK HOMELAND ON HORSE ROAD
Chipchak Turkish homeland bordering the northern horse road to the West.
CASPIAN
SEA
HUNS
Near 400 Christ. Era
PLATEAU OPEN 4 MONTHS
SILK ROAD OPEN 9 MONTHS HERE
MERV
EPHTALITES
SAMARKAND
YARKAND
SILK ROAD BRANCHES TO INDIA & WEST
ANXI
YUMEN
HUNS HERE 1 B.C. -6 C.E.
HOMELAND OF THE HUI DYNASTY
LOYANG CITY
CHINA DIVIDED IN COMPETING EMPIRES
China Divided in three Competing Empires
TSIN DYNASTY -420
SUI DYNASSTY
SONG DYNASTY
SEA OF JAPAN
YAMATO
NEPAL
EMPIRE
PACIFIC OCEAN

TABLE OF CONTENTS

DEDICATION

This book and series took a long time to write and even longer to publish. How do you thank all the many who, for a decade faithfully added their grain of sand or salt to weigh in on the scale of acceptance or rejection in literary work?

THE LIST WOULD BE TOO LONG TO INCLUDE HERE; ALTHOUGH, MY THANKS GO TO EACH AND EVERY ONE OF THEM.

A few names stand out in my mind: Eileen Dauphinee, a writer and illustrator of children's books. She works from her wheelchair and twisted hand to produce incomparable illustrations radically different from my own.

Suzanne McGillivary, whose musical help, casually given and observed gave confidence and instruction to me, before or after Choir practice or Sunday services.

Margaret Ryan is an arbiter of grammar; a seeker of definitions in her super sized Canadian Oxford Dictionary; proof reader and a cheerful corrector of several manuscripts.

Gary Mitton, a retired to a wheelchair, English teacher; who would forget to proof and correct in his enjoyment of the stories.

Joy Martel, who lives up to her name, for her encouragement and suggestions on the original manuscript.

Hazel Fay Thompson, who endured a book-worm husband and captivated writer under spell-check supervision. He's a music lover who can only coordinate one hand at a time. She challenges him in long heated arguments over details and usages with persistence and integrity. Yet she flatters dejected egos frustrated by publication fiery hoops and demands. Hero of the final proofs and the needed reading; she gets top credit and billing in seeing this series through as her husband's eyes slowly fail.

Yesu, the Christ, is the Muse whose inspiration led me to persist in writing the books and seeing them through publication: an arduous task. Words fail me to express my gratitude for the favors received.

The countless publishing services associates of Trafford Publications deserve hearty thanks: they taught me so much.

I cannot mention the rest, whose part I cannot measure, in this endeavor: a word here, an observation there and a smile of encouragement; these are their part.

I really believe that this is only the beginning of encouragement for I know that readers of these books will also add to my pleasure in serving. Truly it is a "world without end' of growing satisfaction and friendship. I write for your enjoyment and pleasure in facing the unexpected facets of life. May your joys be without end.

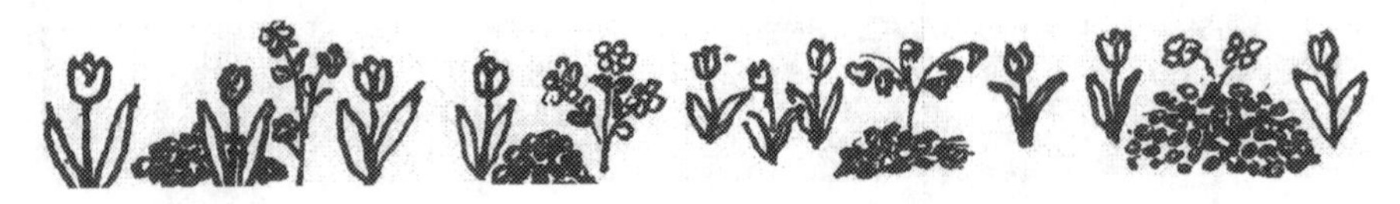

AUTHOR'S REMARKS

This book was a challenge for many reasons: subject, style and conclusion. Most books can't have heroes' deaths to deal with. Heroes are death defying. Only villains are supposed to die.

Life also, has differences and variations of endings. We all find life a sometimes pleasant, yet, nearly always, a difficult process. To finish life well is a real achievement. To me, at least, it makes the difference between the ordinary and the heroic. So, I've written about it. Just as life has many levels of starts at birth and training to maturity; so aging and the moment of death have the same levels of differences. I tried to devise some interesting situations. A few I had to leave to your imagination. Since death does come to everyone and combines in their lives a variety of pleasures, sins, and music; I have also used those elements to create a number of heroic endings.

I hope the presenting of several related, yet autonomous stories, does not produce vertigo and confusion. I have organized a chronology to aid the readers who like their stories separated. You can follow the events concerning Merien Papasian or Miakim and Yuzbasha the Khazar, separately for those who demand such details.

Two stories divided with distinct printing fonts (from the Estrangelo Edessa font, used in the text) for ease in following the stories:

Merien Papasian's letters to Lady Judith: 9-10; 36; 65-66; 85-86; 105; 112-113; 120-122; 124; 136-137; 168-169.

Yuzbasha of the Khazars: **13-15; 25-29; 31; 34; 39; 41; 45; 54; 59; 61-62; 66-67; 70-71; 73-74; 76-77; 82-83; 84-85; 86-87; 92; 99-100; 101; 109-110; 119-120; 123-124; 125; 141-142; 153.**

If you like this manner of treating the heroes, please let me know. I need the encouragement. If you don't like it, I'll know it soon enough. The number of people who make contact for censure is always greater than those professing enjoyment; even when the pleased are in the majority. So read, learn and enjoy, it's for your pleasure.

Marshall B. Thompson Jr.

HISTORIC WRAP-UP

Kaya commands a band of returning mercenary heroes from the conquest of Central Europe under the Huns. Their decision to go home by the northern-most route is governed by one necessity: to escape the greed of Munzur Khan and his grasping generals. They must leave by way of Poland's plains and swamps to find the Volga River as an escape route to the east. The forest tribes are of many sources and make-ups, each with a different religion and custom. Disorganized and weak, they fall easy prey to the mounted Hunnish warriors riding into the land they work.

Kaya's horse-band has little experience in river travel, yet, they must go beyond the forest tribes to the Ural Mountains and farther, as they return home. The Khazars occupy the mouths of the Volga and Don Rivers. The Tartars contend for the control of the Ural Mountains with the East Bulgars. Every road is contested by bands anxious for fees of passage or pillage. If they are able to contact the commercial cities on the Silk Road, there too, instability rules through corrupt oligarchies. A few large cities existed in the old civilized centers. They were usually centers of government and cultural pace-setters for the populations that were controlled by them. Hunnish and Turkish Khanates dominated the grasslands and pressured the civilized communities for land and goods. It was not an easy time to be alive and traveling, but it was better than being dead or destitute. The enjoyment of the essential goods for life and joys of reproduction still hold humans to a desire for survival and a search for any God who will help them maintain it.

The seeking of reasons, results and spiritual truth occupied them even more than it does us. For them life was a day by day, hour by hour preoccupation. Death was a constant reality in the life of every family and tribe. A God who saves was One to be sought by all.

A HIGH LOOKOUT

PEOPLE, PLACES & PLOTS IN CHAPTER 1

Fewsoon: Kaya's bride was rescued and is happily returning home.
Igor: a middle-aged fight manager, freed from slavery to go home.
Kaya: left the Hun capital, a wrestling champion sent into exile.
Koosta: the East Hun is a general sent to conquer the north woods.
Munzur: the Khan finds conflicts between empire and family.
Merien: Governor Papasian's daughter writes scattered friends.
Ozkurt: the lieutenant would like to visit friends in Byzantium.
Sertol: the German-born son of a Chipchak warrior going home.
Yetkin: the princess wants revenge for her defeated champion.

GLOSSARY HELPS

dough roo: that's right; correct; I agree.
hazer ol: get ready; prepare; present arms.
inn'in: descend; come down; go down; get off (a horse).
tope lie yan: collect; gather; bring together.

GENERAL KOOSTA PROCLAIMS

"Keep a sharp eye out for any movement, Munzur Khan has been known to award his favorites and then raid the same heroes for their accumulated wealth." Kaya instructed the agile boy. "Take a bag of berries and some water, Sertol. Let's see how high you can go."

"I'll ride the wind, out of sight, to keep you safe," Sertol laughed, as he chose a huge oak tree to carefully start his climb.

The first concern of rich warriors returning to the homeland is safety. Kaya the recognized leader of these successful men, sent the serving boy , a son of a warrior, up the tallest tree as a lookout, while his father and other men of rank decided on their next move.

"I have served in the Huns' raids past the German Rhineland, where the Franks stand strong against us. The wars in the West are continuous there is no rest or safety there," Sertol's father began.

"*Dough roo*, that's right," said another of the newly-formed band of Chipchak, "I've raided in the Po River valley south of the Alps. The Byzantine and Goths resist everywhere."

A third spoke up. "The lands below the Danube River are being conquered. All the Albanians have taken to the rugged mountains for defence. They would not let us pass."

"We certainly can't return by way of the Ukraine, neither warring faction, Huns or Khazars, would let us pass. Khan Kinner would have us yoked and seated on stakes," Ozkurt affirmed with a grimace. Heads nodded in agreement around the circle.

"That's why I'm here," boasted Igor, "to get you off safely to your own country by traveling through mine. Only the grasslands are occupied by Huns and Turks. The great River Volga flows from west to east and you can leave the river for other rivers or grass beyond the eastern mountains. You'll be able to avoid all the areas you have traveled and see the most beautiful country in the world."

Kaya smiled at his enthusiasm, the band listened with respectful interest, but Ozkurt bristled and objected strongly. "We have only come to where the Danube River makes its great turn to the west. The forest and mountains are already dense and cold. Winter is upon us. We need to move south to warmer weather. We could move through the Greek lands to Constantinople and from there to the Persian Sassanids. There are boats on the Black Sea to transport us as far as the Caucasus shore."

Several men showed disagreement as he spoke. "Those high mountains will be just as cold and difficult as the northern plains."

"If Munzur will give us ninety days instead of thirty we might just make it. The terms and the Yasa are clear; exile or death. Of course, he might not kill you and simply volunteer you into one of his draft army posts in the areas of hardest fighting. That way you might still manage to die a hero." They laughed, the band was finally in agreement; they knew the khan.

They had been released from army service, decorated and enriched to return home. However, home lay a year or more away and heroes save their fame and acclaim for home. Otherwise you were the boy who went abroad to war and never came back. There was no glory in that kind of story. The hero had to return for the process to fulfill the human need for recognition and acclaim. For a hero to return rich and with a whole skin, perhaps marked by a scar or two, was the height of all boys' dreams. To marry the local high-born beauty and become the envy of all others, was to be a success.

Igor and Ozkurt did most of the talking. Kaya, as leader, sat and listened as did all the group. Fewsoon his bride, listened, but cooked to use the time well. She occasionally went to where Altom, the golden mare, was tethered to give her a treat of fruit or vegetable.

It was increasingly clear that the best route lay between the Polish Plains and the Prepet Marshes. Several men had worked north of the mountains and knew the best passes and posts. They would move on the edges of tribal territory of the Balts, Lithuanians and Slavs, moving north until they found a friendly village, to stay the winter.

"*Inn'in*, come down son," shouted the burly father. "We have eaten and are ready to move. There's enough left for two your size." The men loading the horses laughed, they knew the boy ate more than many of the men. As the boy descended, his father asked, "You saw nothing worth reporting?"

The boy shrugged as he went to the caldron for the bowl Fewsoon had prepared. "A squad of ten men went up the Danube, a patrol I think. There was a larger group coming up from Budapest, but it was too early to see which road they will follow."

"Why didn't you report it?" his father insisted indignantly.

"Why?" Sertol gulped an answer, "They're over an hour away yet."

Kaya spoke to Igor, "You lead with the men, Sertol and I will bring up the rear with the kitchen goods."

Northeast they went, over the Carpathian Mountains where aboriginal people hid at their approach and no one would help, hinder or even talk. The Hun camps, where their written pass and seal passed them on, were well appointed at first, but soon, as the weeks passed, disintegrated into roughly-made pavilions where the local soldiery lived by extortion of money and supplies from merchants and passers-by. Patrols became less frequent and more like a tribal levy where patrol duty was combined with the regular hunting and herding chores, centered on the tribe's needs rather than the empire's. They warred a bit with the local population when they became troublesome, and shifted camp and grazing as they pleased. Local khans showed little respect for Munzur's documents even before the granted time expired. The poorly defined frontier was reached. It was convenient to avoid the few posts and to press on in the depopulated forest areas.

The winter's cold sent Kaya's band hurrying as they feared that pursuit rushed after them. Khan Munzur's habit of rewarding men and, afterward, confiscating everything, pushed them on. He or any one of his generals might envy the wedding gifts or the possession of a golden mare and decide to take it.

They traveled from a grassy land of grazing and horses to a marshy land of birch and conifers. Supplies diminished. They were forced to give the horses extra rest and grazing, but the hunting and fishing were as poor as the grass. The birch leaves, were now brown underfoot. The rain and snow had started. Soon they would starve. The grass and leaves started to rot. The ground became frozen and hard, and the surface slick and treacherous. The snow did not melt away by day anymore.

Igor urged them on, "We must arrive at my village before the storms begin. We will be warm and safe there; press on."

> - - - - - - - >

Munzur Khan was accustomed to commanding his pleasure; who would dare to deny him? Yet his perplexity and frustration remained prominent in his thinking. His unrecognized daughter, Sarayjik, was pregnant! Just when he was ready to admit his guilt and had hinted of his mistake in divorcing her mother. He had humbled himself for nothing. A childless widow was a valuable commodity in diplomacy, but a pregnant princess was of little value. In fact it might endanger the line of inheritance. The heir he chose must inherit not another. Furthermore, it was reported that she was writing letters to the Greeks! What next? She was not a participant in state secrets, yet she seemed to foreknow his determinations and decisions. He must alert his agents on the Bosphorus. She was still consorting with Olga, the Queen of the Goths. The Rumens, enslaved, were the object of her concern. She went to Church, that tool of the Latin and Byzantine empires--his enemies! She was said to have a *papaz*, a priest to read to her staff. He groaned.

"Yes, my Khan?" Queried his adjutant, attentively.

"What was that complaint from the Lithuanians of the north?"

"Sir, the forest people are starting to occupy the open woodland and meadows. They are prospering through trade and are starting to build forts for defense." He pointed to some open letters.

"We will burn them out." Munzur growled. Here at least was a problem he was used to handling. "Drive them beyond the mother of rivers, let them know what it's like to touch what's mine." He would teach them a lesson they would never forget: a demonstration of power for the political world to watch with awe. He would wreak havoc on an enemy; farmers, moles who mine the soil with plants. They were not even horsemen, not able in war like the Khazars who press from the east. "Have we a surplus commander or general who lacks assignment for the moment?"

> - - - - - - - >

The princess Yetkin was dressed formally for the celebration in the large reception center. Nevertheless, she managed to separate to herself the object of her search in the small tent which was intimate in setting. The party was in honor of Attila, the boy's farewell; though the destination was still in process of negotiations. Both the Turin Ostrogoth and Byzantine ambassadors were the object of the search. Young princes were habitually sent to live in allied or rival courts to be trained in foreign languages and cultures. Sometimes they were held hostage, or married to seal alliances. By living in the courts and cities of other close or distant kingdoms, they came to a finer judgement of political realities and the conditions of war and peace.

Although there were new rumors that Khan Munzur favored a German prince for the hand of his daughter. Princess Yetkin had other interests which she pursued directly.

"I'm told Commander, that you are to take our forces north to extend the reach of our empire among the forest people. While collecting tribute could you favor me? Eliminate the arrogant upstart, Aya the bear, who crippled our champion. If you do, you will gain other rewards." She smiled as if they both understood what that would be.

"I am only commander of a small expedition of twenty thousand men, my princess. The men will soon be in place to move north over the Polish lands. Wherever we go, we will always consider your wishes as our highest command. Be sure your request will be done." His smile showed that he hoped for much. "I have recently come from service in the east. Perhaps the princess has heard of the arrival of veterans from the Ukraine yesterday. They report that the man with the golden horse, of whom you spoke, Kaya Aya and his friend have served in the Prince of Khazar's Elite Guard forcing the Donetz River's fords. We have traced their arrival to a boat from Crimea last winter. I know them well and have many reasons to hate them. I hope to convince Munzur Khan that they are spies."

"You are a man who will go far in the kingdom, Binbasha, General Koosta" She murmured, "Come let us seal our agreement with a drink." She motioned for a young attendant to come.

"Gladly, my Princess. You know that my command comes with the order to take the demand for obedience and tribute through all the agricultural zones of the north. We begin by raids of subjugation. They must learn that they deal with a merciless enemy. For that lesson it is necessary to wait until the ground is frozen, and the horses can travel through the marshlands. Then, we catch them in their little huts and burn them out. They face the sword in the village or the winter in the countryside. We clean them out like wolves in a sheep corral. After that, they will do anything or surrender anyone in their power. They cannot stand against us; our weapons and horses will destroy them all. I, Koosta of the East Huns, swear it."

> - - - - - - - >

The cry of the hunting wolf pack sounded behind them. It was evening when the howl came again. It sounded quite close as Kaya's band pressed on. It was a cold, overcast end of another day with torches already lit. They traveled over the frozen river ice, trying to make the village before night. Igor had promised that it lay just ahead. The light snow had frozen to the surface, and made a rough but serviceable highway for the group. The horses wore felt overshoes, which increased the size of the hoof and gave support to passing over or even standing on deep crusty snow drifts. It also protected the horses from frozen hooves by keeping out snow and ice chunks that might lodge under the unshod hoof.

Suddenly, a woman's scream of terror cut through the cold air like a knife. A primitive looking sledge and a troika of three lathered, exhausted horses came dashing out of the woods on to the ice. A tall, bearded man stood crouching at the head of the sledge and behind him a woman and child sat hugging in the effort to be safe, not to be thrown off or lose contact with the racing sled. A large half-grown child knelt at the back with a sharpened stick like a spear in one hand while clinging to the back-end of the sledge with the other.

The mournful cry of a gray wolf sounded from the woods behind the group. A large pack of ten huge animals broke cover and tongues lolling, headed straight for the fleeing sledge. About half of them loped along near the bank of the river just off the ice, running parallel to the sledge, cutting off any return to shelter. The huge leader and largest wolves continued behind the running horses. They ran unhurriedly, trailing and exhausting the prey.

The sledge tried to cross the river's width, but the ice was riven in the center stream. The currents and pressures had built a wall of double ice near the open water. The driver shouted a curse and an appeal to the band on the other side of the river as he continued toward them shouting, motioning toward the pursuing pack. The appeal was clear enough even if the language was not.

Igor dismounted, whipped out his sword and ran, but could not pass the open water. Kaya and the band dismounted, stood rooted, open-mouthed watching the action. No man moved except Kaya who slowly armed his bow and drew an arrow. Igor's voice joined the appeal, and the woman screamed as a large hunter broke from the pack, closed the distance rapidly and lunged at the boy on the tail of the sledge. The boy stabbed his heavy, improvised spear at the animal and seemed to make solid contact for the animal tumbled away crying. Immediately, the wolves, scenting blood, turned on the wounded animal and tore it to pieces with growls and snapping teeth. Silently, the Chipchaks watched the proceedings.

The sledge skewed suddenly toward the river in an arc, sliding sideways as the left side, lathered horse fell. Slipping on its belly forward, the horse screamed its terror. The weight of the sledge crashed it through the ice wall. The tail-end rested over the water, splashing the boy. The crouched man sprang forward and, with knife in hand, cut through the lines attaching the horse to the troika, and immediately remounted. He called out to encourage the team, found his whip and instead of using it on his horses was obliged to use it on a wolf sprinting toward the lead animal.

Kaya broke the silence, "*Hazer ol*, prepare fire arrows, quickly," his low voice of command did what none of the Slavs pleas had accomplished. A hunk of wool, used as a wick, from somewhere was pressed of its excess fat and spitted onto his arrow point. The point was ignited by the torch and attention was returned to the scene of action.

The fallen horse was attempting to gain the bank and woods, slipping and sliding frantically. Its muzzle was covered in red foam and its breath labored, steam arising from nose and body. At that instant the first of the pursuing wolves fell on its neck and another caught the soft muzzle. The horse screamed in mortal agony as the bank-side wolves joined the attackers, swarming over its convulsing body. It was difficult to maneuver in the crowd and many a whine and yip conveyed the message that damage was being suffered. But the bloodied, suffocated horse lost strength rapidly.

In the same second a wolf, leaping for the lead horse of the sledge, was taken by the driver's whip and spun in midair falling on its back. The leader, speeding from the occupied pack, lunged at the boy on the tail of the moving vehicle. The back-handed shove of the spear across its neck spun the beast into the water from which the end of the sleigh had emerged. A companion immediately replaced the attacker and with his lunge had received the wood crosswise like a bit in his mouth. The bite carried the crude spear and almost the boy back among the others. The boy on his knees, defenseless, face near the floor, hands feeling round him for some loose stick or stone, waited for the next attack.

Kaya looked at the arrow point now blazing strongly, drew and sent it flying immediately to the end of the sledge, not a foot from the boy's head, between him and the charging wolves. The attackers flinched in their lunge and the boy too, shied away. Then he reached and easily pulled the flaming point from the frozen wood and poked flame and point into the face of the next attacker. With the next assault the point and burning bits disintegrated and scattered among the runners that followed. Now a stream of fire arrows flew before the faces of the pursuers; not one animal was hit. They scattered and regrouped, but they had lost ground. The boy held the bone arrow shaft like a dagger awaiting the next charge.

Torches appeared in the woods ahead. The village was near and the people responded to the cries of distress, but the determined wolves showed no sign of relenting. The hubbub of voices encouraged the horses, as much as the death of their comrade-in-work had done by the terrors of his screams. Their efforts were renewed and they flew past the first line of torches to come to an exhausted halt before the village huts. The yells of the villagers and the wall of flame finally stopped the wolves.

At the kill, some alpha females ran with quivering flesh in their mouths to feed the scrawny, half-grown cubs of the summer litters. They were already gathering in a frantic circle near, but not close enough to eat directly with the mature animals. Their reception of the food was violent in its expressions. They screamed yips and snarls, whining piteously as they snatched at, and fought over everything edible that came near them.

The wolf in the water swam vigorously, but was carried by the current down to the opposite side of the riven ice. After a time, it found purchase to emerge from the cold water. The sopped animal shook its head, then, all its body right down to its tail once and then again. The Chipchak party had turned to face the animal, and they fairly beamed their approval as the male animal did a quick inspection of paw and under parts with a sniff and a lick.

STRUNG BOW & QUIVER

Igor, however, seeing the wolf, ran to grab Kaya's arm and whisper fiercely, "Look, the monster is here, quick, shoot it before it regains its strength." He looked at the men and then to the wolf with horror" "Why do you wait? Why do you approve its presence?" He looked round for someone to appeal to and saw Fewsoon. "Lady," he cried, "can't you move them to action?" Fewsoon, like the others, was staring at the animal with respect, but no apparent fear. He shook his head in bewilderment. Would no one break the silence?

"The grey wolf is their clan animal and spiritual brother," Kaya stated kindly, "they would never consider harming one. It would be murder." A whisper went around among the men. "*Tope lie'yan*."

Then, the men turned to their saddlebags and each produced a bit of dried horse meat, blood sausage or fat, which Ozkurt collected. He took about 15 paces toward the animal which watched silently, quivering slightly from weakness. Disregarding the protest of Igor, the animal stared at the horsemen and then at the offering and staggered forward to bolt it down in three gulps. Again the smile of approval went round the group, and they bowed or nodded slightly. The wolf made a slight humping sound, as close to a bark as wolves, who are a silent kind, ever get. He turned, moved towards the wooded bank and disappeared from sight.

The line of fire on the opposite bank remained on the edge of the village and did not try to drive the wolves from their kill. The wolves finished the flesh and bones of the two dead, and there was literally nothing left but stains in the snow, which the whelps lapped at. Now that the blood lust was satisfied, wounds could be licked without danger to the wounded. Some drew near the riven ice that separated them from the Chipchak horses, but it was too wide to jump. They were strengthened, but not satisfied and would hunt through the night. Suddenly above the village there came a long triumphant call from the leader. It was a call to continue the hunt, and the pack silently disappeared from the river side, entering the woods and skirting the village.

The Chipchaks urged their horses to a place opposite the village where the ice healed and passage was safe. Igor, subdued and thoughtful, led them into the village and safety. Kaya received a grateful welcome from the village leader. Igor established his relationship with the village. They knew his parents and welcomed him home. Kaya and his men were given the use of a hut. But it was a restrained welcome. The kind one species gives to another that it does not fully understand, trust or approve. The women came while their men were present and brought food, but none stayed in the two room hut to cook for the strangers. The hut owners, young and newly married, had moved in with the father-in-law, next door. As quickly as the villagers had come, they disappeared, leaving the newcomers to make their own accommodations and arrangements. They did, by

taking the horses inside the hut with them. The horses got a room with straw and a dirt floor. The travelers rearranged both rooms, pushing everything to the wall, as if it were a Chipchak yurt.

> - - - - - - - >

Merien Papasian looked over her letter with care. It would be the last of the year, for winter sailing on the Black Sea was very dangerous as she knew by experience. It would accompany the letter to her father at his new posting in Yalta. The Don River would be freezing up by now. She felt uneasy about the gift of territory between the fighting forces of Khazars and Huns; each attempted to win the favor of the Basileus, Emperor of Byzantium. Yalta was the Hun's present to the East Roman Empire. The town had the advantage of being able to pass letters to either camp. They would be read by other eyes, but the vital information was important to the receiver. It was addressed to the Lady Judith, wife of Prince Ilkin at The Estates on the bend of the Don River. She read it aloud one more time.

Greetings, in the name of the God of Peace and our great Savior who loves us. Your letter fills me with joy. Your refugees were happily dispatched. They were thankful for your intervention and I am convinced that they all will prosper in a new unprejudiced environment. The rabbi praised your name. Unfortunately, their goods were plundered and cannot be reclaimed without greater loss.

I delight in the reports of baby Daniel's health and growth. My only sorrow is that I did not know you previous to my departure from Kertch Port. In one season, could we have become the friends we are now? No, probably not. Race and Religion, those great separators of peoples, would have prejudiced us and blinded our eyes against each other, yes. As I told you after your first letter's request; it has led me into travels and contacts I would never have made or imagined before. I have met a most fascinating young man, the son of the governor of Pontus, where many Greeks, Laz and Jews make up the population. He says that envy, not religion is the root of the matter. One's tradition is only an excuse for gaining what others have worked for. Ignorance, like darkness, permits those who don't wish their true reasons to be known, to plunder others. Yes, it's true!

As I told you, Olga is now Queen of the Goths. She is well and has a new Peregrine falcon sent from Kaya for exercise and her hunts with Lady Sarayjik. However, the hunts may be interrupted since the Lady is happily pregnant and waits for delivery within a couple of months. Perhaps a Christmas present, no? They request our prayers.

Sources in the Hun capital say that, after the wedding with the fortunate Fewsoon, Kaya and Ozkurt have departed north toward the mother of rivers. Koosta, your late adversary in the Ukraine, is dispatched north to subdue the forest tribes. I fear that Kaya and Ozkurt may be included in the destruction. Our world is full of fast and fearful changes. By God's mercy we continue to survive. At times I think that the time of Yesu's return is close. How can the world get worse? Our sins weaken us before our adversaries.

I'll not hear from you until spring comes again. But I'll write and send them off as news occurs. I pray for your husband Prince Ilkin daily, that he might again enjoy health. How fortunate you have the giant Gochen to be an adjutant and helper. How sweet that Sherbet will marry him only after the anniversary of Han Lees' death. How touchingly tragic is the story of his deception, yet, he saved her life from slavery and misery. They would be prosperous but for his treachery. Life and death sometimes hinge on such great internal decisions.

I leave you with a parting kiss. If Kaya and company reach the Volga you will be the one best positioned to hear the news, no?

Your devoted friend,

Merien Papasian.

> - - - - - - - >

The mounted troops were drawn up in parade order and the speeches, marches and displays were almost over. The selected troops had trained hard for the arduous task of winter warfare. Khan Munzur and the Princess Yetkin dressed in their finest and warmest, reviewed their troops with pride together with their newest favorite Yuzbasha, now a Binbasha. The general addressed the troops:

"We ride north to teach the wild, forest people a lesson. The earth trembles before the might of Munzur Khan. Everyone's prosperity depends on his good will. We who rule do so by the natural order of the world and those who prove their superiority must rule by the will of Tanra, the creator. Herders and horsemen have the mobility and the knowledge of treating the herds for their safety and prosperity. We pasture them in exchange for our just part of goods and services by those we rule. Wildness and rebellion will not be permitted. Good order demands obedience and the keeping of the rules we issue. Forest people must learn to respect our demands. They must obey our great Khan. They will learn, to their sorrow, that we will not be ignored. We ride with fire and sword to victory." Koosta paused measuring the effect of his speech. Then, satisfied, he proclaimed,

"Death to the forest people!"

The mounted battalions drawn up in parade order obediently echoed the cry of their new commander, the hero of the Donetz River Battle, now raised to the rank of general.

'Death to the forest people,' 'Glory to General Koosta!'

> - - - - - - - >

WOLVES ATTACK

PEOPLE, PLACES & PLOTS IN CHAPTER 2

Captain: delays his boat for a few coins and gets news worth more.
Fewsoon: soon realizes their risky venture is in trouble.
Igor: comes home with trouble for the village.
Kaya: must explain his choices and his faith to the inquisitive.
Luvya: serves guests drinks in her father's house.
Merien: in Constantinople meets a past suitor unexpectedly.
Stefen: the curious little brother of Merien likes to answer questions.
Village head man: hosts foreign warriors unwillingly.
Yownja: clover flower, Fewsoon's baby name is preferred by Kaya.
Yuzbasha the Khazar: finds an invitation, a knife, and an old love.

GLOSSARY HELPS

barish: peace; let's be friendly; no more strife or argument.
bin sinni siz-a: a thousand years to you; long life to you; live long.
choke yashar: many years; long life to him.
denar: an ancient coin of the East Roman Empire.
koine: market Greek, the language used in Byzantium.
persona non grata: not acceptable; a Latin expression used to define the diplomatic status of a foreigner.

2 DISCOVERY

A KHAN'S KNIFE

"Oars-men wait up! You have an important passenger with the need of haste," the man in military uniform called out.

"It will cost you a coin more, Sir," answered the tiller captain as the oars-men backed water to bring the gondola to dock-side again. The Golden Horn in the midst of Constantinople, the largest city of the western world, shimmered with ripples and shone in the late afternoon sun. The young man, running to descend to the passenger area of the wharf, was known to them as one who returned late to the Pera side of the city, where all foreigners were required to live. He lived high and though short on cash was full of enterprise and vigor.

Yuzbasha the Khazar had left his uncle's office with a feeling of relief. Uncle was not the easiest man to work under. His family was rich and high placed in the ruling hierarchy, who both trembled, and delighted in the rule of Kinner Khan. That severe man rewarded generously and punished with equal vigor. As a boy Yuzbasha had herded his father's animals and practiced fighting with others his age. His uncle or better stated his mother's brother, Chavush, had spotted him as a potential family booster and prevailed on the General, the boy's father's brother, to have the boy trained and later to use him for an adjutant. Now ten months in the capital with his two uncles, he had explored the water ways, placement of forts, naval sites and regiment locations. All of which was dutifully reported to Getchet on the Volga, and the

Khan's bureaucracy. In fact, his activities were so noticeable that his uncle the sergeant, Chavush, was worried that the boy would become persona non grata, unwelcome and be expelled from the empire.

"Where do you go today, young noble?" asked the captain as they pulled steadily to the harbor shore.

"I've a free afternoon and will be fortunate to make the last boat tonight." He proclaimed to all. There was appreciative laughter around.

"Then you have been paid your wages?" questioned the captain.

"No, not from 'Kinner the Skinner'. He only receives never gives."

"Then from another, for you reek of wealth this day."

The boy laughed and winked conspiringly at his inquirer answering, "Yes, there are always alternate ways of earning."

The captain agreed knowingly and wondered which of his sources would pay best for his new information on the young foreigner's activities.

"If you've money to spend, why not stay on the Pera side? Where various communities live side by side, the laws are always interpreted loosely, giving room for indulgences," he stated wisely.

"But where the top of the line, the absolute best artist is concerned, the capital is the heart of the matter," Yuzbasha interjected. "Tonight I shall dine and be entertained by Miakim, the goddess of dance and song." He waited for the wave of envy and admiration to subside before adding, "And I shall share this moment with the minister of... Oh, I don't know what the Greek term means, something like the inside or interior. He is very rich and I'm to be one of the special guests."

The captain and the regular commuters exchanged knowing glances and nodded agreeably. "Surely some good will come of this for your career in our capital," they agreed.

From the wharf he started up the hill toward the Grand Bazaar away from the Golden Horn, where boats were loaded and unloaded by husky stevedores. Then, entering the galleries of the covered market, he passed salesmen and boys shouting their wares in all the languages of the Mediterranean and adjoining seas. Latin, Greek, Aramaic, and even less commercialized, but increasingly important Hunnish, Gothic and Khazar were heard. Yuzbasha, asking his way to the expensive jewelry section of the market, looked about in admiration at the long line of rich shops. They had a wealth of fabrics, jewelry and all kinds of novelties on display. Lacking money or credit, he had neglected this part of the city in his explorations. Here indeed was fabulous wealth.

He found a shop displaying silver and bronze mirrors, and entered to make a purchase. His order was detailed, and elaborate. It would take time. He agreed to return and pick it up before the evening party. Then he continued his exploration of the vast market.

He spoke to a boy trying to sell him a jeweled dagger in his own language. "When was this building constructed?" The boy stared at him open mouthed as if dumbfounded by the question. Yuzbasha tried again in broken Greek, the language of Byzantium or East Rome as local people liked to call it. His Koine was understandable, so the boy answered it slowly.

"It's always been here, sir, my dad says it has lasted for thousands of years and will go on forever." Then he changed back into Khazar to say, "This dagger has been made by the masters of Damascus. It will last for your grandchildren to envy. It will even cut through iron mail links, no armor can stand against it. See the rubies and emeralds. This is a weapon for a Khan! For you only, the smallest gold coin will do. A special price for I must go home now." He looked about nervously and started to put the weapon away.

Yuzbasha stared at the shining piece and knew the price a bargain. It had the curved beak of the exotic African parrots that were occasionally sold at the market. The jewels reproduced the color of its plumage. The beak was obsidian, the eye a diamond. He reached out to take it and sought his purse in his sash and opened it for the coin. When the boy saw it, he snatched the coin and left rapidly saying, "Best put it away, out of sight, sir; there be thieves about."

At a cross street where the boy had turned from sight, he suddenly returned running. A shout had been raised from the other street. "Stop him! He stole a dagger from my shop yesterday." Yuzbasha pointed to the street open behind him and stood blocking it as the security people came running around the corner. He pointed to the next street ahead and they stormed by in pursuit. Patting his sash where the weapon lay hidden he strolled toward an exit.

As he departed the upper end of the covered bazaar, he stopped abruptly. He was face to face with Merien Papasian, whom he had not seen since their voyage on the Sea Witch. The impact of her presence was like a physical blow. She took his breath away. The breeze had swept away the edges of her blue cloak and her white wool dress clung to her form. The sight struck him with a desire he had forgotten. He started to search for words but found none. He stood eyes bugged out, mouth open; overcome with shock.

She was a stunning sight as startled, she stopped and also stared. However, she neither sought words nor stayed even a moment. She turned and ran, with a surprised maid. The old household servant carrying market fruits and vegetables followed. She could not keep pace with her mistress. Yuzbasha, however, was able to keep the maid in sight, without her detecting his following her to the family neighborhood. However, when he came to the top of a street she was gone. A number of impressive buildings stood before his eyes. Which was her home?

> - - - - - - - >

Not for the last time, Kaya discovered that their presence proved a damper to the emotional celebration of life among the woods people. Igor managed to invite Kaya and Fewsoon out alone and took them to the neighbor's house. Sertol, who frequently helped Fewsoon in the kitchen, pleaded to come along and Igor permitted it. There they met the people rescued. After introductions, the young boy was able to

stutter out his thanks, while the man simply held his hand and said thanks repeatedly. It was the only word he managed in Hunnish. The woman lay in a corner with the child too spent for words. "Would your people let the wolf eat your animals?" Igor inquired agitatedly, "Is the beast a god to them?"

"We lose an occasional meat pony to them, but when they become a nuisance, we have a drive which forces them into a river bend. They must swim to escape and they are thinned in number and forced into another land by this. Our people descended from the grey wolf, but we don't let our brothers defraud us." Kaya smiled indulgently, "It's part of the ancient ways and teachings."

"But you are different and don't respond as they do. You would have killed wolves to save a life." Igor's tone was intensely serious. "Why?"

"My teacher convinced me of the value of human souls as the art work of God and of the importance of saving rather than taking lives." Kaya laughed suddenly, "I was a bear before I became human, so perhaps I know the grey wolf as a thief of cubs, and competitor at kills, rather than ancestor."

"I have watched you pray and sing to Yesu each day. How can you, a man from the east, follow the new religion of the Romans?"

"Is truth the property of one people because they come to it early? Don't some good things become the property of all who love them?" Kaya smiled disarmingly, "Things of the heart are like music. It may change time and lilt as it takes each people's affection and admiration, but it spreads on the hearing."

"There are strange men and women who do not live as others. They proclaim this message in our land: the coming of a God who lived as men yet served and died to save lives forever. They are careless of wealth, status and authority, and they are full of selfless behavior, but their claims are fantastic. How can anyone believe in the eternity of life and the end of death?" Igor asked earnestly.

"We are told from sacred writings that humankind was created with the aim of eternal life in view, and that death for humans was not to be as it is now, a painful, lonesome, weakening end of everything. Yesu came to take away the fear and sting of death, for he conquered the power of the grave to hold humans in bondage."

"My people live in fear of life's end and are careless of the lives and rights of others. Does Yesu change these things?"

"The people who obey the Christos, the anointed, appointed leader and savior, bond their lives with his. They serve God as He does. They are forgiven their sins and the power of disobedience and desire is broken in them. It's like the difference domestication makes in a savage animal. It becomes a useful animal. There is a change in nature and a gentle, rather than wild disposition. Their actions are not damaging as before. They come to love and respect the lives of others. They become profitable to their family and tribe. Other people who don't understand or desire this change, fear them and their God from whom their powers come."

"They denounce as sin the way people live, and while they are right in part, about: bad faith, lies, hate and murder. They press it too far. They seem to make all joyful things sin." Igor leaned forward earnestly, arguing again.

Kaya's laugh filled the room and Fewsoon came from the kitchen bearing two steaming wooden cups. She gave one to each man and stood with her face framed in her golden glory, as she smiled at each. "Such an earnest conversation going on in this corner; I sought an excuse `to enter the arena', as the Romans say."

"This kind of excuse is always permitted and welcome." Igor spoke with gentle emotion as he held his cup up to toast her.

"She always seems to know when the work grows thirsty," Kaya stated proudly, "and she is always there with the best."

"Yownja, Our friend complains of the restrictive nature of our faith." Kaya continued, to his love. "He seeks freedom where his personal weakness and desires lie. Child-like, we all do the same. We desire all that is damaging or unprofitable to us. Whims and cravings replace true needs. The wise parent puts limits and overrules. The wise adult learns discipline and self-control."

Fewsoon smiled and shook her head. "It's not an easy thing to do, but all agree it is the most profitable to the soul's happiness."

"Why do you speak about 'soul' rather than 'body', as the prime identity to be satisfied? Surely the material part of us is the most important, as well as the easiest to identify," Igor insisted.

"People lose parts of their bodies and change with the years. It is not the parts alone that make us a being, but the inward core. Our personality and habits, as well as, that part that decides where and how to live, constitute that core. That core or 'soul' is of true value." Fewsoon contended. "It is the essence of our 'self'."

"Lady Philosopher," said Igor with a smile, "I shall owe you my salvation, as well as my life."

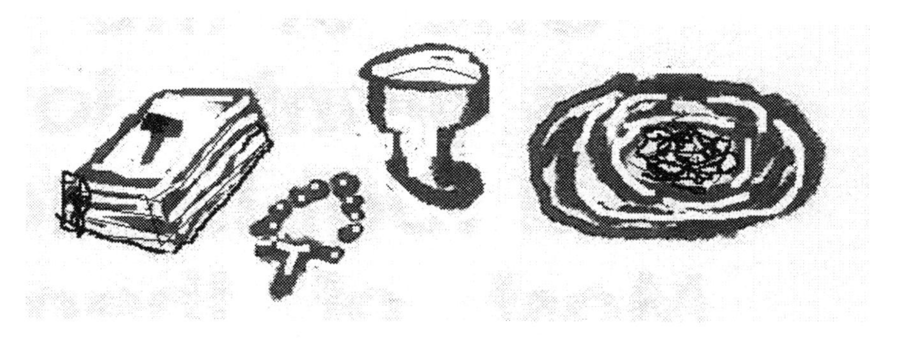

BY REVELATION & KNOWLEDGE

Fewsoon shook her head, as if correcting a child. "Smooth words where true repentance and right deeds are needed." She took their cups. "I'll get you another."

"Yesu saves us by dying for us. To save is an act of grace, an intervention at risk or cost by one for a needy other." Kaya was enjoying the moment.

"What is this salvation in essence?" Igor was serious, "How do you get it?"

"It is peace with God through the forgiveness of sins, and the power to resist sin as we pray. We get it by recognizing our sin, and being sorry for its rule over our will and heart." Kaya was excited, "Yesu makes life different and gives help when needed."

"But you are not all of that mind. Your men differ; not all are believers," Igor insisted.

"Chipchak are free people, we may come and go as we like, and men may join other bands by a simple act of sharing food and giving allegiance. We will respect the beliefs and practices of the tribe and band, but we may not always be convinced of its truth or rightness. We are free to move again, if we do not agree." Kaya smiled, "We pray for all who join my band that God might change their hearts and give power to believe and be saved."

"The religion of the Roman Empire is at war between the teachings of Athanasius and Arius. The churches, schools and monasteries are given to the hands of one party or another, and possessors become dispossessed as this war of religious decrees and riots continues. What do you think of all this?"

"This is the mixing of politics and religion, with men appealing to Caesar, rather than the Christos. I think that the Emperor should not impose his opinions." Kaya frowned darkly. "However, I do think that Yesu must have come with God's commission from the beginning, and was therefore fully of God at all times. Perhaps both men's positions claim too much, for they go beyond Scripture into philosophy."

"I encountered philosophy in Crimea on a trade venture," said Igor smiling. "I fell in love with Aristotle and Plato and spent all my gain for schools and scrolls."

"My teacher understands it well, but I was a poor pupil," Kaya shook his head regretfully. "My brother, Kutch, has ability in these matters, but I lack his good qualities."

"You do well enough," interrupted Fewsoon now returned with the two goblets, "your brother has chosen the Hermitage they say, and it will be a great loss. The tribe needs good heads and Christian leaders too." She sounded a bit resentful.

"He was wounded in an ambush, and missed our herd drive to the Han lands." Kaya's soft answer came. The Hermitage has need of him."

"Barish, peace," exclaimed Igor, "let not philosophy be soiled by politics and family matters. We must supply ourselves and stay till winter passes. Pursuit can't continue in this intense cold. I will find out if we can stay and rest for gold: if there is food enough. We must be rested for travel later."

"Yownja, you might be able to help the ladies, if you continue to serve," Kaya started saying, but Igor shook his head impatiently.

She smiled at his agitation. "No, they are afraid of us and speak little Hunnish," she answered, watching Igor. Then she reached out and held him by the shoulder. "Our lives are in your capable hands." She smiled from her height, half a head taller than Igor. Igor was all eyes and respect, as she led Kaya to the door to take their departure, back to the troop. Sertol left off watching a game of chess to follow.

Igor's eyes followed them and then, with a sigh, he turned back to seek the host, who was deep in his cups. When that one's bleary eyes saw Igor, he roared a welcome. "*Bin sinni siz-a'*, a thousand years to you, Igor Igorovich," he toasted, slurring his Hunnish. "Now that the animals have been sent to their stalls, come drink with the people; wash the horsy smell of them from your throat."

"They suffer as you do from the oppression of the Huns," objected Igor moving to the host's side.

"But the horse turds bring trouble on our people; burning and death by the Huns," the old man shook his head sadly. "In spite of all their offered gold coins and help. Here drink. Luvya come, bring drinks, my daughter."

"Refresh yourself and tell us of your travels, Sir." An attractive, young, light-haired maiden knelt before Igor holding the drinks high on a flat elaborately carved tray-like board.

Igor laughed pleasantly and took his choice of drink and smiled at the girl, Luvya, warmly. He wondered if she were part of the family in the house where he was to stay. Would they share the large stove-top family bed together? "Would you like a song?" he inquired.

"Oh, yes, please." She smiled and others echoed her agreement.

"It is called: My Homeland." His voice was deep and mellow and he sang with the accompaniment of a balalaika:

1. My homeland is deep in the woods.
 It is a summer of green and silver,
 Winter bright lights. I love you,
 Great land of shining lakes and bright streams.
 My homeland is joyful and light,
 It's full of beauty.
 Love it! Love its people and their ways.

2. Songs, laughter, talk, poetry too,
 Contain such wit that is true.
 My people, how I love them! I hear them.
 I see them when at work, home and play.

My homeland is shining and right,
It's full of beauty. Love it!
Love its streams and forest paths.

3. My homeland is rich and is praised.
Love always follows the way of duty.
Honest people, I love you.
Oh, never will I leave this dear home.
My homeland is snow filled and bright,
It's full of beauty. Love it!
Love its lakes and meadow views.

MY HOMELAND

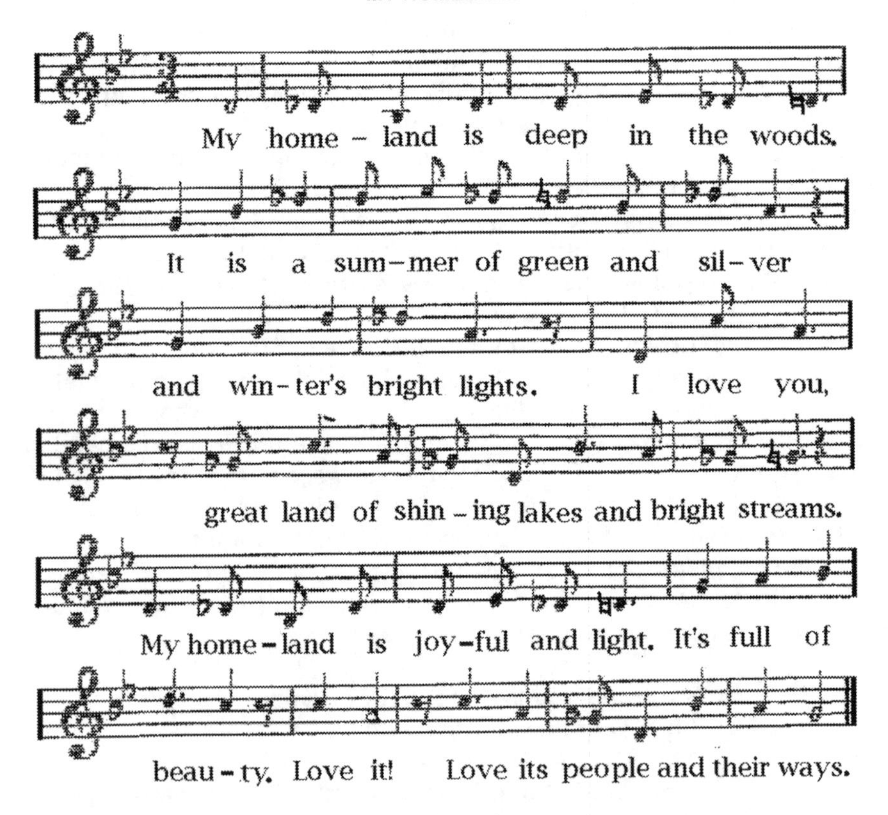

It was a long night full of songs, stories and laughter, toasts and drinking. Igor was the life of the party and did not remember going to bed.

VILLAGE CELEBRATION

PEOPLE, PLACES & PLOTS IN CHAPTER 3

Fewsoon: finds the village ladies to be friendly neighbors.
Ifrah: maid and confidant of the famous actress Miakim.
Igor: learns about farm life again.
Kaya: must hide his troops' training.
Luvya: likes the life of a farm girl.
Merien Papasian: distrusts unknown admirers.
Miakim: the actress finds it hard to be honest, yet rich and famous.
Ozkurt: tries to endure the cold weather.
Rukam: farmer and father of Luvya.
Sertol: gets training and teasing from his father and the band.
Stefen Papasian: takes home flowers from a foreigner.
Yuzbasha: the lieutenant gets to hear his favorite singer perform.

GLOSSARY HELPS

babam: my father; my dad.
papaz: priest; a minister of eastern churches.
Pera: district reserved for foreigners, north of the Golden Horn.
sharkaja: singer; performer.
tamom: okay; I agree; all right.

MORNING CHORES

"Up, up, you can't sleep all day in this house," proclaimed the lanky host of the drinking bout the night before. "We need the stove for porridge." Behind him wife and daughter were busy mixing and pounding ingredients in a pestle. Their happy chatter ignored the confrontation, although the girl stole a glance or two and giggled at the sight of the protesting guest; fully dressed the way he had slept all night. Igor found himself routed out of bed, off the oven at dawn.

"It isn't civilized to drink half the night and then wake with the sun," he shouted. But the host had rolled up the covers and pulled the frame off to set it on the rafters of the hut, out of the way.

"Best get to the milking, Luvya," he shouted to the girl, "Our friend Igor will fork down the hay." He motioned toward the open doorway that separated the animals from the people. Warmth and pungent smells penetrated the room from the adjoining barn. The girl grabbed a pail and disappeared through the doorway. Igor stood irresolute trying to clear his head. The wife and man exchange looks of amusement and the farmer said kindly. "The fork is on the wall behind the door. You'll get the hang of it quick enough." Seeing protest as futile, Igor moved clumsily toward the doorway. From outside came the girl's voice singing as she milked.

1. Farmers work from dawn to dusk,
If they want to eat they must.
Work, they work most all the day.
Night's the time for fun and play.

Chorus:

I just love to work with you
And I know you'll love it too
Work with splendid harmony
We will finish all you'll see.

2. Sing our work songs all day through,
That is what we like to do.
God will keep us brave and strong,
Teach with love, when we are wrong.

Chorus:

Igor plied his wooden fork with vigor while Luvya continued singing. This time he joined her on the chorus and then improvised a verse, which they laughingly followed with the chorus.

3. Sing together as we work,
Try to match the singing lark.
Keeps us working until dark,
Night will come when we can spark.

Chorus:

FARMERS WORK

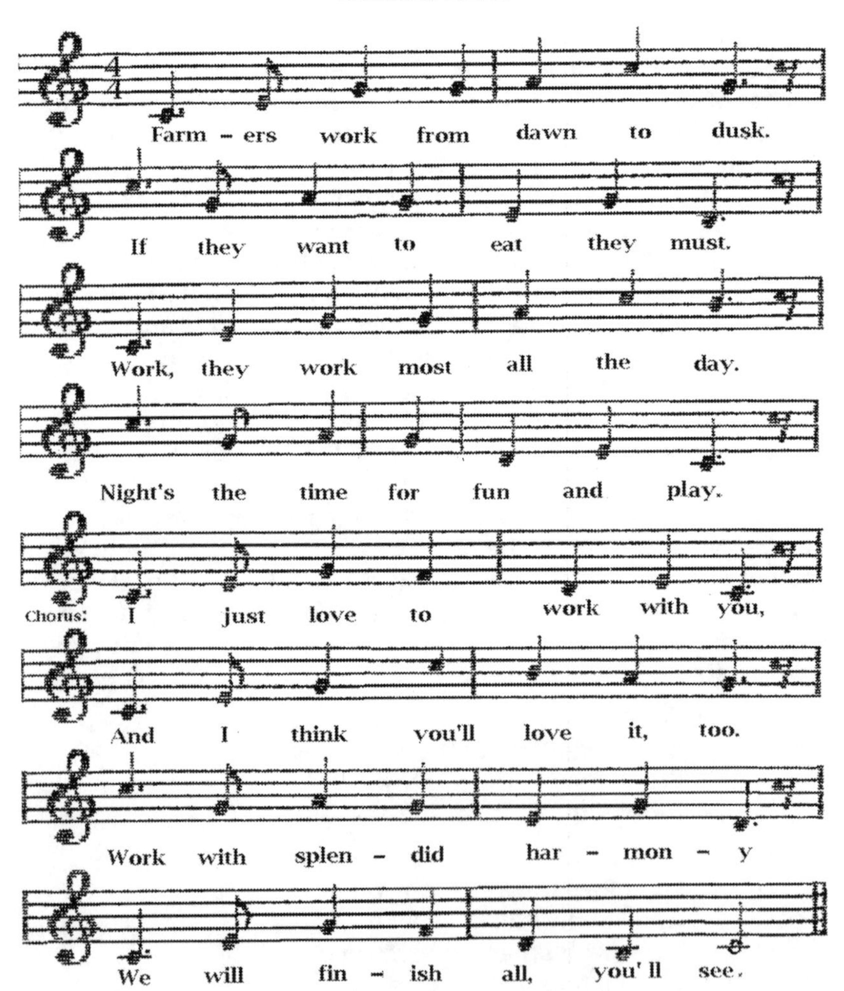

Farmer Rukam came in to muck out the stalls and stack the manure to dry for fuel. Next he went out to cut wood from the pile. Igor joined him with a hatchet. He waved as he saw Kaya and Ozkurt leaving each with a group of men armed for hunting. Kaya rode over to talk while Ozkurt rode across the river and went back the way they had come.

"What are you doing?" Inquired Igor, "You forgot something, left behind yesterday?"

Kaya laughed appreciatively. "He will check our trail to see if we are followed and, also, if we missed any game."

"Then where are you going?" Igor continued.

"We will scout north for game and do some target practice with other exercises. We'll do them everyday when there are no storms."

"Yes, I've watched your military practices coming here this fall, but don't you take time off in winter?" Igor inquired.

"Only if the enemy promises not to attack in that season, and if we could believe his promise." Kaya exclaimed laughing.

Igor waved him away, "Tamom, okay, but don't shoot any wolves."

"You have my word on it, as long as they keep their place. No one likes angry ancestors on their trail, stealing their meat."

Igor knew now that war practice would go on all winter, but not near the village where it would make people nervous. With the men gone he sent Luvya over to help Fewsoon. She carried some butter they made that morning. Fewsoon was cleaning about the yurt-like dwelling. Seeing this, the bride whose house they occupied, also visited. She removed some things from the bridal chest. They comforted her when she cried over the changes and use of furnishings. Fewsoon pointed out that when they left everything could be put back as it had been. After all they would be able to buy many things with the gold being paid. This seemed to make things right and the bride, for that is what they called her, admitted she liked some of the changes. They talked about the increase of refugees and their stories of Hun atrocities. Villages were being burned on the plains and into the marshes. Koosta advanced on a broad front. Everyone was going north. They talked of village affairs and gossip.

They did Fewsoon's hair before they left and agreed to do Luvya's tomorrow. A pattern had been set for the winter.

> - - - - - - - >

Yuzbasha was feeling high and successful as he moved toward the place of invitation. Everything was full of promise, he thought. He had won on his gambling at the chariot races, and at the gaming tables last night. He could look forward to the food, and especially the artist and her presentation. He patted his new knife and remembered Merien's look of shock and the feeling of delight and desire it produced in him. It recalled to mind his boredom associated with his work. He had no opportunity for action or command. Hard travel had its rewards, but little else could live up to the present day.

He had bought flowers that were to be delivered to the *sharkaja*, singer's dressing room door. He had borrowed cash to see her other performances, this time the ministry would pay. He hoped she would remember him from the previous visits. The sun sank and the chilling wind from the west set a cold blue tone to the sky. The streets were emptying of the evening crowds hurrying home before dark. Night in the largest city of the Western world carried special interests, risks and dangers. But young Yuzbasha would have welcomed, confidently, such an occasion for the excitement. The minister's official home was open and guards stood at the entrance for control. A secretary waited to confirm rank and invitations. Yuzbasha was delighted to see several younger men present among the largely mature to elderly figures there. A smaller number of ladies appeared around the hostess at one end of the room. She stood by the door of a salon where the ladies would meet to enjoy talk and mild drinks, while the husbands took the stronger stuff with the other men. Servants and guards, dressed in uniforms stood by to assist the assembled guests. They were there to promote sociability, and to prevent friction.

The men talked of politics, war and smaller victories in work or play. The women talked of marriage, children, and home incidents. Of course, also mentioning clothes, scandal and other women. These two worlds make up a whole society with traditions, opinions and discerning judgment on all matters that affect the common good. This particular group was governmental and therefore, more self-important and keen. All shared a moment of analyzing the person, intent and condition of rival powers from near and far. It gave the invited foreigners a glimpse of the power and wit of those they came to deal with as friend or foe.

The star of the evening appeared dressed in shimmering Byzantine fashion, daringly dressed in royal purple velvet trimmings and a fur cape. Her jewels shone in the oil lamps' light. A jeweled cross adorned her neck, and there were rings on every finger. She dressed extravagantly for the women, but would sing for the men. Her hair was a mass of curls spilling in artful confusion down her neck. Her voice was a mellow contralto, warm and passionate. She poised before the small orchestra which struck up a lively introduction. She swayed and shimmered with the rhythm of it. Her hands floated before her artistically. The men, collectively, sighed in admiration and the women in envy. Yuzbasha stood paralyzed and unconscious of those around him: his heart in his face.

1. From my window, I see your face.
   You look and sigh as you pass by.
   A hundred times, here in this place,
   I wait to cry, and wonder why.

Chorus:

Life is so full of sighs and whys,
First your heart sings, and then it cries.
Foiled by deceit and stung by lies,
Yet, I see passion in your eyes.

FROM MY WINDOW

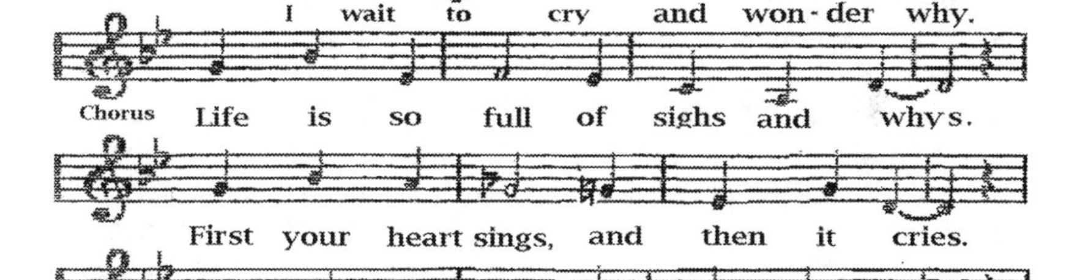

Foiled by de - ceit and stung by lies,
Yet I see pas - sion in your eyes.

2. Sweetly my bird sings in her cage,
   Water and food I all supply,
   And yet her wings she beats with rage,
   To see wild birds go flying by. Chorus:

3. Spices and flowers grow in pots.
   They show from my window all day,
   Each needs its care, I water lots,
   They send their warm color your way. Chorus:

All were mesmerized as she paused and circulated, while she still kept rhythm to the music and cast glances that feigned shyness or coy love play. She danced near the transfixed Yuzbasha and from only a few feet away kissed the tips of her fingers to blow him a kiss. Envy flashed across the men's faces. She laughed and returned to the orchestra. Her shoulders quivering as she danced. Every eye was fixed upon her.

4. Small boats that ply the Bosphorus way
   From big ships, wisely keep away.
   In my small life, my joys each day,
   Must with your passion fear to play. Chorus:

Cheers of approval erupted. The minister himself led the star, Miakim away through the admiring, congratulating men, to the waiting ladies. They whisked her away to the powder room for a discussion of dress and hair.

The pause was only that, the orchestra struck up a new number. A dancer appeared with tiny cymbals fixed on thumb and middle finger. Clicking the new rhythm, she attracted the chattering audience to her slinky entrance with long, low steps to begin from a half-crouch a series of swirls and gestures. Then she went into an athletic display of splits and stands to settle into a rhythmic belly dance. The bouquet of small ribbons on the hip emphasized every shake and twist. All the men and even a few women gave her the once over before dividing into two interest groups again. The men watched the gymnastic art dancing with amused approval and good-natured jests. But the sessions of gyrating display evoked hypnotic fixation.

Miakim soon found reasons to leave the admiring women and to find the room reserved for her use. There, her little maid waited to bring her the news. Three gifts had come and she had them on the vanity before the silvered mirror. Miakim reached for the long jewel case with only a glance at the rectangular porcelain pot of blooming lavender. A small silvered mirror was fastened to an axel that rotated. It was supported by two arms of bronze cyclamen flowers. The stems rise from the ends of the ornate rectangular pot, where bronze leaves completed the design.

She, however, preferred her larger fixed mirror. She gasped at the string of pearls in the jewel box, and hastily dropped them over her head to admire. She opened the ring box and added its content to adorn her already glittering fingers. The emerald stone matched her eyes. She sighed in contentment. She opened the door, and stepped through it to return for another song to her appreciative audience. She turned to give last instructions to her obliging little attendant. "Ifrah, tell the prince that the night is his for a song, and promise the general a future date; after Sunday, when I have had time to have my soul wiped clean by the papaz. Who sent the flowers?"

"A Khazar Yuzbasha, he's a regular at your theater showings."

"Five years ago, it would have been a great treat, but life is passing and I haven't time for the star-struck. I have to make my pile now, for later." She shook her head, "You take it or return it to him as you like. I can't be bothered." She ran to the stage entrance as a young man in uniform approached her. His face wore a strange expression. It made her afraid.

> - - - - - - - >

Yuzbasha was silent on his return to the Pera side and the Uncle's residence which had small rooms out back for the servants and dependants of the ambassador's staff. He placed the pot of flowers with the mirror on the table in his small room. He had retrieved it later, stealing in and out of her room, as he had in earlier days when he possessed himself of a comb she used, for his treasure. Now he regarded his retrieved mirror and grated out his vow. "I have received double insults from the bitches of this town." He addressed the mirror as if it could hear his vow. "You have opened my eyes to the shallowness of one, now you will close the eyes of the other that I may have my full vengeance on both." He would put a plan into action after work next day. A desire for inflicting pain and fear became the object of his focus.

> - - - - - - - >

"Well done Sertol." Kaya proclaimed, "You haven't forgotten the uses of the round shield. On horseback with a bow, you can't handle something large and clumsy. This alone will give you the protection you need. It's also handy as a weapon of offence. The edges leave a cut or bruise where they strike. Let's do the exercise once again. I'll shoot the wood knob arrows and you deflect them."

"Let me do it," Sertol's father offered. "I'll teach him to keep a sharp eye out. There'll be no moody dreaming, when daddy takes the bow." The father laughed, adding, "I'll give him a drubbing."

The boy lifted his head proudly. "You'll find no bruises on me today, *Babam*."

> - - - - - - - >

A young boy was walking toward the door of the house when Yuzbasha standing on the street asked. "Can you tell me the name of the street here? I'm looking for the Papasian house."

"This is the Papasian house on Tulip Street," Stefen indicated. "My father is in Yalta, Aunt Magda handles all business. Why do you seek us?" The boy studied the uniform and face of the man. "You're Khazar aren't you? You must work at the embassy here."

Yuzbasha pressed a wrapped package on the boy, "This is a gift from one of my comrades. We're guards. He's too shy to come himself, but he maneuvered me into bringing it for him. He won't let me give his name, but the package is for the lady of the house. You must carry it just as I gave it to you. Don't tip it over, understand?"

The boy nodded but objected, "You had better stay while I go tell her all this. She may not want to accept a gift from an unnamed admirer. She is fussy about some things."

"Let her give it to another if she scorns it. It's a woman's thing: useless for me. I have a duty to perform and must be present soon." On this he walked away leaving turmoil behind him in the Papasian house.

GIFT MIRROR

PEOPLE, PLACES & PLOTS IN CHAPTER 4

Fewsoon: tries to save a friend's wedding gifts.
Ifrah: warns her mistress of possible dangers.
Igor: overhears the villagers plotting to kill his friends.
Kaya: is forced to leave their winter haven and discourage pursuit.
Koosta: the general leads his army across the Polish Plains.
Magda: her logic leads her to a wishful dream.
Merien: writes a friend about news from the capital.
Miakim: receives an offer for her services hard to refuse.
Minister of the Interior: pays gold for information and hires a spy.
Ozkurt: bored with winter, awakes to find more than he expects.
Sertol: practicing to be a warrior, finds occasion for action.
Stefen: failed to notice the purpose and destination of a gift.
Village groom: suffers when he tries to attack the Turks.
Village headman: distrusts all horsemen, but loves gold.

GLOSSARY HELPS

bar'ish: peace; let's not argue; calm down; be reconciled.
beyler: gentlemen; officers; sir (plural).
choke yashar: long live; many years; long life to him.
hurmet lee: with glory; exalted.
soos: hush; be quiet; don't talk.

4 SPRING RETREAT

EARLY ESCAPE

"He said it was for the Lady of the house and I forgot to ask which, Magda. I told him father was in Yalta and you handled all business. He is part of the Khazar embassy, a guard he said." Magda unwrapped the package, while Merien protested vigorously and angrily.

"You know there were only three on the boat, Magda. I wouldn't touch anything that Yuzbasha gave me, no!" She sniffed indignantly.

"Why would a young man go speak for another and not for himself? Why be shy if you are young and courting? Youth are bold, age is shy. The Chavush had several occasions to speak with me at Alushka and on the voyage after that. He came to my couch to talk at the banquet. An older man would prevail on a younger to do his bidding. Age fears rejection or insult. Let's see what it is, ahh...! " She held up a rectangular ceramic pot of blooming lavender that held the frame of a rectangular mirror of bronze and polished silver plating on the face of it. Magda melted as she inhaled the fragrant aroma and looked into the mirror. "See," she whispered, "I'm really rather well preserved, don't you think?"

>- - - - - - - >

It was in the cold of the pre-dawn darkness of spring when a sound awakened Kaya. He lay half aroused and half dreaming. Again he heard something; stealthy steps moved toward the door of the hut. The horses were awake and making quiet sounds, listening too, from their part of the hut. One or two of the men started awake as the door was pressed experimentally. It was locked, but the bar started to work back slowly.

"Some one seeks to enter undetected," Ozkurt breathed drawing his knife and taking position behind the door. Kaya joined him listening intently, mouth open sniffing the air. The bar slid another inch. It was being opened by a knife point worked through a crack. It

moved again soundlessly. Kaya moved quietly to the barred door and after a wait, listening again, slid it open and tried to open the door carefully without sound. A squat figure stood in the blackness. Kaya breathed the name of Igor, and taking the knife from his friend's hand, stepped back from the door. The figure moved unsteadily into the room as the hands of the troop whisked over his body for weapons. Inside Igor's whisper penetrated every corner of the hut.

"The elders have decided to capture you for reward. An army of a thousand Huns rides two days away, and they are raiding villages where they think we have passed. A man came bearing the news for the village to flee north before their arrival. Now they are drunk and divided as to the best course to follow. The majority think that your capture or death would remove the threat and might be rewarded."
"They told you this?" Kaya questioned.

"I seemed asleep, drunk on the bed while they talked of these things. The messenger was reluctant to give his news because of your rescue three months ago, but it was too important to hide. They are of a timid nature, but fierce when drunk. You can beat them in equal combat, but they will burn you out, and kill those who emerge. They have gone to their homes to prepare."

"We, too, will prepare now," said Kaya, "Take all the food for provisions. Ransack the house for it will burn anyway." Two guards were posted outside while the horses were loaded for flight. The band worked grimly to prepare their escape.

One of the men made a remark in Chipchak, which brought chuckles of approval from the working men.

"What did he say?" Igor asked, worried.

"He said we should be better off had we allowed the ancestors to look after our interests." Kaya shrugged and chuckled again.

"Kaya, come here," the voice of Fewsoon was crisp. "Look, here are her wedding presents and trousseau," she pointed to a small trunk of polished wood. "We can't let it burn."

Kaya nodded, but did not enter the partitioned room where they had slept. He moved toward the barn entrance. "They are doing the burning, and everything will go by Hun or whoever's hand." He turned his back, "The first group had better start now." Ozkurt and four men stood at the barn door with bows strung and ready.

Kaya gave orders. "Remember, a wounded man will distract others and draw men from pursuit. They lower morale and zest; dead men require no immediate attention, anger the living, and make pursuit more determined." He pulled open the door. "Secure the edge of the wood and protect our withdrawal." He whispered gazing into the pale foggy light of early morning.

As the group filed out of the barn with long stealthy strides, there came a muffled shout from the woods adjoining the neighboring house. It was answered by a drunken shouting below the house.

Ozkurt reached the woods as other shouts were raised. From the woods came the howl of the grey wolf calling the pack. Immediately an unexpected, answering howl came from the hill above the village. At the signal a body of horse poured from the barn and ran toward the wood. Not all were mounted. Several led their horses. The last figure ran leaning over as if wounded or burdened.

At the edge of the woods the shape of a tall villager leaped out beside the bent figure leading the horse. He raised a small hand sickle above his head. Fewsoon dropped her burden and leaped back toward the horse, that shied and ran on. She caught it's tail and ran after it. The man running forward, tripped on the burden she had dropped. There was a firm wooden thump and a howl from the village groom as he fell sprawling in the shadow of the wood. At the same moment an arrow passed harmlessly above his form.

The running horse reached the others being urged up the trail. Fewsoon followed unharmed. Kaya had waited on Altom till all the men were ahead on the trail. He helped her up behind him in one strong swing, and then rode away as she clung, laughing, to his waist. He too, started to laugh. “You brought the trunk of wedding goods,” he laughed.

“But the groom has fallen heir to it again. He can never lose her now.” Fewsoon chortled.

“It saved his life,” Kaya observed. “He could have broken a leg.”

“We pray he didn’t break a leg. They might starve.” she added.

“At least valuable goods did not burn. It would have broken her heart.” Fewsoon concluded as they pressed north. Behind them they heard the sounds of cursing, blame and pursuit.

>- - - - - - - >

Meanwhile, in a large elaborately furnished tent, final instructions were being issued to the officers of the Hunnish army.

“The army has crossed the Polish Plains, *Beyler*, but contact with the exiles eludes us. Reports from the army posts and villages they passed make the Prepet Marshes a likely spot for their necessary winter quarters. We must not let the weather slow our advances.

“We will catch and punish the man who wears the ivory swan badge. We are on the edge of the subjected villages. North and east there are people encroaching on land, that should by rights belong to our empire. Tanra has blessed our people with victory. What further evidence of his favor do we need? Horsemen rule the world forever.”

“Keep the scouts out in front of our advance. We will flush them out of the swamps and woods and send their heads to our powerful, all conquering Khan.” At this point, the men took up the challenge with enthusiasm, as they cheered and shouted together. “*Choke yahsar*, long live Munzur Khan! Death to the forest people!, *Hurmet lee*, Binbasha Koosta! Glory to general Koosta! Ride on to victory!”

>- - - - - - - >

"You may be sure the Basileus, Emperor, will make it worth your while," the magistrate of interior affairs said suavely. "Our new ally is growing too fast for our comfort. Prince Ilkin's secret agreement with the Huns is not well understood by us. Khazar gains seem to involve no large battles, but the landings and movement up the Donetz was an easy victory this spring with no defeats for either side. We have secured a few ports in the Crimea from the Huns, but the politics of the situation is unlike the usual terror and slaughter policy of the Huns."

"What does the Basileus expect me to do about such important matters?" responded Miakim, the actress and singer. "My talents lie in another direction," she continued. "Prince Ilkin is ill and has a wife."

"The assistant to the Khazar ambassador is clearly enamored and attends all your presentations. He should be easy to sway. This summer and fall he has reconnoitered most of our navel and military positions. Now in winter he is bored, enclosed in the city with little cash, and time to kill. You fill his eyes. It shouldn't be difficult to fill his time, and we have given him several sources of revenue that he can earn enough to sacrifice a few things for comfort."

"How do you propose to reward me?" she queried, smiling.

"Gold coins for every meeting, and also for the hours spent together."

"Will I be guaranteed protection?" she asked remembering his anger at the reception. "Why should the minister of the interior propose these steps concerning foreign affairs?"

"You will be followed and protected every moment. The public would never forgive carelessness on our part. I direct the police department, the other minister has too many eyes on him to attempt something like this. The young man is simple and venial, as we have already learned. Your task will be easy. He thinks himself the hero of an encounter with pirates. He loves to tell the story. Spring is coming soon; a natural time for love. We require only the information, what you do to obtain it is up to you." He settled back comfortably while she thought over the situation. She had found a white hair at her temple that morning and pulled it with anger, but it was a harbinger of fate. Time was fleeting away and she had not had the urge for security until lately. So, she had not saved.

"I will send him a ticket for a special seat at my next performance." she assured him. "I owe the Centurion, that is, Yuzbasha an, apology."

>- - - - - - - >

Then they all heard it clearly. To the west of the village, a horse whinnied. Silence followed in the band and in the village. Another player had entered the stage.

Immediately Kaya motioned one of the dismounted men to go investigate. Igor, being adept in the forest, went with them. The band now moved silently up the trail. The new danger had saved them from pursuit by villagers.

"How do you explain the wolf call in answer to our `come ahead' signal?" Asked Ozkurt curiously, holding the nose of his horse lest it try to answer the neigh.

"You worry about the ancestors. I'm worried about the Huns. It has to be a scouting group," Kaya replied, releasing Fewsoon to mount her own horse.

"The farmers have regrouped to meet the Huns. They are confused and don't know whether to fight or flee." The rearguard said as he caught up to the group.

"There is an advanced party of ten Huns coming out of the forest from the west. They are uncertain whether to attack the village or offer peace for information. They heard the brawl," Igor supplied as he slipped back to the group. "I left one man there to watch."

"They must not report back to the main body. Take or kill the horses." Kaya ordered.

Ozkurt smiled happily. "So the ancestors get a banquet too, today. They'll find it worth waiting for." He unlimbered his bow.

"There is a trail west that will put us behind them, up by the creek, just north of here," Igor said. While he frowned his disapproval of Ozkurt's words, he was undecided on how to reprove him. He clutched a short handled axe in his hands.

"Lead, we will follow, and silence all of you," Kaya said as he urged his horse after the running form of Igor. "Stay with the loaded horses, Fewsoon, get Sertol to help you. Follow the trail north." She gathered the reins and walked ahead of the animals. Over half the men ran without horses to attack. Sertol took their horses west, after them, to be close for a rapid getaway. He also armed his bow hoping to get in a few shots.

The mounted Huns were distracted in the parley with the villagers. They learned that they had just missed their prey, who had escaped the hands of the village to continue north. They got a description of the party and a head count. Then, while they consulted among themselves about procedure: breakfast, pillage or pursuit, they were hit from behind.

The first volley of arrows from hidden men came with a shout from Kaya. It took their horses from under them. All was confusion and dust with the scream of wounded horses and shouts of men trying to control the plunging and falling animals. The mounted herdsman who guarded the spare mounts and pack animals behind the main body found himself pinched between two mounted Chipchaks who lifted him bodily and threw him over his horse's head. The riders wheeled and took the whole herd off, before the guard could regain his feet. Two other Chipchaks came behind yipping and urging the herd away. The few mounted horses who survived the first volley went down in the immediate second. A few of the guards who reacted and armed too swiftly, suffered slight wounds as the attackers melted back into the forest.

The villagers rushed forward as if to defend the Huns and drive away the attackers. Then, helping the wounded, they triumphantly led them to the vacated house. Some returned to butcher the dead horses, to feed the extra mouths. The wolves would not have it all. The bride's box was moved, happily, to the father-in-law's house. The village that sheltered Kaya's band all winter would be safe now.

>- - - - - - - >

My dearest Lady Judith,
Thanks for your early note. I'm glad the spring has opened the river for boats, yes. Here we are enjoying a brilliant social season and Aunt Magda is suddenly a social lioness. She dresses richly and goes to all the international functions and parties, yes. She even talks to the Khazars, whom she vowed never to speak to again, after our boat ride on the Sea Witch over a year ago. Bomba, no?

There is talk again of establishing Kertch Port as a neutral city of trade. This excites me, but Magda doesn't show much interest yet, no. Sarayjik reports that General Koosta plans to reach the Volga in his pursuit of the forest people, but the gains for empire are few. Expenses and jealousy grow in the capital. Princess Yetkin has recovered, somewhat, from her winter illness. There are rumors of marriage for her again, but politics always changes marriage plans, no?

Olga, queen of the East Goths, waits impatiently for her baby's arrival, yes! We pray that the so called spies have escaped Koosta, and are somewhere over the Volga River. They could come as far as Getchit City, on their return, no? Their escape is always at risk with costs, yes. I would love to know Lady Fewsoon, yes.

If I return to Ketch Port, I will come to visit at Don River Estates. We will have much fun ,no? I pray your peace and prosperity.

Merien Papasian

>- - - - - - - >

They pressed northeast through the frozen marsh lands and into the sandy hills and forests, yet their pursuit stayed doggedly on their trail. Rations were controlled, and they ate the weaker extra horses first, but their dry food ended and they rode hungry. Even the few remaining strong horses suffered as the meadows were lost to an increasing number of coniferous forest and bogs. They were entering the taiga.

"We are all dead if we don't get to the great mother of waters and away from this watershed. We will get a raft or boat and escape east. Once on the water they will never catch us," Igor promised, trying to keep them traveling into the unknown north. Away from the steppes the Chipchak tended to get as depressed as their horses.

"We may have moved too far north," Igor worried. People fled them, and villages were only empty huts. In one they found a fat, old hag, too weak to hide. She consented to talk. She was Suomi from a Finnish tribe, and spoke bits of Slavic as well. She welcomed Igor to Portageland. Lake Ilmen was northwest she directed. The west flowing Drina was near and the brooks flowing east were going to the mother of rivers, the Volga. She sent him southeast with advice.

"You are hungry, and I have no food. You will find your food there and your guide to the great river," she promised. She indicated Kaya and Fewsoon. "Your leader is destined for greatness. And you too, are destined to serve greatly." She paused, peering through hooded eyes, "He serves best who gives all. One who searches finds a magic word," she said enigmatically. Igor emptied his ration bag into her lap and empty, moved away.

Within sight of the hut, they saw a herd of elk passing a hilltop trail. The animals were migrating east the way the band was sent and the hunt started enthusiastically. They spread into a crescent moon formation and walked leading the horses. They would not frighten their prey too soon. They needed to be close before stalking or rushing them. They moved through a forested valley where the stream moved eastward. Some of the men stalking, shot two yearling calves from the herd, and that week they ate well. They stayed in an abandoned village as the days grew longer. When the meat finished they moved on always toward the rising sun.

Before them a large river flowed east, the current was too fast to be frozen over, but the edges and marsh areas were ice. They took the easy but exposed south bank as highway and continued looking for a spot to cross. When they did not find it, they started to believe what Igor had been continually telling them; "This is the Mother of Rivers. There are men who live by taking people across the river. We must find one in order to get to the north. They will also know if there are rafts or boats going east," Igor assured them. There were river meadows of withered old and bright new grass and the horses started looking better.

LIFTED AND LEFT

PEOPLE, PLACES & PLOTS IN CHAPTER 5

Fewsoon: endures the retreat and raid, gathering treasures.
Ifrah: the maid fears and distrusts all foreign soldiers.
Igor: avenges the village women and hunts boats.
Kaya: passes from horse play to serious confrontation.
Kove: the Tartar takes time to confer with the enemy.
Miakim: the actress has confidence in her ability with men.
Ozkurt: finds excitement in an alien environment.
Sertol: has an opportunity to learn warfare.
Villagers: are caught by the Huns, yet wait for freedom.
Yuzbasha the Khazar: plans revenge and conquests.

GLOSSARY HELPS

barish: peace; cease hostilities.
has zur'ole: get ready; be prepared; word used to start a game.
hoe'sh gel deniz: welcome; happily you've come.
hoe'sh boll duke: happily we've found you; thanks for the welcome.
so'ooze: you promise? Your word on it?
so'ooze-um: my word on it. I promise.
who-jews': charge; rush forward; have at 'em.

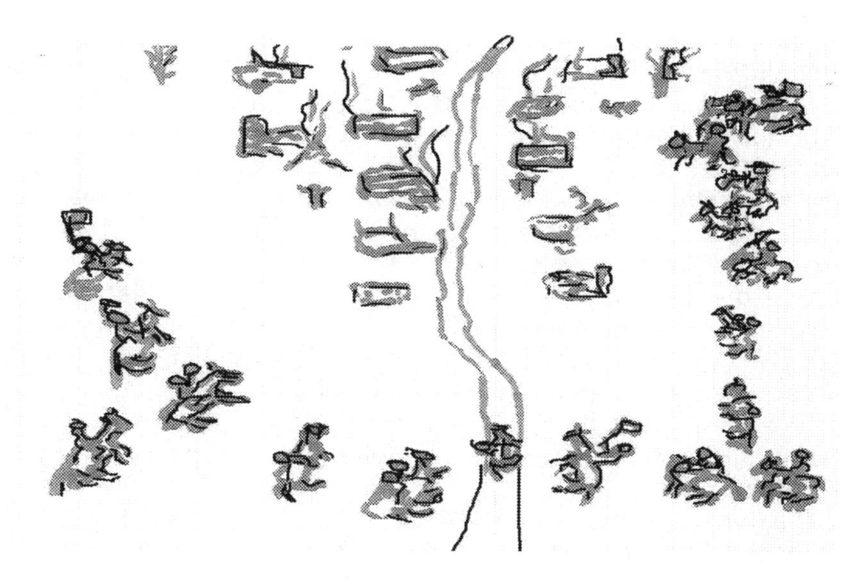

THE BURNED VILLAGE

"It's generous of you, Yuzbasha, to forgive my slight. I regretted it almost Immediately. I tried to send a note, but the message surely went astray. Thankfully, I welcome your return to your favorite seat." But she discovered to her surprise that she was nervous and apprehensive with this strange northerner. He was staring at her now and she was uncertain if it was passion, or controlled hate that blazed in his eyes. He spoke haltingly and again surprised her.

"Your slight was deserved. My gift was not worthy. I presumed too much. I left it for safe keeping with a simple soul, until I collect it later."

His voice and body conveyed humility, but the eyes blazed with pride, a vein pulsed in his temple. "I'm a man who always takes care to collect what's due me."

"You must feel free to visit me here back stage before or after a performance," she invited, and wondered if she would be afraid to have him in her dressing room. "Come," she urged, "tell me something about your homeland and work. I've always lived in this city."

>- - - - - - - >

"The Huns have been here before us and have left nothing useful." Kaya stared at the smoking remains of a charred village. They had seen the smoke as a tiny smudge on the eastern sky with the sun behind it and now in the afternoon the site reached, they could see the damage.

"Perhaps they have withdrawn with the loot," ventured Ozkurt, hopefully. Fewsoon moved her head up in a Chipchak negative

"They would stay a day to enjoy the gains and to sort the valuables. The forest folk are weak, and they would fear no reprisals. It is good that we are in battle formation, husband. You will have need of it." Her eyes scanned the visible part of the crescent moon of which they four formed the center.

"Look, a scout waves a flag. What does it mean?" asked Igor. Ozkurt raised a square flag of material in answer. The scout waved another different colored flag and Ozkurt answered it and the whole right wing of the moon wheeled and shifted forward quickly. They now faced the wood and meadow by the river. From that area they could now hear the sound of screams and shouts.

"*Has-our' ole*, get ready. No quarters." Kaya stated. Fewsoon armed her bow and Igor took out his hatchet. Kaya raised a triangular piece of colored cloth and two men left the formation to face away, behind them. They were rearguard to keep the backs of the warriors safe.

"*Who-jews'*, charge," was said in a soft whisper, for Igor's benefit, as Ozkurt held up another square of cloth. Command was by sight and not by sound here.

The Huns had not even posted a guard, so great was their confidence. Masses of drunken and unkempt warriors were wandering between tents of merchandise and tents of women slaves and a guarded mob of children to be sent off to camp centers. The Huns compared the small treasures they were allowed to keep, and they passed to admire the large treasures that were separated for the Khan. They massed around the tents where women, screaming, crying and gasping, were gang raped. But largely they drank: captured beers and their own supply of beverage. Drinking, they gambled their small gains, for the village was poor by their standards, and the goods near worthless in their estimation .There were over a hundred warriors in the Hunnish force, but they were scattered, and some sleeping and resting from their hard marches and dawn attack. The horses were hobbled on the meadow, grazing new and withered hay.

The flag of death was held by Ozkurt. They would take no one prisoner. The horns of the moon formation and body rode forward at a run. When the horns of the moon reached the river they turned in toward the river banks and in line they swept the water front till meeting they turned toward the center, as they swept in by surprise. Men died.

The horsemen dodged among working old women, carrying buckets of water, and Slav men lifting bundles. These were bypassed and only armed men were shafted in the body or neck. Before the tents the body of horse drew up and fired another volley into the mass of soldiers, before deflecting to the right and on to the meadow where feeding horses were now rearing and excitedly nickering. Some broke their bonds and thundered off. Others were cut free of halter or hobble and scattered after them. One herd was stampeded through the tents by Kaya's core of troopers, who then sent other volleys of arrows into the crowds thus exposed. Everywhere men died in a hail of arrows.

The camp had sobered rapidly, but the wounded and armed alike were in no condition to fight. The children had run screaming to the woods and the working captives had taken arms and followed. Some were avenging themselves in the process of arming from the dead or wounded. The ravaged women tried to follow the cries of the fleeing children, calling as they ran or dragging themselves away hardly able to walk.

Igor had dismounted by the tent where the women screamed and ran. He laid about him with the axe and carved a path to the mouth of the tent, where he remained and killed every man who emerged from the brothel. A rumpled, but richly dressed woman emerged, bearing up another. She spoke to Igor briefly, and then he helped bear the woman away to the woods. No warrior dared bar their way.

Behind them, the remaining Hun tents were set fire by the main body of attackers. One of the troops of Kaya's men took possession of the armory tent. He carried off all available arrows, firing the tent. The other troop took over the kitchen and its goods. Again burning the supplies, all withdrew, loaded with plunder, to the meadow. There they sat down and ate.

>- - - - - - - >

"The Khazar is back in his usual seat, and with these flowers, my lady. He is again at your feet." Miakim's little attendant reported.

"Yes, Ifrah, it seems all is forgiven. We're going out for a picnic to the forest on Sunday. He promises a gift and surprise worthy of me." She smiled into her lamp lit mirror.

"I would be nervous to go out to the woods so soon madam. He is an impetuous heathen from a barbaric nation. Can you trust him?"

"I'm confident that I can manage men of every kind. Don't worry."

>- - - - - - - >

SPY'S REPORT

Kaya's rearguard and some of the younger men, avid for glory, gathered to harry the Huns who had survived and were grouping around the burning armory. Wounded and well, the Huns gathered to arm and repel further attacks. About thirty men stood back to back while wounded limped, staggered or crawled to get to the growing circle. Both groups made forays to plunder the dead of weapons or valuables, while shouting insults and engaging in short bursts of fighting, but the Chipchaks on horses had the advantage of that as well. In a short time the Chipchaks had finished their happy victory celebration meal. They joined the harassment of forty well and wounded Huns in a position on high ground. Most with gut wounds would die during the night. Those who had lost much blood would be tormented by fevers and infection, suffering agony without water. But they would hold their position. Twenty mounted warriors couldn't force their lines now that they were ready.

Kaya had again posted sentinels behind the village. He had no desire to be taken by an unexpected arrival. He waited for Igor to reappear. He needed his spokesman in this new northern land. He dispatched a third of his force to take the horse herd and move eastward, but there would be more Huns soon. They will have seen from afar the smoke of the burning village and will expect good news. If some Huns reached the woods unharmed, they will carry the unexpected news and bring in a cloud of raging horsemen.

"Why is he taking so long? Has he abandoned us?" inquired Ozkurt, irritably. "He must know we can't stay long. It will be night soon."

"Igor will come, don't fear." Fewsoon spoke soothingly. "The Huns cooped up here will not move without horses, unless they are sure of surprise."

"They already outnumber us. What if they are reinforced?" Ozkurt looked round uneasily, "Igor's gone. I never trusted him; losing us in this forest."

"We must keep the Huns penned up, so no word is sent. The Slavs will keep the forest clear of individual messengers. Igor will search out a boat." Kaya looked completely relaxed and was humming an evening vesper. He knew the risk, but chose to ignore it for now.

He started riding Altom toward the river below the camp from the meadow side. His guards moved with him as they rode within shouting distance of the defensive circle of the Huns. The murmur from the camp rose to shouts of defiance.

"Come closer, bastards. We have accounts to settle with you." Shouts of agreement and menace followed. "You caught us with our pants down. You can't screw us again. We're ready now." A growl of agreement followed. "Send over the girl. I have something special to show her she'll like." Course chuckles, laughter and catcalls followed. "I'd like to get my hands on her." There was vigorous agreement by the crowd. One held up a long knife, "I've something long and sharp to put in you, too, commander." A defiant shout followed this statement.

Kaya's group paid no attention and moved to the river where several mounted guards were posted to keep the river side clear of Huns.

"Come," Kaya said, "grab a bucket and lets get water from the river." He rode to the river's edge and dismounting gathered two abandoned buckets and filled them. Fewsoon followed with another. Ozkurt motioned one of his men to help, but remained on horse, following with bow at ready. "Compassion for an enemy is always a weakness," Ozkurt announced to the world in general, "to renew his strength is to weaken your own." Ozkurt had put on his most sour expression. "We are fewer than they, and they are now armed."

"Water, food or music calm the wildness of even the trapped beast," Kaya quoted a saying of Maya, the medicine woman. He smiled his big, easy smile. "Besides, Yesu commands it, and we need information from them." Six buckets were carried by the three toward the circle of wounded. They stopped just at the edge of bow range and set down the buckets on the ground.

The eyes of the wounded had been gazing at the river and now had fastened on the carried buckets. The entire group had one focus; the water carried toward their defense ring. Even the groans ceased for a moment. Everyone licked their lips with dry tongue, and clutched their weapons. They were prepared to rush forward and seize the desperately needed water. It was life to them, more precious than gold or blood. It was as precious as life itself.

"*Barish*, peace, send three men for the buckets." Kaya shouted.

Hastily, several men shambled forward and one of the wounded, dressed as a lieutenant, hurried up. He looked from Kaya to Ozkurt and back, paused uncertainly and said: "*So'ooze*? You promise?"

WATER FOR WORDS

Kaya looked hard at Ozkurt, who turned his head to look at the beach. "*So'ooze um, bar'ish*, on my word, peace." Kaya repeated the words of assurance. The lieutenant was wounded near the collar-bone and did not carry any of the buckets. But he turned to command his men from where he stood. The Yuzbasha said, "Those with cups will get the first ration." A frantic search for cups started. "Those without will have to wait to borrow from a comrade." The men avidly started to dip out their drink. The Yuzbasha raised his voice once more. "Stay in your place. Don't crowd the buckets." Some were taking two dips. Pushing started near one bucket. A sergeant laid one man out flat and some water spilled. The lieutenant looked disgusted at the fray.

"By your accent you must be Turkish," said the man. "You're far from home. Why do you help the forest people?"

"We are Chipchaks from near the Altai Mountains. We feared you were pursuing us, though we have a pass from Khan Munzur. We know that there are a thousand troops following."

"They are closer and more than you know. We were to take the village and its provisions, and the column will arrive tonight. My men were over-enthusiastic and burned one hut and the whole village caught fire. They have no discipline and were plundering when you came." He turned and looked closely at Fewsoon for the first time.

Light came into his face as he took a sharp intake of air.

"You were Princess Yetkin's attendant. So you are the man who rescued her." He turned to Kaya again. "This is an honor, Sir. Your victory over the giant is told and retold over every campfire. I feel less humiliated by my loss."

"I doubt your binbasha will feel the same, if it is us whom he pursues." Kaya smiled sadly at the man. In his forties he was evidently lacking some essential qualities needed for command.

"Koosta forgives nothing and now may have my head as well as yours," the man said realistically. "My name is Kove. You must be Kaya, some add the title: The Bear." They laughed and bowed.

"*Hoe'sh gel deniz*," greeted Kove.

"*Hoe'sh boll duke*," returned Kaya as if there had been no conflict.

"I penetrated your land as far as the hermitage," stated Kove. "I was there about fifteen years ago."

"I was trained at the Hermitage," replied Kaya. "Tell me, did you travel with camels, Bactrian? The ones with two humps, you know?" His face was anxious.

"Of course what else can live that far north and still carry such loads," Kove replied. " I had a good commander whom I loved to tease, but I was not an effective officer. Too much escaped me."

Kaya smiled enigmatically, then corrected the man. "The yak carries loads farther north and in high mountains," he shrugged. "I remember your hunt. It's good for some creatures, that all men are not as perfect and strong as they would like to be. Otherwise nothing

would escape." Kaya's face was troubled and he looked pale. The interview had become awkward and he looked away.

>- - - - - - - >

"I am told you have a helpful prescription for every need, Doctor." Yuzbasha affirmed. "I have a friend who is too bashful to come. He is celebrating a 40th anniversary but wonders if he will be able to perform the necessary love making at his age. He wonders if there is something he or his wife could take to remedy the situation."

"Aphrodisiacs," laughed the doctor. "Spanish fly would do it for either one, but he must come here to be examined, there may be other complicating factors. I can't give a prescription without seeing the patient. Professional ethics preclude it."

"I'll tell my friend, Doctor," Yuzbasha concluded, "but as I said, he's dreadfully shy." Outside, Yuzbasha grinned in satisfaction as he walked toward the closest pharmacy, composing the story he'd tell. If he had lost his prescription and it were urgent... He'd need some kind of soothing tranquilizer as well. A savory sauce would have to be concocted to cover the taste.

>- - - - - - - >

"Boats on the river!" The hail of a lookout came clear. The men conferring on the riverbank parted hastily, both Kaya and Kove ran to the circle of their own men and held council. The situation would no longer be a stalemate: action would be required. All attention focused on the river. The dugouts were being swept by the current to the shore by the meadow. A man with a double-bite, hand-axe stood in the center of one. As they neared the shore, he picked up his recurved bow and armed it. Igor had returned.

BOATS FOR RESCUE

PEOPLE, PLACES & PLOTS IN CHAPTER 6

Fewsoon: finds trouble gathering jewels and choice treasures.
Ifrah: the maid worries about the safety of Miakim.
Igor: the guide disappears and returns just in time.
Kove: a Tartar captain, a mercenary in the Hun's army, but deserts.
Kaya: stays in touch with his men and the needs of the moment.
Miakim: an actress and singer in Constantinople goes on a picnic.
Ozkurt: in his glory, but discovers a stubborn streak in himself.
Sergi: a leader of the village children on the Volga River.
Sertol: gets a taste of war and an attack from Huns on the river.
Yuzbasha: the lieutenant has plans to become the lover of Miakim.

GLOSSARY HELPS

ayran: a cool drink of yogurt and water.
bar'ish: peace, truce, cease fire.
bash ooze too nay: Yes Sir; I obey; literally, it's on my head.
do'er: stop; cease; halt!
do'er-mah: Don't stop! keep on; move on.
git shim day: go now; leave immediately; take off.
goo-re'sh: fight; wrestling match; struggle.
hoe'sh gel de niz; Happily you've come; Glad you're here; Hello!
hoe'sh boll duke; Happily we've arrived. Good to be here. Hello!

RAIN OF DEATH

A mounted Chipchak guard came at full gallop across the meadow and pulled up beside Kaya shouting. All the men in his group looked suddenly to the horizon. There, above the tree tops hung a pall of dust and the sound of disturbed crows cawing, came to their ears. Something vast was moving there; an army of fighting men.

Ten of Kaya's remaining warriors ran to the meadow to change to fresh mounts, staked out there waiting. Kaya rode to the beach to await the boats. He sent Altom with Ozkurt to travel with the remaining horses, east along the river. Fewsoon and Sertol were walking by the exposed treasures, designated for the Khan, picking some jewelry; the choicest stones with gold or silver settings.

The Huns in their circle of defense saw the dust and could now feel a rumble beneath their feet. They seized their last hope of redeeming themselves with their command. When their circle broke open, the sergeant led a charge by about twenty men down toward the beach. Kove and a couple of wounded men ran toward Fewsoon.

Kaya and his two guards at the river saw the mob form and break toward them. They started a flow of arrows toward the rushing men as soon as they were in range.

Ozkurt was with his men at the meadow and they opened an enfilading, high rain of arrows shooting at a 45 degree angle up and the flights turned and fell with increasing velocity to rain among the rushing men. There was no pin point accuracy, but like rain it was hard to avoid. A good archer could keep five arrows in the air at the same time and continue it for several minutes.

The Huns were cavalrymen. Many were short of leg and heavy bodied. Their small round shields were to intercept a direct shot aimed at close range. It did not cover the body from head to foot.

The number of running men under the rain of arrows was halved once and again.

The sergeant at the head of the men was pierced by Kaya's attendants, and fell dead. Now those who tried to break out of the mob were picked off. The rain finished the others, and the charge was ended.

Kove and one of the wounded did manage to reach Fewsoon, and they took shelter behind her. They held a knife each to her throat. Kove spoke to her first. "We will not hurt you, Lady. This is to make a bargain with your husband. Stand still and don't try to run away." Kove smiled in a self-satisfied way. The charge had taken their attention while he had reached his prey.

"Kaya Bey, Order your men to stop their attack. I will not hurt your Lady, but we must talk without danger," his voice was loud and clear and the response from Kaya was equally positive.

"*Do'er*, stop," he shouted. "Gather the arrows," he indicated to the two river guards. "Go now," he shouted to Ozkurt. Seven of the men moved their horses off running east. Ozkurt and two men remained and rode nearer. Kaya moved close to Kove to talk.

The dugouts were beaching now. Igor waded ashore from the lead boat. Huns who were wounded, but not killed in the attack, walked, limped and crawled toward the defense ring on the slope, where the wounded who had remained, watched them. A few came to help.

"We have failed in our last chance of winning a reprieve for our defeat. I have no future here with this army. They will kill me if I stay.

I long for home. Take me with you, and I will see you safe through Tartar country on your trip home," Kove sheathed his knife. His wounded companion did the same as Kove continued to talk rapidly.

"Let us go in your boat. Koosta is upon us and will kill us all. We can expect no mercy, but you are a Christian, you can save us and we will be useful to you. My old commander now lives near this great river far to the south. The Tartar Khan is my relative; my family is rich and I will provision you for your safe return." The man's voice had assumed a pleading tone.

"Don't trust him, Kaya" came the voice of Ozkurt from his horse. "He is a treacherous Tartar, raider of our people, a killer of innocents." Ozkurt was beside himself with anger. Kaya wheeled round and shouted angrily.

"You are a dead fool for lingering and interfering. Their scouts will catch you this hour. *Git-shim'day*, go now." Kaya's eyes blazed black fire. One of the beach guards ran up and gave two full quivers of gathered arrows to the two guards. Ozkurt looked shocked by Kaya's outburst.

"*Bash ooze two nay*, I obey." Ozkurt called as he and his guards galloped away, following the trail of the original group.

From the wood a horn sounded and a group of advance guards emerged, leisurely, from the trees. They had expected a camp set for them and not a battle ground strewn with dead. There was stunned silence as they tried to take in the panorama of boats and fleeing horses.

"Come quickly, we've room for you," Igor's voice cut in sharply. "Two in the other boats. You, Sertol and the lady come with me in the first. The Tartars in the second and the two guards in the last." Kove matched his action with the words and running, helped Fewsoon with her bundle to the dugout.

The hill of wounded Huns burst out in boos and catcalls when they saw the two Tartars run and enter a boat. "Traitors!" "Turncoats!" "Treacherous bastards!" "Cowards!" and other insults were launched at them. Several who had bows tried to close the distance and shoot arrows.

The advanced guard divided into two bodies and one descended on the river while the other galloped after the fleeing horses, arming their bows for action. As they crossed the meadow the camp wounded gave a great shout of triumph. They danced and cheered.

From the river side the riding band launched arrows, the dugouts were already in the main current and rapidly moving beyond arrow range. Kaya leaned forward with his small round shield and deflected an arrow from Fewsoon. Another dug into the prow. From the second boat a cry of pain announced that some arrows from the advance guards had found a target.

The boats pulled parallel to each other and the wounded Tartar, now dead with an arrow through his chest, was lowered into the water to lighten the boat. From the river side they could hear the sounds of hard riding and the occasional twang of bow strings. Twice came the scream of pain and death and the fall of bodies or horses in the woods.

Suddenly there came the multiple twang of bows, and a shout of surprise. Then came more screams of pain and death. The pursuing Huns had been ambushed by the seven as Ozkurt and guards had passed by, running hard. From the confused sounds of battle came the sound of two or three horses retreating, running upstream again. They would return soon with reinforcements, Kaya thought. He shouted toward the woods. "*Do'er-mah*, don't stop." He bellowed to be heard above the hubbub of congratulations, laughter and comments of the ten men. "Another squad is coming. Get on with the herd." He had to yell twice to get their attention.

"Lose them, no more fighting. Build a protected fire facing the water tonight, we'll seek you. Move." They were almost out of range when Kaya saw the face of Ozkurt, smiling broadly, waving an acknowledgment from the river bank.

>- - - - - - - >

"You really are good warriors. After the slaughter of the horses at the village, I thought you wouldn't kill your enemies. I wondered how long you would last." Igor was smiling broadly with his hand on Kaya's shoulder. Kaya laughed appreciatively.

"We would have endangered the village if we had destroyed the band and there was no need." He shrugged. "This last affair was entirely different. We avenged the destroyed village and the ravaging of its inhabitants. The leader we killed in the last charge would kill me and my Yownja as well."

Fewsoon, sitting behind Kaya smiled, "We are told to help the innocent, Igor. So we fight to protect people, but we prefer that people leave us in peace," she said, clinging tightly to Sertol and the boat.

"That is the wish of all people, Lady," Igor added, "but there are conflicts of interests."

"Christians are permitted self-defense, personally and collectively, but our laws are to protect the society by protecting the individual and families from attack," Kaya stated. "So private offenses are judged by the authorities. Personal revenge is not permitted. It would disrupt the community life. It would also destroy the natural development of the soul as a part of a community."

"You got yours back on Biorn. That was personal revenge and something I approve of, but is that why you were so reluctant to act? Fear for your soul?" Igor frowned.

"One cannot be too careful with that part of your life which will live forever," Kaya responded slowly. "Just think how tragic it is when an old person loses his memory. Yet, soul is that part that involves the whole being of the person: will, decision, choice, attitude and values all in one package. That package is submitted in spirit to God or is contrary to Him. To lose that core of self, is worse than loss of awareness of personal history, feelings and past activities. To kill for personal reasons is a damning thing."

"Then why did you change, so suddenly, at the end of the *goo-re'sh*, death fight and devastate him?" Igor asked. "I thought you had killed him when you finished."

"He said he was a bear. I realized that he was not fully human. Animals obey their nature. They have no choice. They cannot repent or turn to God. They act by what they are, each according to their species. He was a danger to Fewsoon and to others. I had to leave him helpless to prevent his damaging others." Kaya's face was intense. "There are bears that become dangerous to others of their own kind. His human body held the spirit of the white bear, and a rogue at that, but for my soul's sake, I'm glad he didn't die."

Fewsoon passed over a bag of *ayran* mixed with water to Kaya and Igor and smiled her prettiest.

"Too much talk dries the tongue and slows the flow of action. We need to camp soon and eat. When will you visit the horse herd and Ozkurt?"

"We must find rafts to carry our mounts. Are there any available, Igor?" Kaya asked.

"You must visit the chief of the woods people, whose dugouts we are using. You will have to offer part of the herd for the protection and transport we need. They will not be happy with the Huns' raiding and will blame us, so be generous." Igor's face was troubled.

Kaya smiled largely. "It cost us nothing. We can give it all. The rescue of the village people should merit us some consideration."

"It may just save our lives," ventured Igor.

>- - - - - - - >

The red headed village boy stood half a head above Sertol and surveyed him scornfully. "You horsemen are reputed to have powerful bows. The one you carry looks child-size to me, like your shield. Can such a puny thing be what they speak of?" A crowd of children gathered around.

"Mine is a hunting bow, but it differs little from the warriors bow." Sertol answered with dignity. "If you have an archer's field I can show you its reach and power. I would like to see your weapons for I know what they use in the Rhineland and can tell you the differences.

A girl of Sertol's height with spring flowers in her golden hair pushed the redhead's arm. "You heard him, Sergi, let's go to the meadow and learn something useful."

Sergi stopped to arm his bow while Natasha, who seemed a born leader, carried the whole party to the meadow. Sergi caught up where Sertol was arming his bow.

"Let's move up into range," Sergi suggested, again taking command. But Sertol shook his head in a negative nod, drew and loosed an arrow at a distant tree stump. The arrow struck with a thump and all the children let out a whoop of astonishment and started talking in their language. Then Natasha spoke Hunnish and said, "Do the warriors shoot from farther away?"

Sertol shrugged, "The men of our band can hit it from the tree line twenty paces back." Translated this produced a buzz of comments. Sergi's face had assumed a look of respect. Sertol yielded his weapon to the boy as he traced the reverse curves of the two ends flexing them with difficulty. "It makes a hard pull," he observed pulling the string, "but that's where the power lies. Why is it so small?"

"We hunt mounted in open meadow land like this clearing. The Rhinelanders are a forest people like you. They hunt in the woods and use wooden bows like you do. They use a horn insertion on each end of the wood that gives a slight recurved effect and takes their wooden arrows further. Go ahead you can shoot now," Sertol encouraged.

"Let me shoot one of your arrows," Sergi requested, "How do you make these arrows?" he added. Natasha held Sergi's bow while they examined Sertol's quiver.

“We make them of bone from a horse’s shin, they’re short, but strong. Shoot the stump,” Sertol urged.

Sergi grimaced as he pulled the bow taut. He released the arrow at a high angle and all watched in disbelief as the arrow overshot the stump. Several small children whooped and set off in pursuit of the arrows. “We should go to the lake and shoot swans,” Sergi said, full of enthusiasm. “I could bring them down with this bow.”

“Our leader, Kaya, wears a swan emblem of office. He doesn’t like us to kill them. His family motto is: ‘The leader must decide when and where to descend, for the good of all, in order to feed his flock.’”

“A flock of swans will make a feast for a whole village,” Sergi protested. “Why refuse an opportunity, just for a good motto?”

“Tanra has other ways to provide for a village’s needs,” Sertol replied seriously, “Why kill something so beautiful just for a feast.”

“Hunger takes place before beauty; need consumes prohibitions, my father says.” Sergi boasted, “I can love them in the air or on the platter.” The circle of children voiced their agreement.

Natasha turned to look over the vast river whose shore touched the village and provided its life and dangers. She pointed west, upriver, and shouted, “A raft with horses! They’re coming here to land them,” she gasped, “Huns!”

The children screamed and turned to run to the village, while Sertol motioned Sergi to come and they ran toward the meadows edge. A thin line of woods fringed the river bank and from this shelter they could see the huge raft with ten horses and Hun warriors. Forest people lined the raft’s sides to row and the tiller was manned. They were headed in, to land on the river’s bank.

“We can’t let them land on the meadow -- anywhere but here.” Sertol said in his most determined voice. “It’s only a squad. I’ll try for the tiller and the onbasha. You must take care of the horses. Move constantly, don’t stay in one spot.” Sertol’s arrow took the tiller in the leg and he sat down hard. The onbasha was ordering his men to arm their bows, when an arrow took him in the side. Sergi’s first arrow caused a horse to rear and whinny, a second brought one down, and it knocked his mounted rider into the river. Another caught a warrior who jumped his horse into the river to try to swim for shore.

“Kaya Bey says that wounding is more disruptive than killing,” Sertol shouted. “*Doer ma*, don’t stop.”

Sergi did stop after the third arrow. His arm was raw and red from the bowstring’s lash against his arm and wrist. An incoming arrow nicked his elbow. He dropped the bow to clutch his arm.

Natasha, who had followed him closely, snatched up the bow.

“You’re wounded. I can do it without the string hitting me. I’ve watched father and your teachers.” She feathered an arrow.

“No,” Sergi protested, girls aren’t supposed to use the bow. Fighting is for warriors, not for women.”

“All Chipchak women learn to defend their yurts. Go for the horses, Natasha.” Sertol called.

She did! Another rider hit the water. The horses were panicked now, rearing, breaking halters, kicking; some fell into the river. The rowers were disorganized and the onbasha was silent. Most Huns did not swim and the breastplates were heavy.

The Huns were pouring their arrows into the riverside brush against the unseen attackers. One of them cried out: “Turk arrows and wooden ones too. We’ve met a patrol.” Another cried, “We’ve been ambushed!” They left four horses and two riders in the water.

The tiller-man leaned heavily on his oar and the raft moved away.

Noise now came from the village down river where the raft had to pass. Guards, alerted by the children, made the defeat of the Hunnish squad complete by their action. Boats were launched to loot the raft.

Back in the meadow the two tiniest children were waiting with the two arrows used on the stump. Then all together they proceeded to gather the arrows the Huns had shot at them. Three exhausted Hun horses swam to the bank and emerged, dripping and cold, to be taken into hand by the children. Their riders never appeared.

Joyously the children returned to the village to tell their story, bind up Sergi’s scratch, show the three horses and join the celebration.

Sertol’s father smiled contentedly at the excited retelling. “Some day, when you become a warrior I’ll give you my bow. You can’t pull it to full drawn now, but you’ll be strong then,” he teased gently.

“Let me try it now, *Babam.* My arms aren’t as long as yours yet. I’ll bet I can get it back to my cheek,” he proposed excitedly.

“Never mind,” his father laughed,” If you could, you’d be trying to borrow it on every pretext. You’ll have to wait until I’m dead to get it.”

>- - - - - - - >

The local authority, a Hetman, was richly dressed in tailored and sewn cloth and fur. His long coat came below the knees and his jewelry spoke of power and command. His beard filled his face. His words were grave and smooth.

“We thank the life-giver for your rescue of the women and prisoners from the Hun’s camp. We suffer from their pillaging and destruction because we resist their demands for taxes and submission. They leave the villages they rule nothing of value, nor sufficient food for winter. Our people die on every hand.”

“We were prisoners in the Hun camp,” Kaya explained. “We won our freedom and return to our own country far to the East. We need rafts to take our men to their homes. We regret that our coming has been at a time when the enemy attacks your villages. We are happy to have been of help to your people.” Both Kaya and Igor bowed low to the Hetman who returned the bows. Kaya motioned Igor to continue the conversation in their own language. So the bargaining began. Each side had much to gain, and equally much to lose. The need was to get both to win and no one lose.

>- - - - - - - >

The rafts' crews of men were plainly reluctant to venture out at night, though the Hetman ordered them. They complained of the dangers of searching in the dark, and the small chance of finding a horse herd unmolested. They talked of ambush and the fierceness of the enemy. They were an emotional and superstitious forest dwelling boat people, dependent on their chiefs and shaman for all important decisions. In spite of the afternoon victory, caution now ruled their hearts. Two things attracted them irresistibly, however: horses to ride and carry burdens and gold to buy goods, power and prestige. The gold had come to them with the seven strangers. Four were foreign warriors with a wife and boy. There was also a strange Slav from the south. They might have fought and kept it, but the horses lay across the river on the side the Huns raided. In spite of all fears, they found themselves captive to the idea of obtaining the herd.

>- - - - - - - >

"I'll leave the horses here in the meadow," Yuzbasha explained. "We'll go over under the big trees to eat and rest. I've brought my instrument for music." He scooped up the large hamper and pillow.

"Bomba!, wonderful!" Miakim exclaimed happily. "I have the spread for the ground cover and some treats from the pastry shop."

They quickly settled their burdens under a great oak tree and they opened their hamper, and brought out the dishes.

"Smells great." Yuzbasha commented, helping himself to a drumstick from the chicken. "I brought bulgur like mother used to make. There's a special dish of sauce; you'll love it." He added. "It will soothe your nerves. We can enjoy it all in the quiet of the forest, away from your audience."

"Wonderful," she laughed, "We'll spend a safe and quiet afternoon together here. What a pity Ifrah misses all this because of her father's death in the village. Now, you can tell me all about life in your country."

>- - - - - - - >

It was near midnight when they cast off and started up stream to search out the fire beacon. It would be small and hidden from the land side. It took two hours to find it. On a hill overlooking a flat bank-side meadow, they saw a bright beacon. The fire, however, was in some kind of cleft or ravine and the light went out over the water, but was masked by the hill behind it.

There they found the herd and the remnant of men, waiting anxiously. They had skirmished interminably, with the pursuing Huns pressing them. Ozkurt and several more were wounded. About a dozen men remained of the original twenty guards.

"We expect a dawn attack," Ozkurt interjected even before the greetings were concluded. "All the reserve arrows are spent, and we have only a half ration each in our sheaths." He pointed to his quiver.

"Enough for the first rush if you wait, pretend sleep, set an ambush and don't start shooting in the dark." Kaya chuckled quietly, "Why are you so nervous? Did you get any sleep?"

Ozkurt stiffened and stuck out his chest. "I had the sentries out. They wouldn't have caught us unaware." He motioned toward the camp. "The horses were between us and would have warned us." He felt Kaya's arm round his shoulders, could feel him chuckling.

"I asked about sleep, Tiger-man, not preparations." Kaya hugged him. "But quick, send out the herders and quietly drive the horses to the rafts. We must not delay."

The men circulated quietly among the horses speaking softly and urging them toward the river. Sertol rode behind Fewsoon on Altom to the rafts. Some walked with their arms around the necks of the leading mares while urging them to the rafts.

Ramps were quickly built of earth and brush. Kaya led Altom on. The other mares were coaxed across. Some were nervous and nickered when they felt the motion of the raft, but they remained in place. Others followed. At the end, the men stood between the horses and the water, a living fence, and the more docile horses were now prepared to leave. The shy, frightened animals that broke off, rejected the ramps, and returned to the meadow were abandoned. Without sound the men withdrew. The horsemen seated themselves on the edge of the raft, but none touched the water; most could not swim and were afraid.

The fourth and last of the rafts with Kaya and Ozkurt in it, pushed off for the opposite bank. The dawn light showed the small remnant herd and in the distance a few watching Hun advance riders. As the raft men plied their oars vigorously there came a shout from an oarsman. Turning, Kaya and Ozkurt saw behind them two dugouts cutting the current to swing out beyond them, as if to cut them off from the opposite shore. Another shout came and arms pointed to the shore, at the same moment a wall of sound hit.

There was a wave of motion and sound that came with the attack. The horizon was filled with a double rank of mounted archers. Arrows made from the shin bones of horses notched the small double recurved horn bows. At the head of the column rode a beautifully dressed figure in armored breastplate and spiked helmet. Commander Koosta, the hero of the Donetz River Battle, who had come to see the destruction of this force of cavalry and collect the heads of the spies for the Khan, gasped in surprise. No enemy force trembled at his call to charge. He rushed into a meadow empty of all resistance. Seeing the escape of their foes, the charging line screamed a battle cry, and with this challenge leaped forward, scattering the horse herd. They drove to the river bank and released a cloud of arrows that hummed like angry bees. Those bees carried the sting of death toward the rafts.

PEOPLE, PLACES & PLOTS IN CHAPTER 7

Fewsoon: gives up her treasure to make a good deal.
Igor: plays warrior, diplomat and ambassador with distinction.
Rurrik: supply and intelligence captain of the woods people's fort.
Kaya: distrusted as an alien, yet needed as a friend of the Volga fort.
Kove: holds a position of wounded war prisoner, yet, allied friend.
Luvya: tries to help Igor, but only has time for a brief farewell.
Miakim: the actress is in trouble with an admirer.
Merien: writes of her hope to return to Kertch Port and visit Judith.
Natasha: warns Luvya of personal danger.
Ozkurt: distinguishes himself as Kaya's chief lieutenant.
Prince Oleg: a troubled ruler of a local tribe, forced to flee north.
Sergi: an admired leader of the village children in Volga fort.
Sertol: by swimming he pushes the raft out of arrow range.
Yuzbasha the Khazar: plots his way toward revenge and vindication.

GLOSSARY HELPS

babam: my father; daddy.
buck'tal-lar :depressed; bored; uninterested; weary.
do'er: stop; halt!
fu'hush: a woman sold for men's pleasure; prostitute; whore.
git shim de: get out of here now; go now!
shim day: now; at this time.
Yesu gel : God help us; Come Jesus; have mercy.

7 RAFTING

RAFTS PURSUED

"Quick, all who can swim get into the water. Dive under the raft and push," Kaya called. He knew only a few of the horsemen had grown near the great rivers and had learned the art of swimming. He called once again, "Swimmers into the water. Push from beneath." He shoved Sertol and the hesitant Ozkurt overboard and dove under the raft. Sertol had learned to swim in the Rhine River. Fewsoon followed them.

The shock of cold numbed their bodies and their minds as they kicked and shuddered. They surfaced in the head-wide space between the great logs laid three to a side and the deck that bridged them, holding them together. Above on the deck he could hear the panic of the horses as the arrows fell among them, wounding some. The drumming of hooves and the scream of horses and men gave evidence of the slaughter for the whine and thud of the arrows did not stop.

"*Yesu gel*, God help us!" Kaya pleaded, as he pushed and kicked the cold water, speeding the raft on the current. Ozkurt and about three other men were with him, and they listened with awe as the carnage on deck continued. Wounded and dying animals and men plunged over the deck and fell into the river. Blood dripped between the boards of the deck and the chill air was polluted with the noise and smells of death. The men below deck were weeping, cursing, praying and crying as they put all their emotion in kicking the water; cold hands on the great logs that lay crosswise to the deck boards. The raft seemed to speed miraculously forward on the white foam they caused.

A feeling of betrayal flooded Kaya. Men had died and he had lived. He wondered if he could face those still on deck without shame. Whatever good had been done by their action -- little or much -- there was still the feeling of hiding, desertion and cowardice. The pull toward dying with those who had died, of sharing their fate -- the solidarity of humans who suffer similarly -- caught at all their hearts.

The whine and thud of arrows had ceased. They would be out of range now. Those pushing from beneath were numb with the cold and gradually were ceasing to push and swim. Kaya pushed several up to get them out of the water's chill. Kaya ventured up and out of their place of safety, his teeth chattering and his body shaking. There were two horses still standing on deck. Both bore wounds. Altom, located at the end of the line near the prow of the raft, had a hip wound. The arrow was sunk three fingers deep into the muscle. Two more were down on the deck shafted to the feather, with several dead men. One man stood soothing a horse. Another sat vacant eyed, cowering in a spot of refuge behind a dead horse. One groaned on the deck, an arrow in arm, shoulder, hip, thigh and legs, like a pincushion. It was Kove, still living. The survivors seemed utterly exhausted, as if the last few minutes composed a lifetime of draining effort and soul-shattering experience. They did not notice him, nor did any expression change. They were frozen in their own special moment and were lost to time, while Kaya helped more swimmers up onto the raft. Fewsoon came out to sooth Altom at the same time. "Babam," a muffled sob came from her side. Sertol knelt almost at her feet, beside the body of his father, who lay with two arrows through his heart, "If he'd ever learned to swim he'd be alive," the boy murmured, "but he laughed at me for learning. He called me 'Otter'."

Kaya scanned the water for sight of swimming horses or men. The two dugouts were pulling closer to the rafts. They were beyond bow range from the bank. There were wounded among them. The third raft also showed signs of dead and wounded animals and several swam in the water after the raft. Dead animals and men floated in the current behind Kaya's raft, but none seemed alive. The devastation had been complete; it made Kaya feel worse about his own safety. Altom was quiet while Kaya extracted the arrow; she seemed too exhausted to move. One of the apparently dead men groaned and moved a hand to his head. Kaya, joined by Ozkurt and Fewsoon, started to look to the wounds of the raft's survivors. They cut their wet shirts up for bandages, and used plucked hair from the horse's tails to sew up the gaping wounds.

In two hours with the current, they had covered the distance it had taken most of the night to travel. The people awaiting on the shore were eager for news of the battle and the escape. Fewsoon and the

tribal women took care of the wounded and fed them broth. The first two rafts had suffered few casualties. Kove, however, required many bandages and the extracted arrows were saved by his bed. Altom limped badly. She would have to heal before anyone could ride her. Kaya led her to pasture. The band helped Sertol bury his father with their other casualties. The Slavs buried their own dead, separately.

Sergi and Natasha came to the grave site where Sertol sat and after a long silence he spoke. " My father once told me that his war bow would be mine some day and he wanted me to be worthy of it. Now that we were in battle together, I have my inheritance, but lost my father." He paused before continuing. "Father heard the story of our encounter with the raft by the meadow. He called me a hero and challenged me to give my best effort for my friends. So I give you my hunting bow, Sergi and challenge you to be an expert with it and share it with your sister."

"I'll do more," proclaimed Sergi. "I'll give her my bow and we'll share both of them, like we do the horses. Father gave one to the Prince, but kept the two for our family and put us in charge of their feed and exercise. Now we will learn to use the bow on horseback."

Natasha smiled warmly, "Whatever happens now, I'll always remember you, Sertol, and I'll not be afraid of horsemen again."

>- - - - - - - >

A sneering Yuzbasha knelt beside the drowsy, prostrate form of Miakim stretched on the great pillow.

"Shimdi fuhush, Now, whore, this is my surprise, you proud little bitch. I'll show you how we use women like you, who profit by playing the whore and showing your body for money and the admiration of lustful men. To sing is one thing, to display yourself is another. I'll explain the dos and don'ts when we get home to your house -- I mean our house. Here, open your bodice, now doesn't that feel good? You're purring, little kitten; you need some special stroking, don't you? We'll have an evening of it. You won't need any of my special stimulants in the future. You'll be mine as long as I need you. Resentment and resistance will just make it more fun."

>- - - - - - - >

Fear swept the Slavic camp! The fear was that the Huns would continue the pursuit and press the people further north and east into more strange lands. Yet it was easier to contend for the land with the northern tribes, than to stand against the dreaded raiders and their swift horses. The badly wounded raft horses were slaughtered and food prepared for a large meal before fleeing or fighting.

Prince Oleg complained, "Our condition is critical. We must make peace if at all possible. Our palisade is feeble, we have just enough food for ourselves, but your Chipchak friends have provided us with welcome meat and treasure. However, by renewing the battles, we are losing men and are again endangered." Oleg paused for breath and considered the face of the consultant, Igor. He was once a slave

and trainer of athletes and now an ambassador. Could he trust this foreign Slav who had enriched him? He listened skeptically.

"Generals need easy victories and much spoil to keep an army in the field. Koosta stands on slippery ground. If they win too much, there is envy and suspicion. If they win too little, there is grumbling and insubordination. They have done both in early victories and now have suffered many losses. Already there are desertions and yesterday, more defeats. They, too, are eating their wounded horses and lack supplies," Igor smiled. "You now have their treasure hidden."

"I would give the treasure for peace and a return to our old home grounds in the south, from which we have been scattered." Oleg sighed and looked up. "I have duties my Hetman awaits me," Oleg stood. The consultation over, he walked away with his retinue toward the supply area. There he spoke with his master-of-supply, Rurrik.

"There is news from your opposite, great chief." The little fat man smiled ingratiatingly and continued, "The general will let treasure go for the heads of the Chipchak spies, but he must have one or the other before his return south in peace." He looked at his leader shrewdly trying to calculate what he would decide.

Indecision racked the face of the chief. Seeing this, Rurrik ventured, with another smile, "A waiting game might be the best policy, Lord Oleg. We have three reasons to wait: food and a palisade in a defensive river position, desired treasure and war horsemen equal to Koosta's own, dependent on your good will."

"Perhaps he would be more disposed to wait if I sent some of the Finnish girls we captured to keep his bed," Oleg ventured.

Rurrik smirked and answered with a chuckle. "I hear he uses girls only as cooks and servants, but young boys are much appreciated." He shrugged when Oleg stared at him. "It is common talk. The great are under constant scrutiny." He smiled as Oleg eyed him carefully.

"Do you spy on our guests as much?" He asked the question cautiously.

"The woman is pregnant and just beginning to show a few of the signs. The men are worn from pursuit and battle, but they are an easy match for the Huns. If you kill the spies Koosta wants, you must kill all. Not an easy task. Unfortunately, they are a lump in our throats; our ways and speech are too different." The fat man rolled it off easily as if talking of barley and flour. Oleg grunted and turned to go, his brow still wrinkled. He still had others to consult and time flew.

"Too many wounded for a good defense; too little food for a long siege. If any rival river tribe provided a crossing for the Huns, they would be on us tomorrow." He sighed deeply, life was so precarious and the gods he knew were so capricious. He must find out what to do; the future of the tribe depended on it. "We will call the council of tribes. It will delay things for a month until summer."

>- - - - - - - >

"We must be ready to act for our own good and safety. The net closes and we are to be taken in exchange for guarantees and treasure. The tribes that edge the grasslands are being driven further into the woods and they will give us up for peace." Igor's face was serious as he spoke to Kaya and Ozkurt. "We must follow the river east passing the Finnish forest tribes until it turns south where it joins the Kama river. From there it continues south into the grasslands. You can't go to Gechit City, you say, because of Khan Kinner. So you'll come to an elbow where the river turns strongly east around some hills and then west again. When you see the river turn west again, look for a small river joining on the southeast side near Samara. Enter it and travel east as far as you can go. There you will find a road that passes the Ural mountains and leads to your homeland." Igor looked in Ozkurt's eyes taking his hand. Igor smiled as they stopped to take measure as they had done before.

"We have not always liked each other, but I know you will see our friends safely home. I pray you will, and stay well." They squeezed hands and nodded. It was a solemn moment.

"When do we break off?" Ozkurt inquired, worried. "We will need two or three rafts and horses."

"During the feast for the council, your men can give a display of horsemanship and war skills. When you finish, ride straight to the river and launch the rafts. The women will be singing a welcome to the boyars and councilors and most people will be watching it. Swamp the big dugouts so they will not be able to launch a pursuit immediately. Leave the smallest boat, however. I will be able to follow with whoever is late or delayed. As your representative I will be expected to sit with the boyars, but will have to get down to the river at the end of your demonstration." Kaya listened with admiration to Igor and took him into his arms in an embrace.

"You have a good plan, and you are our brother. Risk not yourself, for you are dear to us. We will think and pray on this matter."

>- - - - - - - >

"The manager is complaining, my lady," said Ifrah, Miakim's timid attendant, while combing her hair. "He reports that Yuzbasha has insulted several men attending your presentations. He protests that you lack the enticing qualities you usually show. He says the public knows the foreigner stays in your house. He threatens to end your engagement here unless you do something about it."

"What can I do? You know how possessive and jealous Yuzbasha acts when other men are around me."

"I'm afraid of him, ma'am, I'd ask for protection."

"I can't do that now, it's too late. He'll kill me if I drop him. He has sworn it. He's passionate, madly in love. He brings gifts every day."

"Mad is a word I fear, ma'am. You have high placed friends in the government who could send him away, or move you elsewhere. "

"No, the men who engaged me are happy that he is selling every secret of his embassy just to get money to spend on me. They're getting him to recommend changes in policy and to remit Kertch Port to our control. Everyone is happy to have such a willing agent planted. Now, I can afford to take the summer off - go to the Prince's islands."

"But he'll be with you, ma'am, watching with those hunter's eyes."

>- - - - - - - >

The spring floods delayed the meetings and kept everyone busy preparing. The Chipchaks kept to themselves. Only Igor and Sertol were frequently with the villagers. They did practice regularly the routine for the opening display to the chiefs. They were left to tend the herd. Not all the horses had recovered. Altom, among others, was to wait near the rafts.

When the Chiefs arrived, the Chipchaks took two each of the best horses onto the meadow where the exercise was to be held. A red target ball was attached to the tall, trimmed top of a birch tree to bob in the breeze. The visiting boyars were invited to the area of honor to watch the display. The yelping troop with their queue of plaited hair, rode in a circle and changed horses at a gallop. Each rider armed his bow and sent two arrows into the red ball of wool in eye-blurring succession. Then they seemed to disappear behind their horses while continuing to ride at breakneck speed. They lay flat or hung behind the animals, touching the ground to rebound astride them again. Several changed horses, or stood on their back at full gallop.

The crowds watched in profound silence, this practical display of the prowess used by the enemy conquerors. The Huns, had used it against them. Such skills they could not hope to match. The silence continued as the alien allies rode off.

The young women, dressed in their finest, formed a group to sing and dance their greetings to the visiting celebrities seated before them.

1. We welcome all our noble guests now,
The choicest chiefs of all the tribes.
Whose blood from heroes great descending,
Guide all the forest people's lives.
All hail the great and strong defenders,
Rule o'er our weakness, make us wise.

2. We bring allegiance, loyal service,
Our furs and ambers, all the best.
Come and defend us from the horsemen.
Save all the forest people's lives.
Salute the heroes of our wanderings.
Rule o'er our lostness, be our guides.

FOREST WELCOME

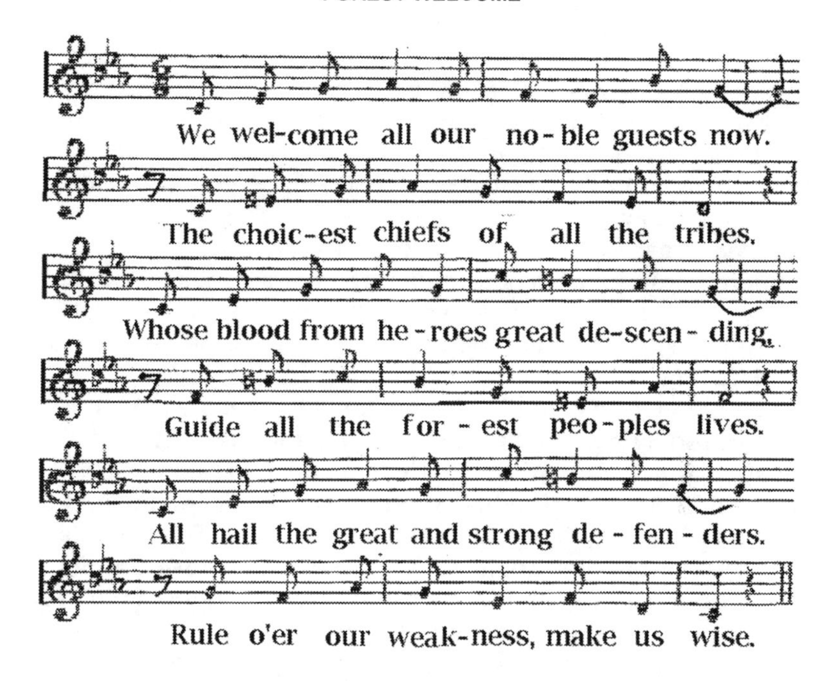

The horsemen rode to the river below the meadow. The river was up and the currents swift, so the rafts and dugouts had been dragged up on the banks to be free of danger. The horsemen dismounted where Kove sat waiting, lifted and moved the rafts out to the water's edge and loaded the first three with men and horses. A dozen Finnish slaves, both men, women and a few children, helped put them in the water and took position as rowers. Kaya helped move the small boat to the edge and motioned the three rafts away with Ozkurt in charge.

But water carriers and tribal workers saw the departure and carried the news to the audience who watched the dancing and songs of welcome. There was no time to swamp all the dugouts. There was only time to load Fewsoon into his small boat and to shout encouragement to the running form of Igor who had broken away from the mass of spectators. He gained space, before the audience with a roar drew weapons and ran toward the riverbank.

The Finnish prisoners of war had been recruited with promises of freedom. They were actually the best oarsmen and with their women were rowing the rafts and four were ready to launch the small boat. Suddenly the arrows started up from the pursuing warriors on the bank, their large wooden bows had less range than recurved bows, but killed very effectively within it. Some arrows found their running target and Igor fell with a grunt and lay as dead. The intent crowd whooped in triumph. "The traitor is downed." "Stop the Huns."

"They're escaping." "Kill the bastards." Thus the mob gave voice to their hatred and frustration. Their hostages were escaping.

"*Beck'lay*, wait," Kaya screamed, but the four Finns did not understand. The arrows and fallen man were clear messages of doom and they pushed off. They dug their paddles in to clear the bank. The excited crowd behind them ran to launch the dugouts and stood sending arrows after the small boat. Kaya gasped and fell forward on Fewsoon, a wooden arrow protruding from his left shoulder.

The small boat shot into the current and was soon gaining on the ponderous rafts, but the dugouts were just a bow-shot behind. Everyone in the larger crafts were bending their backs to gain speed and overtake the small boat. There was no space for shout or shot, just hard pulling.

The Finnish oarsmen pulled for the center of the river which at this season was foolhardy. The fierce current tossed the light craft about like a leaf on angry waters. Only their skill and experience kept the thin planked boat afloat. The Slavs were no less skilled and put their dugouts in the same millrace, with the same results. Both were swept past the rafts before they could move to the slower side currents. The small boat spun out first and the two ponderous dugouts followed. Now they blocked the rafts passage and two more dugouts came cautiously behind. The fugitives were blocked from both sides.

Oleg came in the last boat and stood up out of bow range to speak to Ozkurt in broken Hunnish. "Why all you flee camp, take camp slaves, steal rafts, like bad men? We feed you good, no damage. You pay bad for good."

"We saved your people, gave you horses, gave you all the treasure. We go to our homeland now. You keep horses and treasure, we take three rafts and two horses each to ride and men to row. May there be no anger between us."

"You leave us face enemy alone. Huns come take horses, take treasure, take slaves, kill people. Why you start fight? Take away peace, lose land to Huns." Oleg looked disgusted. He knew they were helpless to retake the rafts without heavy loss of life on both sides. It was a draw. He needed his men for war with the Huns, if it came.

"You wound our Prince Kaya, and take our friend Igor, who is of your people and would do you no harm. How can you expect us to trust you now? You intended to give us over to the Huns for peace and treasure," Ozkurt bellowed.

"Is lie. You speak crooked. We think right, but you hate us, no faith. You thief." Oleg shook his fist. "Igor die, Kaya die, good. You go to Christian hell, bad men."

Fewsoon had the small boat tied to Ozkurt's raft and had helped move Kaya past the horses that faced inward in a circle and laid him amid the few bundles of supplies in the center of the raft. The horses shied with the smell of blood under their noses, but soon settled down. The horsemen trained their mounts to accept the results of a good hunt.

As the ire of the two parties increased Fewsoon walked to the plank boat, untied it, and released it with a push into the center current. She lifted her hands above her head, and facing the setting sun shouted; "Yesu, stop this madness. Give us peace."

The empty boat shot into midstream and the dugouts pulled over to successfully intercept it. The current took them across to the opposite side of the river while the rafts continued their majestic trip down the north bank of the Volga. The trailing dugouts then let them go with their curses.

>------- >

Dear Lady Judith,

Spring has arrived, everything is in bloom. The tulips and fruit trees adorn our city. What a beautiful time for a wedding, yes. But anytime is wonderful for a wedding, no?

Your Don River is open for letters and we will have much to write about, no? I look forward to your letters, yes.

It is with great joy that I hear of the wedding last fall of your dear friend Sherbet and the giant commander Gochen, yes. What a lovely wedding they must have had in the church. And the reception in your home would lack nothing, no? Now, this spring they have a baby on the way, how great a delight, no?.

I, too, have news. My father has been requested to return to Kertch Port and to reestablish the neutrality of the port. He will serve all nations in commerce and repair of vessels. Father writes with joy that it is great to be in the old house. He is inviting Magda and me to return. Magda is so eager to go. She is bored with our great city. A romance she hoped for has not developed. She is all ready to return, yes.

My friend in Pontus, you remember, no? He has done work for you with your people and his father is applying for his entrance in government ministry. His hopes are high, no?

Olga is still waiting for an heir. The Goths have q hard life under the Huns, but she finds happiness in high fort.

Lady Seraijik, has not only her baby boy, now four months old, but is starting an orphanage for Rumen children. Her father show great anger, no? She name Munzer Orphanage for father, daring and funny, no?

Our news say that Koosta continues raids on north woods, burn villages and towns, poor people are hungry, no? We do not have much to show for efforts. We pray Kaya and friends be safe, yes. I would so love to know Fewsoon, yes. Kaya wrestled a giant to win her. The story made me cold with fright. Now they are lost in the north. We must pray, yes.

Kiss your dear husband, the prince, and the baby. I wish them well.

I pray your peace and prosperity.

Merien Papasian

>- - - - - - - >

Igor groaned as he felt the water on his face and lips. It was dark and he was behind the log where he had fallen. He had been forgotten in the excitement of the chase. He looked at the face of the woman whose hands tenderly cleaned his face and helped his thirst. He asked her name, for it was dark and he was not sure. "Luvya" she whispered, and kissed his feverish forehead.

"How often I wish I had asked your father for your hand this winter, but my life was too uncertain to risk your happiness."

"I held that hope in my heart, especially when we decided to move north to join the exiles. The first patrol of Huns were good to us, but those who followed were worse than the wolves. I was glad to follow you to these shores."

"Listen, there is gold for you near the plundered village. Go with your father to the west woods. It is at the foot of the largest birch tree between the large rock and the shore. Two scars on the bark form an arrow to the burial spot. Ten gold pieces in all, it will be for your marriage. Name a boy for me - to remember."

"You will live and dig it up. I want you to see and enjoy it. It could buy your freedom," she cried now.

"Lovely fool," He sighed, "My head is all Oleg has to send to Koosta for peace. It will be the minimum acceptable to satisfy the Khan. They may have to give the treasure, too. Keep what is yours. I am bleeding inside and will not live, but I did find the magic word. The old Grandmother said I'd find it. Remember, I told you? It can open the gates beyond. Yesu knows, he said. 'My word is faithful and true,' Kaya, my friend showed the way." His voice weakened and stopped. Luvya cried on. Natasha came quietly and called her away. "The boats are returning," she whispered.

Now the boats returned, and they dealt with him as a traitor and enemy. His body was hung, twitching, to the stake, but he did not speak to any of them, disregarding the torture. He died within the hour.

>- - - - - - - >

"I'm sick of your trying to run my life," Miakim shouted. "You're constantly jealous and harsh. Nothing I do pleases you now; you're unreasonable." She slammed the bowl of mixed fruit down.

"You need someone to teach you manners and humility. You act like you're trying to seduce every man you meet," Yuzbasha roared.

"You'll leave me when you go back to your own country. I'm no good for you there. We both know that." She shook a finger in his face, "You'll go back and marry a local bitch who'll milk your herds."

"She'll be pure and honest, something you don't manage."

"I've had enough of you. Go back to Khazar lands," she cried. "You nasty little boy, sulky and demanding, forever complaining and incapable of pleasant conversation or fun. Your only interest is in bed-time games." She picked up the bread knife from the table. "Don't ever come near me again or you'll take scars home to show from your posting here in the largest city in the world." She shook the knife in his face. He leaned forward daring her to strike.

"I don't have to take your insults and complaints. You only want to know what I do and what the Khazar plans are. Well, I'll tell you. We Khazars, or people like us, will some day rule this city and you effete, corrupt weaklings can suffer the consequences. Then you'll have to go along or get out. But you belong to me. I'll not let you go, never. The men who lick their chops and excite their imaginations over you will never have you." He stomped out of the house. It was time to force a change in his life and depart the embassy. He planned his plea.

>- - - - - - - >

It was necessary to beach the rafts every day to allow the horses a night on the meadows. Hunts were planned to supply meat. Birds had migrated north. The land bloomed and green sprouts filled the land.

The Finns stayed with them for a week, each nationality using the few words they knew of Slavic for work, but all the Finns disappeared one night after they had seen tribal hunters on the passing meadows.

Kaya remained weak and pensive during the time spent on the raft. The shoulder was slow to heal, and the days fled by as the voyage east continued. They stared in wonder as the great Kama River from the northeast joined the flood and carried them south, back toward the familiar steppe country. They clung to the east bank for the river was wide enough to be lost on.

Finally, when the river turned definitely east again for the great elbow, they knew they were near the end of their travels by water. Here before it turned west again, where grassland started, they left the liquid uncertainties of rafts for the firm and familiar joy of riding and hunting daily as they covered the miles. Only Fewsoon, now starting to show her condition, complained of the difference. Kaya and Kove too, looked pale and tired, but they did not complain. Everyone was happy to be back on the summer grass, pressing east.

PEOPLE, PLACES & PLOTS IN CHAPTER 8

Basileus: King or Emperor of the East Romans in Constantinople.
Bata: the thirteen-year old son, named for the Tartar Khan.
Binbasha: a general, head of the Khazar embassy.
Chavush: Sergeant, a maternal uncle of Yuzbasha in the embassy.
Fewsoon: is expecting her baby, loses her knife, but finds haven.
Hock'dale: a general, is holding a fortified tower on the Ural River.
Ifrah: attendant of the actress, Miakim, repeats bad news.
Jonny: a Tartar corporal, a nephew of the wounded Kove.
Kaya: wounded and ill after the river rafting and travel.
Kove: has come home, but still has matters to settle with his rival.
Magda: hopes to meet her secret admirer, but finds a fraud.
Miakim: is angry, tired of spying on Khazar activities in her country.
Minister of the Interior: as chief of security, faces a tragedy.
Ozkurt: tired, but still able to enjoy fighting on patrol.
Per'ihan: fifteen-year-old daughter now considered marriageable.
Sertol: ignored by Bata, plays with young Yuzbasha.
Sev'im: eleven-year-old daughter, named for Kaya's mother
Vash'tie: mother of Fewsoon and foster mother of Kaya.
Yuzbasha: practical, thoughtful nine-year-old son of the General.
Yuzbasha the Khazar: scheming to leave the Khazar embassy.
Yownja: the baby name of Fewsoon, used while in the Tower.

GLOSSARY HELPS:

ga'la or ka'la: a fort or stronghold.
gu mul ta ma : Don't move !; Stand still! (Tartar)
Ku mul da ma: Don't move!; Stand still! (Chipchak)
kil'im: a woven woolen rug for floor or wall.
onbasha: corporal; a warrior in charge of ten soldiers.
persona non grata: not acceptable; a Latin expression used to define the diplomatic status of a foreigner.
sandal: a small rowboat used by merchants for deliveries.
vah'she: wild beast; a woods child living in the wild; savage.
yala: a summer home; a mansion on the Bosphorus shore.

8 SUDDEN CHANGES

TARTAR SURPRISE

The Chipchaks traveled in two parties. The forward group, nine men, took the baggage and readied the camps. In the second group were three wounded, one pregnant woman and a child: the people and all animals that could not be rushed. They arrived at camp late after dark. Gradually they saw mountains rising in the northeast. They were at the southern end of the Ural mountains. It was well into summer now and the grass, once so green was now brown and maturing. Tension had developed in the camp. The forward riders were eager to arrive at home, while Fewsoon was both bigger and louder in her complaints. Kaya was more grim and tight lipped. Altom still limped slightly. Several of the horses were on their last legs and the land was bare of herds and people.

One night, a worried Ozkurt went out to meet the late party and talk to Kaya. He rode beside him a while and finally spoke.

"When I was a boy, we had but one old horse for me to herd with. He was fine for all work and steady, but any evening when we neared the corral he would become eager and uncontrollable. He ran for home where there would be grain awaiting him. He often threw me, even jumped over me, and left me to walk. No punishment helped. I had to camp out or start home early to control him." Kaya looked at him knowingly.

"What would you recommend in our case?" He smiled, "Will you join the race for home?"

Ozkurt replied slowly and thoughtfully. "*Yo, buck'tal-lar*, no, they're depressed. Divide the supplies and send them on their way. We will ride north and seek any who live there to rest and replenish. There may be grain growers nearer the mountains. Sertol will stay with us, as his father requested."

"Arrange it tonight." Kaya ordered, "I too, have seen the danger of desertion or rebellion and loss for all. We cannot hold them by force or threats. They have been many years away and chaff at delays. We must send them on with our blessing." So it was arranged and done the next morning. Farewells were sincere and heartfelt. The band was out of sight in an hour.

>- - - - - - - >

The day Kaya turned north, one of the horses died in the afternoon. He simply dropped dead. They had covered half the normal distance and camped early in rough country. That night the sound of predators on the corpse made the horses nervous. Kaya spent time with Altom and the other horses, talking and humming to them. Ozkurt took the guard duty, but they lost the horses, anyway, just before dawn. They could not tell at first what had spooked them, but then they found one of the hobble ropes cut. Altom had not run away with the herd. Someone had robbed them. From here, they would walk.

They had loaded themselves with the most necessary supplies and were trudging north up a slope when they heard the sound ahead on the track they were following. The sound came again.

"*Do'er*, Stop," The D sounded more like T, *To'er* for stop, but the arrows in the drawn recurved horn bows in the hands of the band of small, dark, fierce, slit-eyed men was a clear indication of the meaning. "*Ku-mul-da'man*, don't move," with the K sounding like G, as well as the d-t switch: *Gu-mul-ta'man*, underlined the fact they were held at the mercy of aliens.

>- - - - - - - >

"You've been missing work days this summer, boy, what's wrong?" the Khazar binbasha groused to his assistant, who had come in late with a hasty excuse.

Yuzbasha paused and then sat down before the general. "I have some things to say that will perhaps, not come as a surprise."

The general smiled benignly at the troubled youth. "Pretend we are in the yurt, a paternal uncle and a favorite nephew. Now is the moment for plain talk. You are having an affair and it is troubling you." The youth nodded as the general proceeded. "Does she demand marriage or money, now that the thrill has diminished."

"Neither, uncle, She has boundless curiosity about my work, my country and the principal figures there; their wealth and politics. I have found my papers mussed and I caught her at it this morning, before I was supposed to be up and about. She doesn't love me and I have nothing else to attract her. She is a spy and I regret the infatuation of this spring and summer." The general looked concerned. "She insulted me and laughed at my accusations. Called me a stupid, little boy."

"I'll call Chavush, we must learn how much she knows and if it hurts our cause." Binbasha rose from his couch.

"Does he have to know? Mother will find out about it and everybody will hear about it." Yuzbasha protested.

"Trust your uncles, son, there are things that never arrive at the home yurt. In the business of espionage, friends or foe are all alike."

>- - - - - - - >

The weary band halted and looked dumbfounded at their new challengers, whose faces tightened and bow arms drew slowly to the tightest position against the cheek. Kove, painfully bringing up the rear, spoke quickly to the nearest of the men surrounding them. Again they heard the strange brogue of their captors. It was neither Hunnish or Chipchak, but somewhere near both. They saw the men relax a bit as Kove continued speaking.

"They think we are renegades or criminals exiled from a wandering tribe." Kove chuckled nervously as their captors lowered their bows and began to chatter excitedly to each other. One man, the Onbasha, came forward and again engaged Kove in conversation. Another came to take the men's bow quivers, but left everyone's knife. The hostility had now evaporated, and it was evident they were listening to Kove with interest, then they laughed and relaxed.

"They're Tartars. My old commander has a *Ga'la*, - pardon, a *Ka'la*, a tower, north of here, we will go there now." The relief made his face bright. He laughed with glee, "They'll bring horses for us. The Onbasha, Corporal Jonny, is my uncle's son." All looked happier, only Kaya frowned. Behind the band a horse whinnied. It was Altom. The horses offered turned out to be their own faithful animals. Now, it was the prisoners' turn to laugh.

Laughter accompanied them on the trail north. Kove was engrossed in telling stories of a soldier's life under the Huns. He kept the surrounding circle of Tartars in guffaws and snickers as they rode. Gradually Kaya and his party came to understand the radical differences of accents, and it became easier to follow what was said. Kove became a new man, confident and happy as they rode six days north.

They were now among the high grass steppe meadows and mountains of the southern Urals. Lush river valleys ran south to join the plains and the Caspian sea. There, on a flat-topped ridge to the north, they saw the tower, grim and beautiful, commanding the upper reaches of the Ural River Valley. Its dominance over the area around it was clear by the care with which the village of yurts below were arranged and policed.

They reported to the day command at the village post. The prisoners were then deprived of their knives. Fewsoon saw her Wolf-

headed copper knife go with regret. They were given the freedom of a yurt, where they rested and soothed their stiffness.

>- - - - - - - >

Kove was the first called out. The General would see him now.

The commander stood erect and handsome to greet his former comrade and rival. Kove humbly kissed his hand in deference and homage, and touched it to his forehead, his face a mask. His voice was smooth.

"Greetings, Hock'dale bey, from my Commander, General Koosta, servant of Munzur Khan of the West Huns. I come escorting the King's champion to his home with his bride." The bey cut him off in his narration. His voice conveyed contempt and sarcasm.

"Where are your horses, fine clothes and riches, bold warrior? Has the Khan's commission carried you to such poverty and wounds? Ah, such are the fortunes of war and pains of experience." The twisted smirk of Binbasha's face showed satisfaction at the sight of a rival abased. He continued in the same vein.

"You passed the Bulgars without incident? Are they the ones who deprived you of your goods? Of course. How fortunate for you that you're here on the western frontier, now safe under my protection. I can't help you, but your family yurt lies two weeks east with Bata Khan's son and grandchildren. They have the resources to be generous to wanderers. Rest your wounds for a week and I will give you a horse for a safe return to your family yurt." The smug condescension of his voice infuriated Kove.

"We have come a long journey by river, which is where I obtained my wounds. Among the Huns, Finns and Slavs of the woods there is much fighting," Kove continued looking for a chance to equalize.

Binbasha shook his head in condolence. "Why would civilized people travel in the wood country where the only roads are water? Rivers and boats instead of grass roads and the horses we enjoy in good open country. Among savage people, how could you talk? What important language could they possibly know? Did you live in their shacks of wood? How could you be comfortable?" Hock'dale Bey continued to prod.

"Our army under General Koosta, moved north to free the open woods of troublesome Slavic hunters and farmers. We took some villages on the east-flowing mother of rivers, but met counterattacks. I suffered seven wounds. I kept the arrows." Kove was determined to impress the commander.

"Your facing of unusual hardships in such cold inhospitable country speaks well of your service there. Your family will be very proud of you." Binbasha gave the praise sparingly, grudgingly.

"My party of Chipchaks needs rest. The lady is within months of delivery. I request your generosity for the winter. They have suffered

much. I will continue east to winter with my family in Booyuke Yurt," Kove smiled slyly.

"Yes, but I will expect recompense by Munzur Khan." Then remembering the distance and seeing the hope of reward fade, Binbasha added. You can speak for my part to Khan Bata." His face went blank, and he tried to smile.

"He will expect a complete outfitting of your guests because one of them is the famous *vah'she*, wild boy and child of promise of the Altai Chipchaks. You have not forgotten our frustrating hunt for the wild phantom of the woods? Such failures stay with us. Perhaps, for his safe return, old Erkan will pay you something: some of his superb golden horses?" Kove enjoyed thoroughly his prodding of Binbasha.

"You are serious?" questioned Binbasha, suddenly red of face and excited. "The *vah'she* is here?"

"*Evet*, yes, he is the great Khan's Champion. Ask them," said Kove, now feeling completely confident.

"I will tonight, with all of you present at dinner."

>- - - - - - - >

"I never knew the pressure would be this heavy. The Basileus wants Kertch Port returned to its previous status of an unoccupied port, free to treat with all nations. We would have to change our river terminal to Port Azov that we got from the Huns. This leaves us with no control over the inlet to that sea. Khan Kinner won't like it. Also, our family document has fallen into the Hun's hands. That Olga or the Papasian girl is the only one who could have taken it...unless the ship's mate works for them." He paused.

"I don't trust any sailors or sea-going people. It must be a hard way to make a living. They have no honor."

Chavush waited patiently for the general to run down. "***Dough rue***, right, Binbashim. If the document gets to the hands of Kinner bey, we will excuse it with the explanation that we were working for his interests. Because of the troubles he's had, first with marriage, and then the wounding of Ilkin, his heir. We are working for one who has not earned his father's anger. Yes, he will excuse it, since it has in no way endangered the kingdom or the present succession. It is prudent policy to groom a second heir if the first fails." They both exchanged knowing nods.

"Our nephew is another matter. He has been indiscreet, accumulating gambling debts. They let him win much and now have taken him for more. I'm sure the woman has drained him dry of information and cash. It may be the proper time to send him back to the family. He has done two summers here. He has finished his usefulness in visiting bases and armament supply factories. He can give the home office a good account of all they have and its location. We can send him off as a hero or the Basileus will send him home ***persona non grata***,' as they say here, 'an unwelcome diplomat'."

"A spy, who has seen too much," laughed Chavush.

"Exactly," continued Binbasha, "Khan Kinner may promote him."

"How about marriage for our hero? Has the family made any arrangements?" Chavush inquired.

"They've paid a bride price and have picked a girl from a good military family. Her family is securely entrenched, but not distinguished. We'll promise funds to help launch the marriage. They'll welcome a 'destroyer of pirates' and 'member of the first embassy to Constantinople.' He's met the Basileus and the famous artists here. He should have a distinguished career with our army."

"He will be a new star on the town's circuit and a hero that's easy to live with, since he's as venial as the rest of us," observed the sergeant. I'll get his passage on the next boat while you write a praise-worthy dismissal and new autumn posting."

>- - - - - - - >

The tower was simple. A small staircase led to the storage and supply rooms in the basement below. On the ground floor were located the command center and the kitchen quarters. They ate in the dining room, which was the shape of the tower, almost like a yurt.

There was the entrance from the winding staircase between the outer and inner walls that encompassed the building. Leading from the storage and supply rooms on the ground floor and basement to the administrative level, the kitchen and garrison areas then going upward to the assembly or dining area and above that the private living quarters of the commander and family.

The rough wood floor was cushioned by cut grass topped with rugs. *Kilims*, colorful woven wool fabrics, covered the walls to absorb the condensation on the stone.

As the guests gathered, the required tea ceremony was conducted by the mother and girls. A dark haired girl of about fifteen years and a blond of eleven helped their mother of about forty to do the honors passing the porcelain bowls. The guests sat around the room, backs to the wall, on the covered boxes and chests that held the family goods. All the travelers were present and served in turn starting with the oldest man, who was encouraged to talk of his experiences and travels. The commander sat with a boy of thirteen on his right and one of nine on his left.

Conversation followed the ancient formula: inquiries of health and family, standard replies or explanations if some new death or birth event had occurred. Hunnish was used by all present to the relief of the Chipchaks. Urging and polite refusals were required by etiquette at the time of serving food. Relations, goods and tribal status were revealed gradually in the stories of adventures, triumphs and defeats. Only evil people hide their doings from the judgment of others. Hiding secrets was practiced as an art.

The large communal dishes were brought to the door by the kitchen help, taken by the mistress with thanks and praise, and placed on a large cloth on the floor. The invited ones sat in a circle and pulled

the cloth partly over their crossed legs. At the open-handed bow of the host, they started eating. Wheat loaves baked from a single thin disk of dough and puffy with air were served with mare's butter and bulgur, steamed cracked wheat. Side dishes were served with both horse meat and wild game: partridge and deer. Wild onion, cress and other herbs were sprinkled on the main dishes. The silence that followed was broken only by the hostess pleading that her guests sample a bit more of this, that, or the other delicacy. Ayran was served in large horn or skull goblets. They all ate to repletion.

Reluctantly, they returned to the divans. Kumiss, a fermented drink of mare's milk, was served. It is a clear potent beverage which tended to loosen the tongue. Completely relaxed after several jokes and cups had gone around, the commander turned to Kaya.

"I hear from lieutenant Kove that you were the wild boy we hunted in the Altai, about sixteen years ago," he stated ruefully. "I realized that you must have been terrified, but I did not intend to hurt you. I knew of your existence and wished to capture you. Were you hidden by the hermit?" He attempted a smile. Kaya sat dumb.

"I understand that he found his own hiding place, though the Hermit may have known it later," Ozkurt said, interrupting the expectant silence. The three boys stopped to listen avidly.

The women sat together near the door. Some sat on the floor and talked to Fewsoon about her condition. There was an outburst of joy as the lady exclaimed and the girls clapped their hands exuberantly and laughed.

"You are from Erkan's band of the Chipchak nation? You know Maya and the hearth of the medicine yurt? I am Vashtie, my daughter had red hair like yours. Can it be? Yownja? My little Yownja?" Crying and laughing, the two women and the girls embraced. The excitement drew the men's attention. The younger girl called, "Yuzbasha, come hear this." The little boy ran over to his sisters, laughing.

"So, the daughter is found. Then you must be the Khan's heir, breast mate of Yownja." Binbasha indicated Kaya who managed to agree silently. The older boy regarded him with care. "That is the reason I sought to capture you. I realized you still lived in Altai. I had believed there was little chance of survival when your boat drifted into the river current the day I first saw you." Binbasha nodded to the attentive boy. "Remember, Bata, a careless moment causes much confusion and regret." The boy nodded solemnly, his face a miniature of his fathers.

"I should have followed the boat and rescued you. She would never put you two from her mind: 'little Kaya did this' or 'Yownja did that.'" He imitated a high voice and then laughed boisterously. There was a grin of derision on the child's face as he joined his father's amusement.

"She lives far too much in the past. She still dreams of the attack of the Persian marauders and the murder of her owner." He snorted his contempt of female weakness. The thirteen-year-old, Bata, reflected his emotion.

The women laughed, cried and compared stories for a long time. Then Vashtie came to Binbasha and drew him aside. He returned to interrupt one of Kove's stories of service with the Huns, to inform them that they were invited to winter with his family. This way, the birth of the child would be in the Ural tower.

Kaya reluctantly accepted the offer. He felt he would have to pay in more ways than gold, but they were all in no condition to continue traveling. He urgently wanted to talk with and hug his foster mother, whom he only remembered vaguely. He still feared the man, the hunter, whom he remembered sharply. He was his enemy and the killer of his brother, the stronger bear twin, Bronz.

>- - - - - - - >

Kove went on after a week to Boo'yuke Yurt, after filling everyone's ears with praise of his cleverness and accomplishments. He avoided a clear cut accounting of his joining up with Kaya and his wounding. He conveyed the idea that his service was of utmost importance to the Hun's successes. As the departing hero he made all promise to visit him in his father's yurt on their way east.

Yownja and Vashtie were constantly together with the girls, and Kaya and Sertol were invited to sit with them. Kaya was often pale and withdrawn, even with them. Sertol was companion to the younger boy, for Bata was usually otherwise occupied.

Ozkurt, who showed a strange reluctance to seek the company of the women, was active outside, traveling with Binbasha or the boys. They found him willing to answer their questions, hunt, fish, or to see their treasures. Only Perihan, the older girl, seemed to miss his presence. She was always first to greet his return.

>- - - - - - - >

Yuzbasha had packed and placed his trunk on the ship. It would depart at dawn. He was on the Street of Tulips, facing the Marmara Sea. He had waited for an hour when the boy, Stefen, finally appeared. He was running toward the house at the head of the street. He paused as the man called.

Yuzbasha smiled warmly, "You remember an admirer sent a present by me last fall? Well he would like to meet her in the church garden this evening. He has something special to say. Please have her come and he will be there. You understand don't you? I think she liked the present, right? It's important that she come." He stood aside and let the boy resume his run. He was late no doubt, but would use the message as an excuse for it.

The Khazar chuckled as he moved toward the church emptying after the vesper service. Few would remain late. The garden was darkening now. He would have her alone. He felt for his parrot-headed knife. He would need it, after he finished with her. Meanwhile, Miakim would be in the theater until late and would sleep late as she always did. She would sleep alone. He had registered at the inn next to the port. He would be there for breakfast with the uncles and their farewell.

He heard steps coming and hid under a dark tree. She had not delayed. He waited, ready to pounce, and heard the movement into the garden.

"Where are you Sergeant?" came the whispered words. "Oh, Chavush, you were so polite and formal at our encounter at the embassy party. I wondered when you would get the courage to speak up." The vast form of Magda blotted out the stars as she drew near the tree. He gasped while trying to keep quiet. Then, he panicked and bolted, tripping over the stone bench and sprawling on the graveled path. She turned toward the sounds and moved forward, concerned. "Are you hurt? What happened?"

He groaned and scrambling to his feet, ran.

She recognized him and shouted after him. "Yuzbasha, why are you here? Where is your uncle?" The second gate was open and he hobbled down the street. Behind him he heard a hiss of despite:

"Khazar scum! Barbarian dog! What evil were you up to?"

BOSPHORUS BOATS AND YALAS

PEOPLE, PLACES & PLOTS IN CHAPTER 9

Bata: Hockdale's arrogant, older son, named for the Tartar Khan.
Binbasha: 1.a Khazar general and ambassador in Constantinople.
Binbasha: 2.Hock'dale, a Tartar commander in the Urals.
Fewsoon: delivers her baby, enjoys her mother and sisters.
Hock'dale: a general holding a fortified tower on the Ural River.
Jonny: Tartar corporal, nephew of the war hero, Kove.
Kaya: though wounded, tells Shanla's story to the tower ladies.
Magda: Aunt of Stefen and Merien leaves anger for fear.
Manga bey: Tartar warrior originally from Erkan's Chipchaks.
Messenger: an old man, carries orders, spies and collects ransom.
Miakim: murder is not always the end of a love affair.
Nevaz: the new baby boy is center of interest in the tower.
Ozkurt: still able to fight on patrol, feels safer than at the tower.
Perihan: fifteen-year-old daughter of Vashtie, named for a friend.
Sevim: eleven-year-old daughter, named for Kaya's mother.
Vash'tie: mother of Fewsoon, and foster mother of Kaya.
Yownja: baby name of Fewsoon, meaning clover flower.
Yuzbasha: 1.Tower Mother's favored boy, friend of Sertol.
Yuzbasha: 2.the Khazar is in the right place for a timely deed.

GLOSSARY HELPS

ay'ran: a mixture of water and yogurt to drink.
bash'ooze-two-nay : as you have ordered; I obey; yes sir.
bulgur : hulled, cracked, and cooked wheat.
goon-eye-toon : Good afternoon
ka-la :tower; protective keep; area of last defense.
ga-la: tower, in another (Tartar) accent.
kil'lim : woven thin coverings for wall or floor.
kumiss : clear, fermented milk for festive occasions.
nevaz: courtly; to do a kindness; to pet, caress or stroke.
peck'ee: agreed; I'll do it; okay.
vah'she: wild; savage; wild child.

TOWER HOSPITALITY

Fewsoon's prompt confinement and labor were hard, but the boy-child was strong. They gave him the name Nevaz-- Caress. The infant prospered, a favorite of the family. The winter settled in soon and lasted long. The food was plain, yet abundant.

Patrolling the western border line was required and clashes with the Bulgars were frequent. Ozkurt, healed, was constantly on the front, but Kaya made excuses and stayed with Fewsoon. He truly did not look well. Kaya wondered that on their coming, they had escaped the Bulgar patrols without strife. Both tribes showed no mercy in their warring. There was no news of the other party of Chipchaks.

The spring lingered uncertainly. Nevaz, the baby, was a hearty six-months-old and the center of the tower's activities. As the traveling time drew near, so the reluctance showed on all but Kaya. He seemed pathetically eager to move on.

"Erkan, my father, will be so happy to see us. Our return with the new 'child of promise' will please his every hope for the future of the tribe. We will travel to visit my brother at the Hermitage by the valley of the chase. They will be surprised and delighted. It will be good to pray in the chapel and to hear the sung praise." He looked dreamy-eyed as he sat near the ladies as they worked.

"Peck'ee, agreed," Yownja nodded and spoke her thoughts as her hands knotted the last row of the rug, her winter's work. "Would you like to go with us, Mother?" She inquired, "Everyone would love to hear your story of the Tartar capture." The women exchanged smiles.

"I know my man would not let me go. He can't stand my absence even to visit Booyuke Yurt." She smiled modestly. "He acts hard and calloused at times, but he is really very dependant and affectionate. "He plays with the children when no one sees." She smiled to herself. "He is jealous of the girls, especially when a corporal is near."

"The Onbasha is conceited and brags about his family," fumed a red faced Perihan, "I prefer a true hero."

"But, Mother," interrupted Fewsoon, "You can get permission to travel. You have handled three husbands in your life." All laughed together nodding vigorously.

"So you say, but the first was as self-willed and determined as yourself. The second was a wonderful gentle tribesman who suffered unjustly, but I never heard more of him after his yoking and exile." Kaya drew a sharp breath. "But foster mother, Erkan's wife told me there were messages brought by the musicians," Kaya objected.

"No friends of mine, those wild wanderers brought me nothing, though they did return to the camp several times after their first appearance. Keke is a liar."

"A broken harness piece, a measure of silk, a gold Byzantine coin, a piece of broom straw, brick and a few blue flowers, all this was in a bundle," Kaya was distraught.

"A message bundle never received by me, but I do remember Keke wearing a beautiful silk shawl, but she was wife to the Khan. I envied her, but thought nothing of it." Vashtie shook her head and smiled at them. "Keke was vain and vindictive. I hope fame has brought good changes. I have continued to pray for her all these years."

"She is often ill, with the lung complaint, they say. She cannot appear in public without creating a stir, so she stays home and cares for her invalid daughter. Her nightlife is theater centered. She misses the hunts with the Chipchak," Kaya reported.

"She loved hunting and killed without mercy," Vashtie frowned, "She knifed her master and killed a Hun in the woods outpost. She was jealous. Ondar was going to trade her for the stallion. She left the knife to condemn Yuzbasha, but I got there first and took the knife and the two gold coins before someone came."

"Were you very frightened, Mother?" asked Perihan. "I should be paralyzed with fright."

"I had no time to consider anything. Someone came through the brush and the knife was Yuzbasha's. I still have dreams of pulling the knife out of him. He wasn't dead, but I couldn't stay. The Hunnish arrow was in his shoulder, and the intruder lay dead with Chipchak arrows. I feared to be the next." Her face reflected that early turmoil.

"What did you do?" asked her youngest girl, Sevim.

"I ran, hid the knife and went back to wait on the hilltop, where Yuzbasha left us." She shivered pressing her hands together as if cleaning them. Her breathing was becoming heavy.

Kaya changed the subject. "You seem to maintain your faith despite your living so far from others," Kaya complimented her.

"She commands all the believers when Ghen-chair is traveling with the chapel wagon," teased Sevim, the dimpled, with a laugh, as her mother reacted with shock.

"How can you say that? The church is for the ministers to command. I am but a servant, Ghen-chair is the *apostolos* around the Urals." Vashtie's face was red, tense.

"But you run the orphanage here, and everybody comes to you for advice or finances." Sevim hugged and kissed her mother. Still amused, she turned to the others. "Mother is patroness and mover of more than you would think possible, for one who never travels. Ghen-chair makes no decisions without consulting." She laughed and hugged her again.

"What position does Hock'dale bey take to your many activities, Mother?" Yownja asked carefully, tactfully.

"My husband respects, even admires our faith, and he listens to the morning prayers. Even sings a bit at vespers, but he equally retains his old attitudes. He says our faith is too good to be true: a heavenly vision, too hard to live on earth. I continue to pray for him, but he changes so slowly. He loves the security of wealth and power."

"That God should give so much, on the basis of our submission to His Grace and Will, seems too generous," Kaya stated. "It is the joy of believers and the doubt of unbelievers. 'A good God in a bad world seems a contradiction, unless we can understand our own sinful nature'." He smiled modestly, "Those are the Hermit's words, not mine."

"May we sing something for our guests?" inquired the girls who had grown restless with the talk.

"Yes, my dearest, what will you sing?" The mother's smile was proud as she hugged the two beauties.

"Your old favorite, Mother, about the blind *bulbul*, the nightingale, it's so beautiful and sad." The girls spoke out enthusiastically. Then they sang simply and charmingly in what they called gallop time:

THE NIGHTINGALE

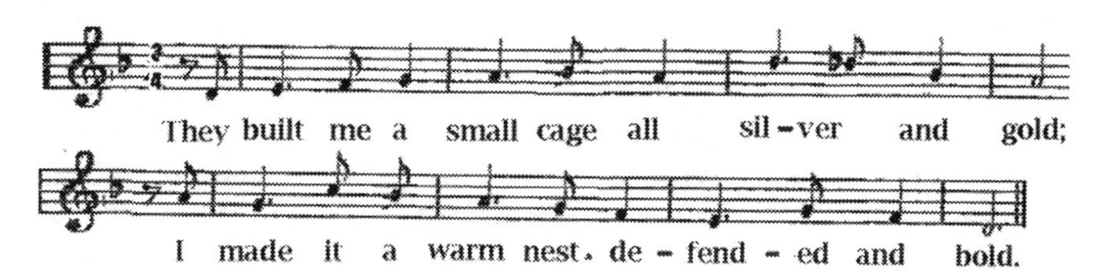

1. They built me a small cage, all silver and gold;
   I made it a warm nest, defended and bold.

2. They dug me a dungeon, deep down and pitch black;
   I made it a den with all comfort and tact.

3.They named me a *bulbul*, a nightingale blind;
God made me a songstress in Christ blessed sign.

4.They shook heads in pity and hid me away;
I found strength for love, joy and hope day by day.

5.They called me a prisoner, a plaything for fee;
I found God in praying, and faith made me free.

6.God gave me four children, the pride of a wife
I taught them to love our Great Giver of Life.

There was a brief silence as the two sweet voices finished the song. Then, the Mother kissed both, hiding her tears and Fewsoon did the same; while Kaya beamed his approval. After all, the youngest bore his mother's name. Then, a servant interrupted with food. In this way the winter passed pleasantly.

>- - - - - - - >

We have a concern of magnitude, Majesty," began the minister of the Interior. "You must hear it before it becomes common knowledge and the rumors start. Our leading actress Miakim is dead, murdered and robbed."

Shock registered on the face of the Basileus, who stuttered saying, but I heard her last night. She sang 'From My Window' in a balcony scene."

"I, too, was there, Majesty, but the fact remains: her throat was cut and her house trashed. Valuables are gone and none knew until dawn."

"Thieves would not have killed her. Perhaps bound her, but this can only be a matter of love or hate."

"Both, Your Highness, we were aware of the departure of the young Khazar officer with whom she shared bed and secrets. None too soon for we have written out a denunciation and were ready to issue it next week. They have anticipated us and sent him home. His boat left at dawn. The embassy was there to see him off. He is reported to have retired early with the attention of a doctor. He was in pain with a badly-bruised knee. It was swollen and the doctor doubts he could have walked to their house. He was able to walk to the near dock, while others carried his hand luggage."

The minister made a gesture of despair. "He is the obvious suspect for she reported that he had accused her of reading his documents and prying for secrets. She was also convinced that he loved her. He had reluctantly left for the inn the day before the sailing."

"Still he is a man with important facts he spied out, and we should recall him for inquiry. The ship will not have cleared the mouth of the Bosphorus yet. Have it pulled over." There was a long pause.

"Majesty, the ship is a Khazar vessel with Captain and sailors of that nation. He has diplomatic immunity and we are in delicate negotiations for the return of Kertch Port to its former governor and neutral status. His alibi is good and will hold up in a court of law. There is another mystery in this puzzle." He leaned over to speak confidentially, "A pot of lavender and a broken mirror were found at the water-gate door of the house. It was thrown just after sun rise.

"Who would throw a pot of lavender at an actress' house?"

"We wish we knew, Majesty, Our security agent reports a large man in a sandal, with only one paddler, came and smashed the object against the door and left without delay. Our agent pursued the boat from the shore, until he found a sandal for hire. Then, he states that it entered the Marmara Sea and was lost near the old city. It was misty, and too far away to overtake the boat. He returned to his station to discover the death. He had been gone over an hour. The maid, Ifrah, comes late, to give her breakfast in bed. That is when they discovered her in bed, dead, a bread knife was found near her. But it was not stained. The house was in disarray and the valuables were gone."

"The pot of lavender was a distraction to lead your man on a false trail. Were no others observed near the water-gate?"

"Ships were sailing and boats rowing in all directions. Boats were seen by neighbors from their yalas, but no one watched to see where they put in. It's the hour vendors and delivery people make their visits. We will question some, but the Khazar ship will not delay at the Bosphorus mouth."

"We will accuse the tall man. Let the Khazar boat go and take their hero home. They will have to grant our wishes for Kertch Port. We will bury our beloved lady with appropriate honor, and her favorite chaplain will preside. With time, God willing, another songstress will appear to fill our sad hearts with music."

>- - - - - - - >

Kaya was exercising near the stables at the foot of the tower, when the man rode in and, dismounting, left the servants to attend to his horse. He was as tall and lanky as a Chipchak hill man and his speech to the servants had foreign echoes. Kaya put down the rocks he was lifting and sat to observe this man more closely. The man walked to the kitchen to receive a ration and came back to eat it in the warming sun.

"*Goon ay toon*, good afternoon. We've not met before. I'm Kaya of the Chipchaks."

The man looked him up and down carefully and answered slowly, "I understood that you were wounded and not outside the tower." He looked around uneasily, then continued, "You have grown much more than I expected."

One of the servants came out of the stable and said, "Your new horse is fed, and groomed, Man'ka bey. He is ready to travel when you are." The man nodded his agreement.

Kaya spoke quickly, "You were taken in the Tartar raid on the home yurt eight years ago, Man'ga bey." His voice was sympathetic and warm, but the man's response was confused.

He was bolting his food down like a hungry wolf, as he muttered. "Yes, uh, no we moved our family here, Erkan bey was angry with me. I left before the raid. That is, I was not in the village when they left for

tribute in the north. You were in E'peck Kent," his voice faltered. He stopped eating, put down his bowl.

Kaya nodded and said, "So you were assigned to the western edge near the Bulgars when Hock'dale bey was moved west." Again the man agreed and moved toward his horse. "As a Chipchak you were free to change bands and move where you would. Do you still enjoy such freedom?" inquired Kaya. The man mounted and rode off to patrol, without another word. Kaya shook his head in wonder and turned to exercise Altom. He would take her on a short walk and run everyday. Patting her nose and giving her a treat he said, "You would never sell your herd for a promise of a better pasture, as this man has, would you? What advantage is there? You must measure the loss as compared to the meager gains. If we choose, without prayer to Tanra, we suffer the results. I chose hastily to distrust Oleg and to attempt an escape with the rafts. With patience the boyars might have been persuaded to protect us. If so, Igor might still be alive. We would have parted friends. We still suffer the effects of my choice. Manga too, chose badly."

>- - - - - - - >

The mist curled around Yuzbasha and he knew he must be back at the yala on the Bosphorus Channel. Again he heard her voice, soft and plaintive: "I thought you loved me." Miakim's face and form slowly emerged from the surrounding mist. He saw her beautiful figure filling her filmy silk negligee. She reached out a hand to touch his face. He instinctively flinched. She repeated the question, "Didn't you love me?" She was coming closer. She reached out again to touch his face. Then she would kiss him. His breath came raggedly, his heart raced. Her hand was as cold as the ice on the rivers. He feared her kiss would be death. He struggled to free himself. The words: 'Love forgives, pride kills!' echoed in his head. He sat up gasping on the bed in his little cubby hole, the bare quarters of a junior officer. He was chilled by his sweat. Getting up he dressed in the pre-dawn cold of first light. He dared not sleep again.

Yuzbasha stared at his uncle's letter written to the family in Getchet. He had already opened it and inserted the number one before the sum uncle had offered to give to finance his nephew's marriage and career. He hoped the distractions of duty in the largest city in the Western world would cause a man's memory to be vague about dispatched letters. Now he wished to erase the insertion, but it would be noticed. He would need the money he assured himself, and the dream was not a warning, only a nightmare to be shaken off. The other letters had been taken by his new commander at Port Azov and forwarded by messenger to Kinner Khan. The Khazar military boats were now using the interior port and avoiding Kertch Port. The Don and Donetz Rivers were frozen and his return to the capital was delayed, countermanded by the Khan himself. Generals came to debrief him. Within the military routine, he had regular lectures briefing the commanders on the location and strength of Byzantine posts. Sometimes he ended by reminiscing about the great city, while answering questions. Between envy and acclaim, life was not as unpleasant as it could have been on winter duty. His stories of fighting pirates were listened to with interest. Yet, while the military data interested his fellow officers, the fact that he had spied them out, gained no warm congratulations. On the contrary, many showed scarcely veiled contempt for a spy.

>- - - - - - - >

Ozkurt and Kaya rode with the Commander on the south edge of the escarpment looking out over the newly–green, rolling plains. The figure they had been watching for an hour was now close upon them. The messenger drew up before them and shouted a greeting. He rode to them and bowed slightly to Binbasha.

"Our Khan Bata sends greetings and requests that the hostages be sent to him at Booyuke Yurt. An escort will be waiting at the halfway station in a week."

"*Bash ooze two nay*, I obey. What news, messenger, are there caravans on the horse road?" The commander asked.

"A small east-bound caravan from Gechit Kent passed far to the south last month, but was delayed by sickness and some were brought into the camp for help."

"What nature the illness? To take such into the camp is dangerous," Binbasha looked stern and disapproving.

"Fever, discomfort from the brightness of light, and great thirst." He shrugged, "The shaman treats them in a medicine yurt with aromatic smoke to keep them sweating. He promises a cure, and the merchants pay well."

"May the spirits of the ancestors guard you," responded Binbasha. "What of the promised moneys. I have waited two years. Accounts need to be settled."

"Obedience comes before rewards," quoted the tough little rider who lived on his horse as naturally as men at home. "I've waited three years but this summer I get mine."

"I hear and obey. The prisoners will be sent." The angry words of Binbasha were correct, but not submissive.

"The Khan expects as much. I have messages from the merchants to the great river town, a request for medicine money from the families." Here the little man smiled proudly, happy to be an agent collecting ransom. He rode away on the southwest road to Gechet.

>- - - - - - - >

Dear Judith,

In a week we will leave the city to go home, yes. Kertch Port will be small, but beautiful. Everything is settled and father is fixing up the house. The city is in a festive mood, yes. He says everyone asks about me, and wants me there now. I could wish to close my eyes and puff, home, no? Magda is getting everything ready. She is nearly frantic to get away from here, yes. Last Spring she was at all the festivals and parties. Yet, now, she says no to all invitations. She almost never goes out of the house, even to church, yes. She asks for the priest to visit often and talk about Hesus and His death for our sins. She was never interested in things about God before. She questions me about all who come to the house, even deliveries.

Letters from Sarayjik say that Olga's baby girl is -- oh, so beautiful, yes. The baby has white hair like sweet little grandmother, no? They let the babies play together: golden boy with snowflake girl. He is sixteen months old now and she only eight. I wonder if Fewsoon is pregnant yet. It's eighteen months since they were married at the Autumn Festival, yes. Some say that 'no news is good news,' but I don't believe it. No news is dull, yes.

Hun troops return from forest country to get away from intense cold, deep snow and surprise attacks. Koosta is sent beyond the Rhine River to fight Franks. He has no treasure beyond a few trinkets from north woods and has no standing in court. Sarayjik thinks he will die there on the front. Here I'm waiting, impatient for the day of departure. Stefen is sorry to lose school-friends this spring, but thinks he will become a sea captain, yes. Oh, I forgot to tell you, we travel on the Sea Witch again. I hope it is easy trip without pirates, no? But I think Stefen would love such an adventure. I'll write again on arrival.

In great haste and much love,
Merien Papasian

>------- >

Regimental lunch was over. Yuzbasha walked in the growing power of the sun. He was still heavily clad against the freezing wind. At the river bank he stopped to watch a platoon of men removing the securing ropes and covers from a medium sized boat of ten places. He asked the onbasha, a man he recognized from his trip across the Black Sea in the fall, "What are you doing with the boat? There is still ice covering the river."

The man , a local, looked over and nodded. " Ay, t'would seem so to outsiders like yourself. Do you see the water on top the ice today? T'aint much, but it shows that it's softening." He pointed to a lone traveler with a burdened pack animal, following him across the frozen river. "You see, he'll be okay today and maybe tomorrow. It'll be breaking up before the new moon. Then it'll be too dangerous." He nodded thoughtfully. "Sun's warming, most don't notice, it seems slight at first."

Yuzbasha squinted against the glare. "There's something larger coming over there." He pointed at a mass of dark dots approaching the other shore of the river. "Looks like horsemen," he concluded.

"Darn fools, to try to cross with a cavalcade, must be twenty men there." All the men stopped work to watch.

"Back to work," Yuzbasha shouted. "Get the boat ready. We may need it before they get across." The work speeded as the horsemen, after a pause, decided to follow the lone traveler over the river's surface. They were too far away to hear or heed a shout of warning. The leaders had dismounted to lead their horses across the ice. However, one of the drovers of the pack animals had cracked his whip. This sent his mounted drovers, horses and mules over the ice as a mob. The ice seemed to hold.

"Maybe they'll make it," Yuzbasha murmured.

The boatmen stopped again to watch, but the corporal shouted at them. "Lift the boat off its supports and down to the ice."

Yuzbasha joined the men in the lift, and righting the boat at the bank, they slid it on to the ice. There was a slight tremor as the walking men reached the center of the river. The drovers too had slowed their pace, and followed tentatively. The fact of danger had at last caught them. A sudden crack like lightning and a roar like thunder, announced the parting of the ice behind the mob. All motion stopped, as men and animals found themselves on ice floes or in icy water. Shouting and panic followed.

Yuzbasha entered the boat, while the men pushed it over the ice. They raced to the open water, jumped into the boat, seized the oars and started to rescue the drowning men. Part of the cavalcade had been able to pass on foot, but it took many trips -all afternoon- to rescue the men and animals from the ice floes.

"It'll all be breaking up tomorrow," observed the corporal as the ice shifted and crackled. The whole regiment turned out to watch and to carry the rescued to the warmth of the barracks or stables. More boats were readied and launched. The crews changed when one team tired. The troops sent up a roaring cheer each time the boat landed its bedraggled victims. Yuzbasha waved his arms in response and helped the retrieved men out of the boat. Others led the exhausted horses, pulled to the shore by the rowers, up the bank to safety. They dried, rubbed and blanketed them as they went to the stables. Repeatedly, Yuzbasha gestured a return to the water to rescue more, as the crew manned the oars and the troops cheered. He was a hero again.

TO THE RESCUE

PEOPLE, PLACES & PLOTS IN CHAPTER 10

Bata Khan: does not admit mistakes in his long reign.
Binbasha: Hockdale destroys an enemy and sends a murder squad.
Fewsoon: escapes with her baby but finds no help from relatives,
Hock'dale: kills the oppressor but must condemn others to be safe.
Jonny: the corporal must pursue and kill the released Chipchaks.
Kaya: must run for his life with those he loves, against all odds.
Kinner Khan: humiliates his rescuer and guard before promoting him.
Nevaz: the baby travels and hides with the family.
Ozkurt: takes his part in the escape from Booyuke Yurt.
Yuzbasha: finds himself disciplined as the Khan's personal guard.

GLOSSARY HELPS

ay'ran: a mix of water and yogurt to drink.
bash'ooze-two-nay: as you have ordered; I obey; yes, sir.
Boo yuk Yurt: big tent; big town; capital city.
bulgur: hulled, cracked, and cooked wheat.
goo lay goo lay; good bye; happily go; go now.
kumiss: a drink of fermented mares' milk.
yasa: law; ancient oral traditions: tribal code.

10 BATA KHAN

AN INSIDE JOB

As they rode, Kaya was lost in thought. He felt better because he had been right. They were caught by the hunter, but not killed like his brother, Bronz, and after a pleasant imprisonment were being sent to the seat of power. Mother had cried and pleaded for them. She was unable to retain even Yownja and the baby, Nevaz, with her. Perihan, too, had begged permission to accompany them, perhaps as much for Ozkurt as for the baby. Hugs and crying were plentiful, and Kaya now cleared his mind of confusion about his mother of those early years.

Tribal lore had been correct; the Tartars were old enemies and not to be trusted even with honeyed words and hospitality. Though Ozkurt had helped fight the Bulgars, no gratitude from Binbasha or Kove was expected. When they reached the Tobal river, they would be objects of barter to go to the highest bidder, east or west.

Dispensing with frugality and reasonable passage rates, Bata Khan had become greedy and luxury loving, thus forcing the caravan traffic farther south for safer routes. The vital line between protected passage and piracy had been breached.

East, far beyond the Ishim river where Tartar power thinned out, western Chipchaks lived. There the traditions were still guarded and merchants protected. Kaya had been caught in running the gauntlet. Demands had no doubt been sent to Erkan and how would the band respond? How much would the ransom be for a ‘child of promise’? How would they make them pay?

In the distance the disciplined ranks of Booyuke Yurt could be seen. There was a strange moving haze over the town. Kaya felt a sudden shiver down his spine. They were at the center of the evil empire. In the distance the city seemed to be moving under a spiral of a black, but transparent, cloud. Black dots swirled in the sky. Then, as they drew nearer the sounds reached their ears. Shrieks and caws of scavenger birds filled the air above the city. Booyuke Yurt was filled with dead.

Riding in from the west, the stench of rotting flesh filled the air and the birds flew heavily from their feeding, as they approached. The Khan's yurt and royal tents lay near the river above the ford. There were two old men in the normally crowded courtyard. The commander, Hock'dale, rode forward to demand an explanation.

"What is this curse of death that fills the city of Booyuke Yurt?" One of the old ones responded dejectedly.

"It is a return of the spotted pox that passed from the Han people in my grandfather's day, now returning from the West. I had the sickness as a child for it stayed several generations killing less each decade. Now it returns in power to kill our babies and all who have not paid homage to its terrors. Most have fled the city and only a few of the old remain for the plague will not strike those who mastered it once."

"What of our Khan, Bata. Did he survive the pox as a child?" inquired the commander.

"Yes," they answered, "he is here in the tent, mourning the loss of his sons."

"We will see him," demanded Hock'dale bey. They entered the tent and the Khan lay on the divan unattended except for one man. The Khan looked them over and spoke to Binbasha.

"See what the spirits have visited upon us. But we have offered the sacrifices and obeyed the *Yasa*, code of the ancients. Why should we be cursed now?" His voice was high, irascible and whining. The standing man shrugged.

"You took sick merchants into your town without quarantine or precautions," he stared accusingly.

"I followed the directions of the shaman," the Khan whined. "The spirits approved. Hospitality is blessed."

Hock'dale snorted his contempt and stated briefly, "They had much wealth, and greed overcomes caution." Silence fell as the two men's eyes locked, each glared at the other. Slowly the Khan let his head drop.

"I brought the prisoners. We have kept them safe according to your command," Binbasha reported.

"The ransom has been paid, and we have other preoccupations. We will release them. Jomer of E'peck Kent was willing to give what Erkan would never part with."

"You are excused," said Binbasha to the old attendant. "I have a special matter for your master's ears alone." The old man nodded and left.

"Have you a knife?" He spoke to Bata Khan as he stood near a bowl of fruit. "The pomegranate rind is tough, and we left our knives, by custom, in the outer court." The old man passed over his knife while Binbasha attended to a large red pomegranate. He dropped the knife on the tray and gave half the fruit to Kaya with an order. "Wait for me outside the inner door. I have one last thing to say." Kaya left, eating the sticky red seeds of the pomegranate.

Binbasha approached and extended the other half of the fruit to Bata Khan. "How strong and fine is your brocade on divan and cushions," said the commander.

"It is of the best eastern quality," said the old Khan irritably, "now what is your secret?"

"I bear a farewell message," said the commander and pressed a brocaded pillow down over the Khan's face firmly. The old Khan resisted strongly and Hockdale bey reached over to the knife on the tray. He plunged it into the old man's heart. He left the room when the body under its coverlets ceased to twitch.

"Wait here," he said to Kaya who still picked at the pomegranate in the inner court, "I will see the old councilor in the outer court alone and then, come when I call you." Kaya nodded his understanding and ate on while the commander went on out.

"The Khan would talk a bit with the ransomed man, then he wishes to rest, do not disturb him until the evening meal, on pains of his extreme displeasure." Binbasha's confident tone assured the old ones, and they nodded their approval. He moved impatiently and cocked his head. "Kaya, aren't you finished yet?" he inquired loudly. "Come on." Kaya appeared, sticky fingered, still eating the pomegranate and looking apologetic. "No? Never mind, we must go." Kaya bowed to the old men in the outer court and followed the commander out of the palace complex, where they joined the others of their party.

"We will ride to the river ford. We must waste no time in this city of death," ordered the commander.

At the military tent that controlled the crossings, the commander turned to his escorting troopers. "You will rest here, get some food at the camp mess and feed your mounts. They will need strength. Stay out of the town. Looters will be executed. The abandoned goods belong to Tartar families. Do not rob your brothers."

"Fellow warrior against the Bulgars," he said to Ozkurt, "You have decided to leave my service and reject my offered gifts. I regret but respect your choice. *Goo-lay goo-lay*, go well! May the spirits open your road as you continue southeast to your homeland." He turned to Kaya and bowed.

"Foster son and daughter, go well to your earned rest. Care for little Nevaz, teach him to be a warrior."

"Sir," pleaded Kaya, "we have no food and the horses are weary. Let us eat and rest here."

"Yes," echoed Ozkurt, "As you value our service do give us food for travel and fresh mounts."

"Am I a khan to dispose of great wealth? E'peck kent has bought your freedom, nothing more. So, you are free to go. I have duties to perform. Your guide, Kove, returned to die of the plague; the family will perform the last rituals." He shrugged disdainfully. "So ends the life of our impoverished war hero." He turned to go.

"Foster father, without fresh horses we are at risk with the first tribal patrol we meet. Please reconsider," Fewsoon's words were soft and respectful and seemed to anger him more than ever.

"Procure your own. I know you have money. Ride on now, go by the mess and take some food with you. Kaya wears the ivory swan medallion, your flock waits for you. Go to them. You must be out of camp within the hour." Binbasha was red-faced and shouting now, waving his arms. This was his farewell. It was time to leave.

>- - - - - - - >

"You wonder why you find yourself with Kinner Khan at the Don River Bend, eh Lieutenant? Don't think you saved my life by taking me off the ice floe. No! I was destined to continue my rule as the Khan. My heir is not in condition to succeed me. Tanra knows and governs such things. Don't think any of the benefits you enjoy come from a sentiment of gratitude. You were doing your duty. You could have been assigned to some other work at the time of rescue. Another would have done your work. Entertain no false hopes. You showed initiative. In spite of the weakness which we will purge out of you, I've decided to take you to the capital for instruction. I lost several valuable adjutants and generals on that day of disaster. So I've taken you into my personal guard for training. Don't interrupt me now. I know you're thankful, and well you should be. Learn the discipline of silence when your master speaks. I know of your gaming debts and of the temptations of that hell hole where you worked. I know about the actress-spy and your trip over from our ship to retrieve forgotten personal items from the yala the morning of departure. Did you think the ship's master would not report it? She got what she deserved. The question is do you deserve better? You've much to learn, Yuzbasha. I've had the guide, who led the Donetz River crossing, and the herd-master seated on sharp stakes. I'll have the same fate for you and anyone else who blunders in my service. As long as your actions profit myself and my people, you'll be tolerated. Enjoy being a hero for a season. I'll make you work hard enough for what you get. Remember you're mine, life and limb, now, and into your future; which I'll govern."

>- - - - - - - >

"Come, hurry, we will go now." Kaya was mounted and moving off toward the army camp. "Yownja, you come with me to the camp for food. Ozkurt, you look in the market for animals. Take anything you can get." Everyone knew that there was no market in the dead town,

but he would round up any stray stock and bring it, giving a small coin to any who claimed ownership.

There was hardly two score of men at the camp: a cook and helpers, the ford guards who stayed for the passage money, a patrol off duty, and their own escort. They were bunched in small groups eating round communal basins of boiled bulgur, whole cooked wheat. Some camp followers and survivors from the town huddled at the edge of the camp hoping for scraps and left-overs.

Kaya wasted no time, but went straight to the cook and obtained some of the bulgur, and put it in a leather sack. Several hunks of cooked horse flesh were dumped on top of that, and some bread, was wrapped separately. These would provide food for the coming day. The cook willingly received a small coin for his wares. Ozkurt, meanwhile, rode round the edge of the village inspecting stray stock and appropriating apt, strong horses. Kaya mixed kumiss with the warm cooked grain and fed all the horses the mixture for strength.

They were over the ford and riding up the opposite bank before the hour was past. As they reached the top of a hill beyond, a cry of alarm came from the tents of the Khan. They saw the commander and some men ride over to the tents as the commotion spread. Screams and cries spread, dogs took up the noise that the living echoed.

"Everyone ride now, east, at a run. Something has been discovered at the Khan's tent. We must distance ourselves, lest there soon be a new Khan and new demands," Kaya ordered and the band hurried out of sight.

>- - - - - - - >

The howling of the dogs and the wails of the rump court were beyond description. The Tartars made their anguish known to all the world. All the male relatives and personal bodyguard cut off the last joint of the little finger of their left hand. It was an ancient custom for, now, their anguish was real. They deposited them at the feet of the Khan and burned him with the fingers on a funeral pyre. In burning the body they followed the southern practice of the Indo-European Aryans whose wars, women and ways they increasingly shared.

The Khan's dark contorted face and knife wound revealed violence as the cause of death and the court remembered the presence of the ransomed man whose hands were red with pomegranate juice. The other half of the fruit was in the hands of the Khan. Red stained the pillow of the divan. Thus was the murderer easily identified and Onbasha Jonny and the escort of ten men were sent to hunt out and destroy the guilty one.

Hockdale bey, the commander took charge of everything. The survivors of key families, like those of Kove, his now dead lieutenant, were ordered west to the Ural tower, The heart of the people would now beat on the frontier under a new leader.

>- - - - - - - >

Hockdale bey sat his horse on a hilltop overlooking the river, the setting sun could not fail to reveal his exhaustion. He faced east with his head on his chest, so the moist west wind blew behind him. His horse's head was bowed. Down his hand and horses back a small drip of blood coursed regularly from his severed fingers. He had volunteered even the end joint of his sword hand as well as the traditional left. He had arrived at the end of his trail of servitude to the Tartars. Behind in the camp the howling of the women, men and animals continued. Even the animals mourned their own wounds and amputations: tails or toes. Only those under a vow of vengeance; Corporal Jonny and the escort, their faces streaked with ashes, would escape the wounds. They became a posse to avenge a death.

Hockdale bey, the Commander meditated on the results of his actions and choices. He spoke to the wind which also mourned and sighed.

"Sweet revenge has become bitter in the act. Where has the feeling of triumph fled? The khan was a monster. He was destroying the trade on the Horse Road and was guilty of greedy brigandage against all the needs and good of the tribe. He was heartily hated by the principal families, but will they love me better? Me, the upstart and war captive? If I married one of the old family's daughters would that win acceptance?" No one answered; only the dusk heard.

"One of my girls is already destined for marriage to secure peace on the new western border with the Bulgars. Should the other go to a chief family? If Ozkurt had stayed or wins through, I could offer her to him. She would like that, but he may not win the leadership of the Chipchak, when Kaya is killed. He could have stayed. I wouldn't have to offer one of mine to the Bulgars. How I wish I could have the love and loyalty that he gives to that Kaya. I am rich now and rule a great, powerful people. I'm a great warrior. Why should he leave me for him?" Silence answered him.

"How will I face Vashtie? She will hear it all from others. She will guess. She will look at me in pity and pray for me. I will feel helpless, guilty and furious; then we will quarrel. I'll hit her hard and think her ungrateful. I supply all she needs. Why should she complain? If I take another, isn't that my right?" Silence, only his heart reproached him.

"Didn't I give a joint of my finger on the sword hand? They were astonished when I made the dedication and hacked it off. Who will doubt my loyalty to the miserable Khan? Many will gain by his death. If he were a varmint raiding our animals, wouldn't everyone rejoice? Why should I regret killing an evil beast? Is the killing of a man so different from that of an animal?" Silence gave no answers.

"Now, I rule as Khan, none will dare disobey me. I can renew our coffers with trade. I can persuade our enemies to make peace.

I will have to search out the rebels and those who plot against me first. When Kove's protégée, Jonny, returns I will have to reward him publicly. He will want Perihan. Will his family back me as he has?" None answered, but his heart could not rest.

"I am alone. Ozkurt was a friend, but who can I trust now? Will I always fear the daggers of the nobles or the poisons of their women? Vashtie loves me, but I fear her God, and her presence brings anguish and remorse. Why must I suffer so? Can no one save me from uncertainties?" Quiet came and a breathless pause touched his heart.

The wind moaned around him now. He felt his tears on his hands mixing with his blood's drippings. The horse shivered and sighed. He abruptly looked around. The setting sun's light dimmed. The sound of drunken howls came startlingly from the camp behind him. His dryness and chill touched him first. Fear struck suddenly. His hair stood on end as his body woke to the danger. Anyone could kill him where he sat alone, and never be apprehended. The dark and silence would hide them. He realized he would never know safety again. He raked his horse with spurs and whip and plunged toward the camp like a madman, leaving the silence to rule and wind to mourn.

REMORSE

PEOPLE, PLACES & PLOTS IN CHAPTER 11

Bata Khan: murdered ruler of the Tartar nation.
Bata: the boy feels compelled by duty and custom to sacrifice.
Fewsoon: cares for baby Nevaz and calls for Tanra's help.
forest hunters: know the hand of oppression from Tartars.
Gen'chair: the wise Apostolos with a mobile chapel.
Gochen: as acting commander, guards Prince Ilkin and son.
Ilkin: the heir of Kinner Khan, has another narrow escape.
Jonny: bent on justice and revenge, feels nothing must stop him.
Kaya: has traveled far, and must go yet farther.
Magda: wants to leave the city and return to Kertch Port.
Merien: puzzled by her father's teasing, waits for news.
Per'ihan: feels lonesome and friendless, but will not sacrifice.
Sertol: willingly helps in the tasks of sentry and guard duty.
Sevim: worries about the problem confronting her mother.
Vashtie: there is a price for the dreaded day, yet she is prepared.
Yuzbasha: Vashtie's son, is rejected by his brother Bata, again.
Yuzbasha: now a Royal Khazar Guard, seeks greater things.

GLOSSARY HELPS

ah-ee: ouch, reaction to pain.
ah'bla: elder sister, a position of respect and authority.
bulbul: nightingale.
evet: yes; right; sure.
ke-se-je; executioner; one who cuts.
koor'bon: sacrifice; blood offering.
ool'ack: boy; son; page or young helper.
Tanra's Garden: heaven; after-life for believers in Yesu.
Tan'rum: my God; an invocation in prayer or surprise.
vah'she: beast; wild thing; savage.
Yesu gel: come Jesus; Lord, help us.

CUT SHORT

"Always running, it's like my childish nightmares. The hunter will be behind us again, closing the distance, solving every trick and trace, narrowing the gap," Kaya's voice was faint and troubled as they sat with exhausted horses beside a small draw eating the contents of the bag filled at the cooks' tent. "We will cross on the rocky ground and take our supply of water and walk from midnight northward. They will expect us to go south or east. The sun has set and there are clouds in the west. We will hope for rain to take away all traces. Perhaps the death of the Khan will occupy them." Kaya's face was troubled.

"The Khan is dead then?" questioned Fewsoon. She sat with the baby looking up at her from her out-stretched legs, which she moved rhythmically while she ate. She hummed when no one talked.

"I was not sure at the time, but now I know something sinister happened after I was sent outside to wait," Kaya hunched his shoulders and shivered. "The man is greedy for power and control. My foster mother is the helpless *bulbul* in her song." He hung his head in sorrow.

"Mother will be safe in God's hands. She has learned to live in His care. She will bring the man and all her children to Tanra's Garden. Her prayers will prevail. We too, will live, in spite of pursuit. No hunter has ever caught my Kaya." Fewsoon's smile was trusting. Sertol nodded his agreement. Kaya smiled in return.

"The first time caught is usually the last," he stated, but continued to smile. "We will make them work hard and pay dear for our lives. Now we must sleep while the horses sleep and graze. Ozkurt has the first watch. I will take the second."

"I can take the third watch," offered Sertol, anxious to do his share.

"Not tonight, we march on the third watch till dawn. Then, we hide. You'll have lots of watches to pass there. Now, we must sleep."

Fewsoon sat smiling at the baby, Nevaz, both were full and sleepy. She sang gently:

1. Sleep-bringer, hark unto me.
Sleep-bringer, come and help me.
Sleep-bringer, bring your bag of dreams.
Come from your high heavenly home,
You, who dwell above, guard my soul.
Send angels near, keep us from harm.
Shield us from wrong.
To protect our sleep,
Angels, vigil keep at our heads and feet.
Renew our strength for a new day.
You, who give new hope and warm love,
We trust in you. Hear my plea,
Come to me. Bring us sleep, rest and dreams.

2. Sleep-bringer, hear me calling.
Sleep-bringer, calm our fears now.
Sleep-bringer, show us your sweet dreams.
Come dry our tears, comfort our hearts.
You who live on high, give us life.
Send angels nigh, sing to our hearts.
Guard us from wrong.
Angels vigil keep, human needs to meet,
Awake or asleep.
So guide our paths through dangerous ways,
You, who mark our steps and our words.
Help us be true, just like you.
Life is sweet, baby sleeps, softly dreams.

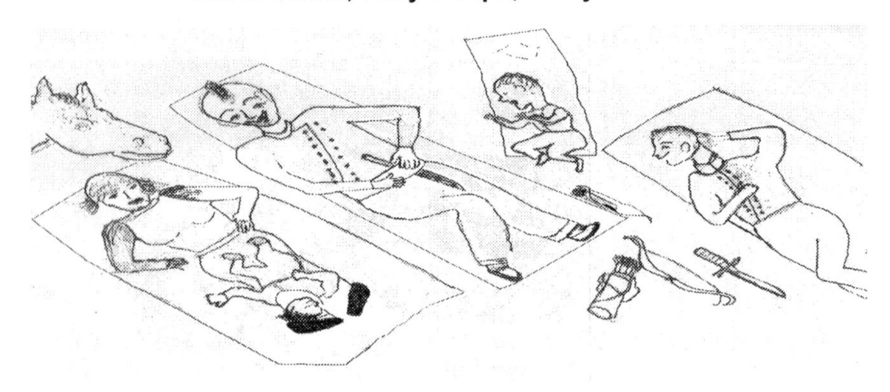

TRAVELERS' REST

SLEEP-BRINGER

>- - - - - - - >

Yuzbasha sent his uncle's family letter off by messenger. Now was the time to act. His uncles had detailed the necessary steps to improve the family fortune. He had found approval and success as the Spirit of the Ancestors had smiled on his trials. Now, he must promote the claims of the heir his family served. If the plans matured, he could expect a reward that included marriage. His people and local culture precluded an arrangement like he had had with Miakim. The bride would be chosen for him. A power of veto could be exercised only for extreme distaste. Long lived grudges could be opened by blunt refusals. Tact was required at each point of matchmaking. However, such plans always depended on wealth and honor. He must please the Khan from whom all promotions came. To help a man become the Khan of the Khazar, was to assure the elevation of the family to near royal status. Khan Kinner would remain at the Bend for a week more. He planned carefully, leaving no room for error.

>- - - - - - - >

Several times Kaya detoured for no apparent reason. At one spot they skirted and took the long way around an extended colony of marmots whose burrows extended for miles. When Fewsoon asked why they didn't take the direct route, Kaya smiled and quipped that they would leave the fleas and holes to bother the pursuers. "Remember Maya always said that the marmot towns were the lair of the 'sweating death.' She is my *ahb'bla*, elder sister who must be obeyed. We will leave the risk and dangers to our enemies."

Forced to trade for fresh horses and food, their progress was observed by local people. What remained of the wedding gifts were traded off one by one. Trails through forest and across steppe had to be learned or guides secured.

>- - - - - - - >

The ten men of the escort, now in pursuit, were circling to find a trail. Their first efforts had been to the south. Now they formed a line ten miles wide moving north, each rider just in sight of the others on each side. All carried a set of signal flags for communication and rode the line. It was the sixth day before they found definite signs of movement northeast toward the taiga, the forested world on the grassland's northern edge.

The Tartar force found the trail and carefully took the short cut through the prairie dog colony. Marmots' burrows are harmless if you walk your horse across instead of riding. If you watch out for the burrows so the horses will not break a leg you can suffer a few flea bites and cut miles off your pursuit. From there they slowly traced the small group.

The Tartars were accustomed to terrorizing the forest people for food and information as they went, relentless in their progress. The Onbasha, Corporal Jonny, was vigorous and ambitious. He was sure of his position and felt free to threaten and to fine tribal chiefs among the timid forest and northern people, users of boats or reindeer.

The trail was lost a dozen times in the freezing and thaw of swamps and forests in the north country. The method of circling and interrogating all humans contacted, always put them back on trail. Though it cost time, every tribal chief and shaman was a mine of information about any activity in their area, even when they lied or left out vital facts.

As sure and relentless as the grey wolf, their ancestor, they would trail on and on. Exhaustion or entrapment would deliver the pursued

prey into their hands. Recognition, promotion, marriage and the future of each man depended on it. Life for life, justice must come to balance the offence. Only the blood of the guilty could cover the crime.

>- - - - - - - >

The river port had opened with the coming of spring. Yuzbasha made it a practice to go and talk to the arriving sailors. Since most Khazar people had little in the way of maritime traditions, it did not touch his pride if he asked questions, and / or confessed ignorance. Though lakes and streams were a part of his early life, he found that boats fascinated him. There were so many kinds with different uses. He tried to learn about them all. He bought models that were perfect replicas of the larger types. Warships, in particular, held his interest. His experiences with the pirates assured his attention there.

Yuzbasha was well aware that there was another person, very important to him, that had the same attraction: Daniel, the infant son of Prince Ilkin. He became Daniel's friend and not only told his story, but showed off his models. The child was young, but precocious. Yuzbasha fought a battle within himself as to the plans he had laid out. He thought his uncles would approve his reluctant decision. He chose an hour when the docks would be deserted. He found Sherbet preoccupied with house affairs, and invited the child out to see a new model floating on the river. It was large enough to hold a boy his size. He assured Daniel it was his to keep. It was tied to the wharf post. He was told that he could sit in it until Sherbet came looking for him.

Without fear the boy crawled into the canoe as Yuzbasha walked down to a docked boat. The captain was aboard and willing to share a bottle of wine in the cabin. The canoe was tied loosely, so that the knot would yield to pressure. It was not designed to carry people, large or small. The canoe tipped over and swamped within a few feet of the dock. It moved away on the current, while the child screamed once and floundered. The captain heard the cry and left the cabin, Yuzbasha reluctantly followed. They ran to the spot closest to the child. And the captain threw a rope. The child was too far away and sinking again, when the giant form of Gochen came running and threw himself headlong off the dock. He sank where he surfaced, after his momentum failed. He reappeared downstream holding the child. He sank again, but held the little one's head above water. He came up again closer to shore, but further down river. He took another breath and sank again. He continued this until they reached the shore. By that time a crowd had formed and men waded in to pull them out. The weeping women took charge of the coughing child. The swamped canoe, below water level and in the river's current, was out of sight.

Yuzbasha came to congratulate the rescuer, exclaiming "I would have done more, but I can't swim!"

The giant looked at him coolly, and replied. "I can't either, I pushed off the bottom."

>- - - - - - - >

The apostolos had come for tea and consultation. The two girls served as the family sat around making the customary remarks and queries. Ghen-chair was just starting to grey in the temples, but his appearance was rugged and tanned with his constant exposure to the elements. His solemnity was belied by his cheerful smile.

"I suppose the commander will be returning soon from his delivery of your dear ransomed ones," he asked.

She laughed heartily, "Evet, yes," overjoyed on being home with travels over. Then he's angry as he thinks of the Khan's stingy, greedy ways and the debt that we incur to expand his borders. He'll feel frustration that the golden horse has escaped, and that the hostage's ransom did not come to us."

"I think he might have released us in exchange for the horse. He loved it more than the baby," he chuckled.

She shook her head wisely, "He needs us for his ambitions; we are beyond price. Who else would tell him the truth yet put up with his tantrums?" As they talked, a hail came from the sentry on the tower top. It froze all action and conversation, as all turned to listen.

"A running rider is coming from the east, an urgent messenger," the sentry yelled.

Bayan Vashtie responded quickly, "Open the gate, but let no one leave without my permission. Send him directly here." Yuzbasha ran up the stairs to the tower top, while Bata ran down to be at the gate. Those who remained exchanged glances, and seemed to pray, each according to their desire.

Sevim's prayer was, "God protect the Baby."

"Lord, help the heroes," murmured Perihan.

"Tanra guard my daughter and son," was Vashtie's prayer.

"Yesu, Your will be done now and always," Gen-chair's voice came. Outside other pleas to other deities would be offered.

Inside the courtyard, came the sound of clattering hooves, and heavy breathing followed. Then the clatter of boots on stairs and a disheveled rider entered, followed by the two boys. He stopped at the wood barrier gate that separated the corridor from the room and extended a roll of skin with the writing. When it was received by the Lady, with a cry of anguish, he drew his knife and cut off the last joint of his little finger. In this way all the tower knew of the death of the Khan. More shrieks followed. Vashtie opened a small door behind a wall-hanging and motioned urgently to Ghen-chair.

"You must pray for them now, at this moment. It will spread unless you calm them." The man rose and in one swift movement had passed her to step on the balcony. His voice dominated the cries.

"*Tanrum*, creator and sustainer of all life, You have taken to Yourself Your servant and our Khan. We thank You for the good he has done, and we pray You forget his sins and mistakes. God grant us a new Khan who will respect your laws and show mercy. Grant us confidence that You will guard our lives and bring future blessings to our people. *Yesu gel*, come and guard our spirits." Inside, the bleeding man had collapsed on the hay-covered corridor floor while outside the cries had lessened and noise decreased. Calm returned.

"We have prepared for this day. Now we must act promptly or the Bulgars will be marching east against us again." Vashtie went to a small chest where the children sometimes sat and brought out a roll of skin. She unrolled it to fix a date to the parchment scroll.

"Have you made any changes since we last spoke of the matter?" inquired Ghen-chair.

Vashtie smiled, "I have prayed much and added little. My dear husband signed it. I must add the date and send it; let us read it now and act," she said.

"To the Blnbasha of the Southwest Front, Greetings: The expected departure of our old Khan, Bata, has occurred as foreseen. We request that those wishing to sacrifice to his memory, be restrained until the month's end and be divided for those remembering to one quarter of the regiment each month. Mercenaries and captives are not required to sacrifice. The horses shall not be bobbed, lest it weaken us before our enemies. Every warrior shall direct his family, without compulsion, according to his decision. Children are not to give the sacrifice. Judges are to witness and record those who offer *koorban* by the *kesejee*, the executioner. Persons who have never met the Khan in person are not required to sacrifice. It is a matter of choice. This order is to be read to the army, every tower, band center and village, by order of the commander in charge of the west tower." Here the signature appeared. She rolled up the document and affixed the tower seal.

The apostolos nodded his approval, but added sadly, "It is a brave effort, but the old families will hate you and many will not obey. The blood frenzy will prevail."

"Those who already hate us will continue the same. Mercy is now possible for all the others. From a frenzied tradition, we move to a permissive law and sacrifice instead of despair and the desire to make the world suffer their loss with them equally."

Ghen-chair nodded, "It's a good start in slow business. Will you offer *koorbon*?" he inquired, with a knowing smile.

"I must, for my husband and the protection of the children," she affirmed.

"And I must for the church and to be received by those who are opening to truth."

"I will take my finger back and my daughter will sew it back on, and I will show them the power of my God. The judge will have it recorded and all will see it attached by His power."

Perihan cried, "Mother, how can I sew on you? It will hurt." Both adults laughed together.

Vashtie held out the roll. "Boys take this letter down to be sent to the commander of the Frontier immediately. The messenger cannot sacrifice until he arrives," their mother ordered.

"Actually a mercenary would be the best choice as messenger," stated Ghen-chair. "He would be calm and less likely to incite the sacrifice." The boys left.

Ghen-chair looked keenly at the two girls, in turn, then, asked compassionately, "What will you do?"

The girls exchanged glances. Perihan spoke first. "No hero would want a marred girl. My father intends me for an important marriage. I cannot be stub-fingered for a stingy tyrant like that shriveled old Khan. I hate these barbaric old Tartar customs." Her lips pouted, but her mother kissed her tenderly.

"Don't judge our people too harshly, dear. The Huns will cover their bodies with cuts and slashes along with stabs and amputations for slaves and mercenaries when Munzur dies. We will give you a glove to wear to disguise your hand for the next months dear. When things calm, it won't matter that it's not cut. Your decision is good, although the reasons may not be fully correct. And you, Sevim, what choice?"

"I would give mine, if you could keep yours."

Her mother embraced her. "How well are you named, my little love. No, you keep yours. God will heal mine. For me there is no escape. They would not let me if I tried. I must as your father must." The boys returned while they were speaking, and the sound of a departing horse was heard below. Both were out of breath and Bata was very agitated and seized her words.

"Father will make the sacrifice and so must I. All my friends will give a finger. They will despise me if I am not like them. Yuzbasha can keep his. He only plays with Sertol, an alien, and the girls anyway. I, the oldest boy, will inherit and rule. Youngest sons are not important."

"Would you play with me if I give my finger, Bata?" Yuzbasha was ignored as Bata rushed out and down the stairs. So he turned to his mother and asked, "Will all the boys treat me as he does? They will despise me, too?" The priest looked at the distressed family and took his small service knife from his belt.

"Come, I will give you a scar, but you will keep the finger. By the time you are in military school, it will not be important. Here I cut the skin over the first knuckle and we will rub some soot and cinders into the wound, and it will scar nicely. It will look real." He took the finger and made a light fast motion across it, and the cut was made. Blood welled up quickly and Yuzbasha stuck it in his mouth after an initial shocked '*Ah*-ee! Ouch!' The Apostolos moved to the brazier and took a mix of soot and fine cinder on his finger.

"Now you must put the cinders in while it is still bleeding. Give me your hand. Now we will wrap it. Some may think it has grown back like your mother's."

Sevim spoke up, "Isn't that deceiving people, Father Ghen-chair?" she asked innocently.

He smiled and nodded his head in agreement. "Yes, not a thing I recommend, but necessary now to prevent something worse."

Noise on the stairway announced the arrival of another visitor. The guard came bearing the body of Bata. The blood-covered hand and pale face announced his act of brave desperation. Perihan quickly unrolled a covered bedroll which was nearest the door. She stared in horror at the half-severed finger.

"Here, put him on the bed and leave," commanded the lady of the tower. "Perihan will have her sewing lesson before I go to the judge. It will give both of us a calmer spirit and steady hand. Bring a warming stone from the hearth, Sevim. The finger must be kept warm. There is clean horsehair for thread with the medicines, Perihan. Bring them. We'll work and pray now."

>- - - - - - - >

Dearest Judith,

Your letter was waiting at the port, fast, no?

Coming home was a precious moment, yes. The whole port seemed to be there to meet the ship. It was a celebration I shall never forget, no. Such dear people, they came with flowers and food; music and dancing.

Papa was there to show us the changes and improvements, yes. He is again my loving Papa and such a tease, no? Stefen got a new sail to captain, but I must be the passenger on all trips and practices. Is a wise precaution, no? Finally we are here and your letter came, yes. But letters are not enough, no; you must come. Your banker, Ebenezer effendi, says a visit for estate business is due, yes.

This reminds me of your story about Yuzbasha. You say he is big hero in Getchit City, no? He brags too much, for others: Kaya, Ozkurt, the uncles, the mate and the captain, did as much to stop the pirates. When in our great city, he bring scandal and wild living to dishonor his post and people, no? I'm afraid of him, he is barbarian in soul, as Magda says, yes. Is strange your story about how he walk on wharf when your little boy fall in. You say child playing, fall in river, and he, Yuzbasha, not swim, no? But on Danube River he swim from beach. Wind and water so cold, he laugh at us, no? I thank Yesu with you, that Commander Gochen jump in river to rescue your little one, yes. Is wonderful his devotion to your poor dear husband, no?

I thank God that the prince can ride a little again. May Yesu give him joy and strength as he takes more active command. My dear father promised me a big surprise here in Kertch Port, yes. He said I will love it, no? Already, I have many such moments, yes.

I wait for your reply, here in my port, yes.

Love always,

Merien Papasian

>- - - - - - - >

By evening half the Ural Tower had given a finger joint in the traditional ritual of the Tartars. It was difficult to restrain the whole garrison. The mercenaries were glad to be exempt and formed most of the able guards. Although Vashtie refused to allow the horses to be bobbed yet a symbolic cut was made that all might share the loss and suffering of the tribe. Vashtie was kept busy during the rest of the day. She was among the last to sacrifice.

At home the unread letter lay unnoticed until night-fall. Perihan who had nursed the feverish Bata and her quietly suffering mother during the late afternoon, picked up the document laying on the writing desk. She held up the skin to the light, with her glove-covered hands, and asked thoughtfully, "Do you suppose they will have the details of the death here? I hope he suffered as much as he caused others to suffer." She opened the skin and rolled it out on the small desk. She examined the document closely and gasped in surprise.

"It says that he was murdered during an epidemic of the pox. It says the war prisoner, Gaya, knifed him and escaped before the body was discovered. Onbasha Jonny has been sent in pursuit of the party to avenge the tribe. Oh mother, what can we do?"

"Pray, my darlings. Our greatest help will be prayer alone. We don't know how much of this is true and what the circumstances were. It could have been self-defense. You remember Bata's rages? The man lost control easily. Let us trust in friends and pray." There followed a long silence and the sound of sobs and sighs for a daughter and son, for the baby. Perihan spoke her thoughts aloud.

"The heroes will be far away now, and going farther," she sighed. She was right.

>- - - - - - - >

The hunter's camp lay on the edge of the dark forest by a stream. Kaya and his party entered riding slowly. They dismounted, showing their empty hands as they did so. The hunters stood around their fire and watched the movement of the horsemen guardedly with bland, expressionless faces. They knew that friendship might be the prelude to demands for tribute or other things. There were no women visible, but a bit of washed cloth was spread on a bush. The strangers came smiling, weaponless. The golden horse took the hunters' attention.

"I am Kaya the bear. I leave the Tartar lands behind to return to Chipchak country," he waited, but the hunters remained stoic and silent. He tried again. "The Khan Bata has died and that has left the tribe in confusion and mourning. The Chipchak will protect your claim to your lands and animals if you will make an agreement with them. For this I come in peace."

One of the grave men stepped forward and spoke. "Even here we know of the things you say and who you are. We know your lion horse tribe. We cannot risk the wrath of the Tartars if we help or make peace. We go now to collect wood, fix traps and do some night hunting. Our camp is open, and if you fulfill your needs in our absence, the fault is not ours. When they come, we will not remember a man, though we have seen a bear. Remember our people when you return here." The men faded out of sight instantly and silence reigned as the travelers took supplies from the tents. Then Kaya began to scatter things about and knocked over a tent.

>- - - - - - - >

Onbasha Jonny with four of his men rode into the hunter's camp with arrows drawn and ready. His shouting was answered by only one old man who came out of a tent.

"We are a party of the Khan Bata, who permits your use of Tartar lands. We require food, and other supplies for our use. We seek justice, vengeance from those who have abused our hospitality. Hear and comply, servants of Bata Khan."

"We hear. We have paid the tax and supply as we have means. Why have you surrounded our camp with hidden riders?" The hunter moved not at all, but the blowing of one of the hidden horses revealed the truth of his question.

"We search for the renegade Gaya who has disturbed our peace. He has come to your camp. Have you supplied him?" The onbasha's voice became hard.

"We hunted last night. A bear has been in the camp. You can see the damage where he robbed us." The onbasha continued, disdaining the reply.

"There are horse tracks near here. Gaya has passed here." The man shrugged and looked about the camp. Then he walked over and tried to straighten the tent before answering.

"When we are away, we cannot be sure. We are busy in the forest. We have seen a bear. We have a few horses. Perhaps you see their tracks. Steppe travelers pass our camp by night, but few stop or sleep with hunters." The onbasha signaled the men to dismount and they entered the tents, and brought out anything that pleased them, edible or otherwise. The old man watched their progress. They neglected the fallen tent. They rode off without further comment or command.

The hunter grinned. "The bear was wise to collapse our food tent. Damned, thieving Tartar scum, may your squad go rot with your Khan Bata forever!"

PEOPLE, PLACES & PLOTS IN CHAPTER 12

Attila: holds a hunt for the officials of Prince Ilkin and visitors.
Av'ja: a Dolgan tribe hunter brings a message to the hermitage.
Fewsoon; worn by travel and worry, has managed well.
Gochen: acts to save his master's life at the hunt.
Jonny: places his troops and waits for an opportunity to kill.
Kaya: arrives harried and exhausted, he would be willing to die.
Koot'sal: Kaya's teacher, the hermit has a vision to share.
Merien: wants information and tells of her plans to visit Judith.
Mookades: the hermit's title, he continues in prayers for all.
Ozkurt: worn out, but willing to face the Tartars.
Students: seek a fight, fiercely protective of their heroes.
Yuzbasha: plans an accident for Ilkin, a rival of his prince.

GLOSSARY HELPS

agha: a moan of grief.
ahta: of the horse; of the ancestors; of the forefathers.
aslan: lion; lion like; lion color.
ark'ah-dash: friend; companion; a person who guards your back.
ben, Ahv'jam: my name is Hunter; I'm a hunter.
boyun: tribe; community; band; people.
gelen: a bride; newly married.
hanjir: a fine pointed knife; dagger; assassin's weapon.
Kim' orda?: Who's there? Who is it?
koot'sal: holy; holy one; saint.
ool-lack: a boy; apprentice; page in court.
vah-she: the wild boy

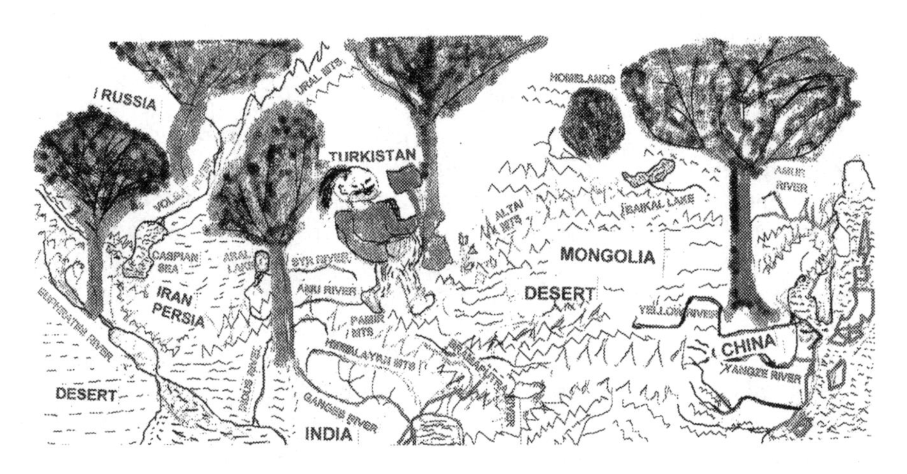

FIVE EMPIRES VISION

When they passed the Barabin Steppes, the searchers became very cautious. They were deep in Chipchak territory, rivals and competitors for the vast grasslands of Eurasia. The search pattern was discontinued and a war footing was displayed, shaped like an arrow head. They now made a bee-line for the hermitage in the Altai Mountains.

"We know the den of this beast. I was an *ool-lack*, a little page and messenger, when our Commander and Kove hunted the *vah-she*, the wild boy, in the valley. Now, we will finish the hunt the way it should have ended," said Jonny. "We know that he got to the Hermitage and was taught there. His yurt lies to the south, so we have to cut him off before he gets there." His men nodded in grim agreement. "His blood or ours, just as we have sworn: blood for blood."

>- - - - - - - >

Atilla the scout, now a rich landlord at the Don River Bend, had prepared the hunt with care. Prince Ilkin was to honor his hunt with his presence. All the nearby villages had suffered the damage done by a herd of hogs. These were devastating the planted fields of everyone within The Estates area. Lords, helpers, and hunters gathered in expectation of excitement.

Yuzbasha got wind of the hunt and hastened to join it, although, his new bride complained of his moving away from the capital city, so soon. He assured her of the necessity of moving and reminded her that their future lay in the west not in Getchit City. He scolded her when she reacted glumly to leaving her home for strange new places. He walked out abruptly. Kinner Khan had ordered his guards to the Bend and he wanted to be there first.

The hunt focused on the known home of the animals, a low bog where the water and mud provided an attraction, in addition to defense and hiding places. These massive creatures stood as high as a horses belly and were fierce, using tusk and hooves for their aggressive attacks.

Everyone knew that the farms' damage would stop as soon as the acorns started falling in the oak groves. However, pride and love of excitement beguiled the sportsmen to the dangerous task of reducing the herd. Some would disdain the meat, but prize the tusks.

A drumbeater and guard were dispatched in pairs to surround the area where the beasts were reported to frequent. The sound swelled as the men moved through the rank swampy growth toward their agreed point of contact; a clearing near a stream's bank. There the sponsors awaited the coming encounter; all carefully arranged for the success of the hunt. The advantage of the excited hunters was assured. Some, in anticipation had celebrated with drink.

The pigs broke cover from the riverside brush and crossed the clearing. A crescent of horsemen came to intercept the escape. The lead boar charged the horsemen as Ilkin aimed his arrow, but his mount was bumped from the left side, and the arrow missed, nicking its back. The prince and horse fell before the savage charge. Yuzbasha's horse plunged ahead and his position spoiled the aim of the left side riders. Gochen, who held the right side, tried to intervene in the boar's charge. His arrow took its throat, but its speed and ferocity brought it crashing into Prince Ilkin. A cry of horror arose from the participants. All attention was focused on the giant, who dismounted swiftly and stood with reddened knife, straddling the massive male. One, of the flight of arrows, was in his leg; the arrow-filled carcass of the animal still rested on the bleeding body of the heir. Only a few of the hogs were downed.

>- - - - - - - >

The Hermitage loomed before Kaya's exhausted, little band as a giant sanctuary. It was an oasis of repose in the midst of endless forests, swamps and mountains.

New boys waited at the gate and operated the stair-way that descended for them when they had laid aside their weapons. The hermit was in his room looking thinner, grayer than ever, but with his customary air of assurance and peace.

"Welcome home, Kaya, again you are harried and harassed. Welcome to your refuge."

"We are in need of help again, just as I used to be when a student. It's always the same, just as you seem to be, calm and happy."

The hermit gestured to the floor cushions and touched a gong to call an attendant. He looked at the travelers keenly: Kaya, thin and dark faced; Ozkurt, nervous and frayed; Fewsoon, hollow cheeked and disheveled with the bright-eyed baby, Nevaz. His name means courtly, kind-acting or caressing. Sertol, too, was new to the Hermit. He noted the boy's interest in his new surroundings and his quiet help offered to Fewsoon in her care of the baby.

"You have come far and with little food. Come, sit and I will send for soup and tea to warm you until supper."

They wearily sank down on the cushions or on the chests that lined the walls. A red-haired, grey-eyed youth appeared and was instructed by the hermit. When he left, Kaya asked, "Who is this boy? He has a different look."

"The son of a Mongol chief from far beyond Baikal lake. They are keepers of sheep and camels as well as horses. Good news has reached them now, and some are interested. Your brother will return next month from a journey beyond Khingan Heights to the Mongol homeland. But, come, tell me of yourselves." The hermit leaned forward peering in their faces with kind concern.

Kaya spoke without further prompting. "I am confused by the events that cause us to kill and run risks constantly. I find no peace or confidence in mankind. I know about sin, but it is everywhere. Why? People make rules and break them." Kaya spoke with his head bent, his tone anguished.

"You no longer are confused about who you are, nor where you should go, nor about the nature of your spirit? You have made good progress. Now, you wonder why others go contrary to the kind of world you wish, and you think God ordains. They are willing to kill you for their purposes. You are forced to kill as a measure of protection. When you avenge a wrong, it becomes worse and more complicated. More are hurt and killed. Is this not the problem?" the hermit smiled understandingly.

"I have grown sick of blood," Kaya nodded.

Ozkurt quickly added, "I weary of wounds and the loss of brothers and good men who sacrifice themselves for the safety of our people. Why is there no honor in leader's agreements and treachery by those rich enough to be generous, but who steal the little from those weak or disadvantaged?" Ozkurt raised his voice and said heatedly, "I curse those treacherous, greedy princes and warriors, and their foul women with hearts full of adultery and deceit."

"They are already cursed. Why add yours? Rather pity them for they are no different from all mankind. Having lost our inward guidance from God, we refuse the outward rules and laws of man's guidance as well. We assume the power of control and choice without the understanding of consequences. We refuse to acknowledge our sins and mistakes that mar the intentions of our best desires. We hide the sins and selfish mistakes by lies and deceptions that become habits. Only a saving encounter with God can change the consequences of our fallen natures."

"But Koot'sal, Holy one, how do you change the act of killing?" protested Kaya. "No amount of repentance on my part will relieve one soul of death. Necessity caused their death. I desired my promised wife and breast mate. Is that the sin that has cost a hundred lives?" The hermit nodded understandingly and spread his hands.

"Does it matter where you start? Even to our first ancestors this willfulness and rebellion against God's will substitutes blundering selfishness to God-ward submission. The repentance of one or a thousand, desirable as it is, will not change the dominance and conflict of human will in world affairs. While few submit to God, sin and death will be the results of human endeavor, wherever you start the chain of guilt and blame."

"When will this chain be broken?" ventured Fewsoon.

"The redemption of Yesu by His sacrifice on the cross has destroyed the power and despair of death. The best of God's creation is sacrificed for the flawed part that all might come into perfection and submission." The old one looked at Fewsoon tenderly, "Even the inequality between sexes that came with the subjugation of women is destroyed. Freedom to be God's child is for all to enjoy."

"But my Mother is subjected as a prisoner in the Ural castle," Fewsoon objected. "She is controlled as a prisoner even though she is a wife and mother."

"The power in Yesu is often expressed in its overcoming man-created limitations, not always in external ways, but in unlikely spiritual manners that no one would expect. If she continues to pray and believe many new perspectives and results will develop under God's guidance."

"Vashtie, the prisoner, is freer in spirit than Shanla, the actress, is in body. Both are successful: one in the spirit and the other in the world," observed Kaya thoughtfully.

"Which fame will endure the longest, that of flesh or spirit?" asked Ozkurt. "I would like to be remembered by my friends as a man of greatness."

"A man's spirit is shown in what he does, and how he does it. Fame or infamy is given on the basis of the result of this interplay," observed the Hermit.

"*Ark'ah-dash*, friend," said Kaya, hugging his short companion, "You are famous in our generation. I pursued a bride, but you are a friend of the bridegroom, who showed equal faithfulness, without the same gain. I love you as my constant companion in battle. I appoint you my successor and heir before witnesses, for you are true."

The hermit beamed his approval. "Come let us eat with joy for you have all returned safely. Also you have brought us a new student. Sertol must stay with us to work. His relatives can come for him."

The rattle of dishes and steps of young serving lads announced to all the arrival of refreshments. The hermit saw to the distribution of portions. They ate heartily. After this, prayer was offered with fervent thanksgiving for the meal and safe arrival, and he dismissed them to rest until dinner. That night they ate with the students in the dinning room. It was habitually an hour before dark so little would be spent on lighting.

>- - - - - - - >

My poor dear Judith,

How tragic that the horse would fall with your husband on a hunt with your guests from Getchit City, yes. Military people are a hard riding bunch and they like to risk to the limit of their endurance and ability, no? I plan to visit you as soon as we are settled here. Aunt Magda says two weeks may be required, yes.

By the way, the summer shipment of religious refugees has been arranged by the young man I spoke of in Pontus. He sends you greetings, yes. He will write directly to you of dates, vessels and costs for your agent here, yes. I will make sure of the food and lodging.

I received the news that Yuzbasha is now married, yes. I feel sorry for the girl, but perhaps he will treat her well. He is such a braggart, no? I'm glad I didn't have to go as an attendant. It was generous of you to help the wife's family sponsor the wedding, yes. You must write me of her trousseau and ceremony. I am interested in such things, no?

In haste, your friend and admirer,

Merien Papasian

>- - - - - - - >

The Tartar band put their heads together in consultation and shivered in the chill night wind. Jonny, whose name means murderer, summed up their situation.

"We have our prey holed up in its den. If we attack with force or fire we will have all the Altai tribes on us in a matter of days. Surprise, speed and subtlety must be our chief weapons. We must avenge our late Khan and be out and away before word of our penetration is known." He looked round the ten men who had traveled so far with him.

"We will post two men on each escape route. That will be eight men. Two will accompany me in a penetration of the interior. Remember that we must kill only one man to fulfill justice for our murdered leader, but any who block our purpose will have to pay the penalty." He raised an arrow over his head with both hands chanting: "May the spirits and ancestors guide our arrows, thirsty for the blood of the guilty, and crown our efforts with success."

That night each pair was settled in the valley and on the ridge, also on the gorge entrance and the ridge above the meadow. Three slept out of sight near the main gate, where they would start the action at first light.

>- - - - - - - >

They sat replete and satisfied, in the cross-blessed garden as the sun set with glowing fires. The chill of fall crisped the air and the colored leaves.

"My change came here," Kaya stated thoughtfully. "Here I learned I was human and took up a new life. The changes have never stopped. I continue to learn, but it is not all pleasant and good. There is much evil in the world."

"We may join it or resist it, but to resist evil successfully we need the resurrection power of Yesu. The willingness to sacrifice seems part of the requirement for victory. God died for men. Men must die for God." The frail face lit with deep thought. "Yet it must all be of God's time and place, not of man's selection. I would gladly die for Him, but He has not arranged it." The hermit pulled his cloak about him as stray wind stirred the bushes at that moment. In the near valley came the howl of a grey wolf, long and mournful, at the rising of a full moon.

"Yesu gave me a vision for your people Kaya. It has come repeatedly in this last month, so I knew you were coming, and I was to tell you. Though it is for the ages to come, you must tell your people. It concerns your end." The pale, faded face of the hermit solemnly spoke this prophesy: "I saw the whole middle earth and a giant tree grew out of the earth near Lake Baykal, and it shaded the whole earth. Then five tall trees grew from its seed: in the east beyond the Yellow river; in the west on the Mother of rivers; in our own land at the heart of the earth; to the south between the two great rivers of Hint, and the last between the five seas of the west near the great empire of the Greeks. Then the Baykal tree shrank away and left the five daughter trees to grow and become great with fruits of jewels and gold. Our people spread with the trees and were respected. Then a giant form filled the sky with the shape of a lame and cruel dwarf and with sword and shield furiously slashed the trees in the center and west destroying them and taking their fruit. The tree among the seas in the west was damaged but not destroyed and grew again to greatness. The tree on the Mother of rivers was utterly broken and scattered into three parts. As the dwarf turned to attack the tree in the east, he died. I looked in vain for the men of faith among our people, they were slain and a new different tree grew up on the Mother of rivers to cast its evening shadow over the heartland in the shape of a cross with clubs on the ends. As I pondered these great things a voice spoke, saying 'A thousand years for the people of faith as promised, then the end and after five generations pass seven times, renewal. The people of the Aslan *Ahttah Boyun*, the Lion Horse Tribe, will awake again to a new inheritance.' Then I awoke frightened and shaking. I ponder these words. The fulfilling of the promise to your father is clear. You are the heir, but the trees where you will shelter and the destructive dwarf I do not understand." A cloud moved over the moon. The howl of the wolf was renewed, and the wind rose sharply.

"Kootsal, let us return to the building. It grows cold," Fewsoon insisted, with a shiver.

>- - - - - - - >

The dawn came with ground fog as cold air blew in from the northeast. The Tartars shivered in their watch. Before dawn there had been the movement of light inside the cliff-built Hermitage. A vigil of prayer was held by all teachers and students; the kitchen was now in full activity.

The Tartar raiding party still hung back, perhaps awed by the vast structure filling the side of the cliff, so much more complex than the simple tents and yurts of the tribesmen. How would one find the prey in the midst of multiple rooms and corridors? So many hiding places!

A savage mountain huntsman appeared before the large gate, as if by magic. All was quiet outside the growing hum of the hermitage building. Then the man pulled the rope attached to the tiny bell.

One of the Tartars braced his bow, slipped the string into the notch, slid an arrow into place, but the corporal, Jonny, pushed the drawn bow down, made a motion to wait and leaned forward to listen.

"*Kim orda*? Who's there?" The childish voice of the door keeper piped the question from the floor above.

"*Ben, Avjam*. I'm the hunter." The mountain man's voice came clear, but frightened. He looked uneasily toward the trees where the Tartars were hidden as if he could see them. As the door cracked open, he slipped between and moved out of sight. He preferred the fears of the unknown building to the fears outside. He waited in darkness as the gate closed behind him and until the summoned authority was present. Examined in the light, his confidence grew again.

"What news, great hunter from the northern mountains?" The Hermit spoke in a slow throaty voice, as if in imitation of the speech of the mountain people.

"Tartar war party watch gate and surround building on ridge side, valley and front. Come from far, horses tired. Men hungry. Long trail, chase end here." He looked about the storage and stables then seeing the worn horses, nodded with vigor and pointed with his chin.

"There, those horses, Tartars wait for riders. They stay, kill." The old hermit stood considering, but the listening boys immediately went into action. One touched a bell cord that rang small bells in dorms and kitchen. As the bells sounded, the young defenders ran to the emergency post calling excitedly. The building was in an uproar.

Kaya left the dining hall with the rush of student defenders. He went by instinct to his old post over the elevator, but finding his post taken by others he descended to the place where the Hermit stood.

"They've found us then? They were closer than I supposed. They'll not leave without blood. Their commander will keep them here till the vow is fulfilled and I die. It would save lives if I went out to them. I can lead them away in the chase." Kaya was hollow-eyed and worn. Fewsoon came hurrying down. "We are safe here. The tribes will get notice of this raiding party, and they will exterminate them. We have but to wait them out." She looked anxiously at the hermit for support and confirmation.

"My pupils are excited and wish to show their bravery. Would you deprive them of this opportunity for defiance and experience in resistance?" He nodded to Fewsoon, with understanding and continued to speak. "You are a hero to these children. They will not give you up. News has come from the West by travelers and returning mercenaries. They know of your match with the great white bear-man of the North. They will not surrender you." All who heard agreed noisily.

"You Kaya Aya, brother of great bear?" The voice of the hunter cut into the noise. There was a hush. He went down on his knees and offered a pouch of dried food. "All hunters know that brother of bears come to tribe, kill shaman with snow slide, help teacher, bring new life to mountain people." The hunter, still prostrate, paused and looked sad, hanging his head. A great moaning started.

"Chavush our teacher dead, go to Yesu garden, Agha, leave poor mountain people alone. Agha. Tribe send me to great house, tell friends. Agha. Find Tartar trail, bad men come here to kill. Agha. Hunters will come fight raiders. Agha. Father of people send teacher? Agha." With bobbing head and mournful cries the messenger and hunter, Avja, finished his news, offer and request.

>- - - - - - - >

Outside the Hermitage the Tartars withdrew from their positions. There was no glory or reward in killing noisy children who just might venture out to hound them. As they went the children shouted at them and visually followed their speedy withdrawal from the roof and garden of the building. A small spontaneous victory chant and dance erupted as the Tartars faded out of sight over the ridge. Cries of joy and boasts of power filled the hermitage.

Everybody was very proud of themselves. Four of the largest boys linked arms at the elbows and with their fists before their chests, in time they lifted their right foot high and stamped one, two, three, four steps forward heads high, with ululating sounds; then, heads down and bent at the waist they backed four. Again, they lifted head and voice as they advanced, tossing their heads like wild horses, but keeping together and sometimes bobbing low and raising the right foot like a pawing horse. Smaller boys jumped about, some acted like bucking horses, and some scrambled out of the path of the advancing dancers. Many imitated the older boys, a few howled like the grey wolf, others made the neighing sounds of horses. The dancers started a tribal victory song.

We are bold ones, see how they run now.
We have frightened off our foe.
We are strong ones, now we will hunt them.
See, we've beat them, off they go!

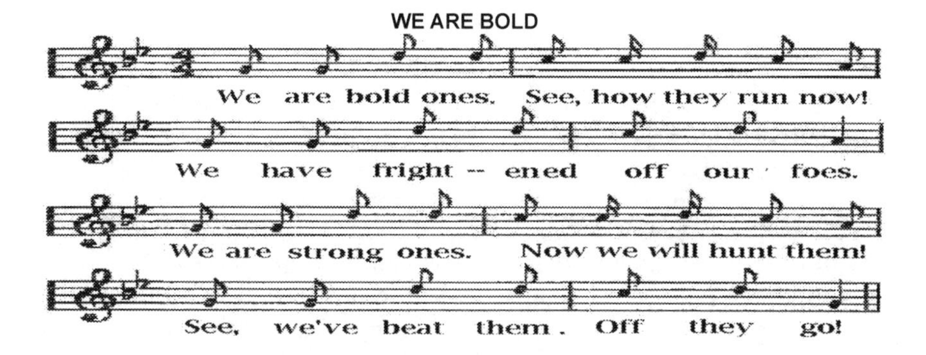

They sang it several times, and the smaller ones jumped around and acted silly. Whatever the older boys hoped for, these little ones knew no one was afraid of them.

The adults, too, seemed contented and happy. They congratulated all on the defense of the building. A day of thanksgiving and celebration was declared with extra rations and a feast for dinner.

In the chapel, the hermit gave a eulogy on the brave life of Chavush among the hunters and the bravery they were learning by their defense of Kaya and the hermitage. He commended them to bravery for God's cause and sent them early to bed. The hermit knew they would be slow and difficult in class tomorrow.

>- - - - - - - >

Out of sight, Jonny called his men together. "We will hunt and rest today beyond the ridges so they will think we have left for good. You saw the children on the roof and ground above. There lies the way into this great stronghold. Tonight we approach before the moonrise to enter by the high ground. We must obey our command to kill the guilty one. Justice must be done and revenge taken."

DARING DANCERS

PEOPLE, PLACES & PLOTS IN CHAPTER 13

Amja: a Khazar general, the paternal uncle of Yuzbasha is angry.
Chavush: the Khazar sergeant knows the Huns are a dominant force.
Fewsoon: finds they are not as safe as she hoped.
Lahlee: the *gelen* of Yuzbasha finds fear rather than happiness.
Jonny: the Tartar corporal continues his pursuit for vengeance.
Kaya: finds he has brought danger and death to the Hermitage.
Merien: recalls her visit to The Bend, and announces her marriage.
Kootsal: at prayers, is martyred at the hands of avengers of blood.
Ozkurt: warns of coming encounters with the Tartars.
Yuzbasha: tells his uncle his plans to become rich and famous.

GLOSSARY HELPS

***am'ja*: paternal uncle, or a name of honor to any older person.**
***binbasha*: general; commanding a thousand,**
***die'ya*: maternal uncle, also a name of respect for an older person.**
***ev'et*: yes; I agree; okay.**
***gel'en*: a bride; literally, the one who arrives; just come; is here now.**
***han'jir*: a thin, pointed dagger for cutting cloth, or holes in leather.**
***Hesus*: Jesus, the h is aspirated strongly.**
***Hristian*: Christian, the first letter is an aspirant 'h'.**
***jevap' ver*: answer me; reply.**
***kim orda*: who's there; who is out there?**
***ye'yen*: nephew or niece; the son or daughter of a brother or sister.**

13 VENGEANCE

SHADOWS SHOW

"Please understand Amja, I was in dire necessity. I was only a lowly lieutenant at the base, without hope of money enough to complete the wedding arrangements. Then, when I save the Khan from the ice floe, everything changed. I'm now a friend of the claimant our sponsor. He is eager to pursue a more aggressive policy on the western front. He now has the favor of many in the government. Our wedding was attended by all the high officials, including the Khan. Your gift did it. I've always intended to pay it back."

"It was fraud and forgery, yeyen. I will not be bilked, even by my own family. I expect to be paid back, promptly, or you will have earned an enemy that will never forget the offence. I know all your excuses and attended the wedding to save the family honor, but hero or not, I'll not excuse it. You are rushing ahead, failing to consult wiser heads."

"But I do consult experts, Amja, I was in Kertch Port before the wedding to pay a debt of honor. However, the one I sought had gone to The Estates on The Bend, and I had to postpone my plans. Then, I was able to visit several bankers and to propose the purchase of the letters of debt accumulated against the estate of Prince Ilkin. Because of his illness, I was able to get them at a discount. The Hristian banker wouldn't touch it, but I found someone who would. He is buying them out. If we apply pressure to pay, they'll lose the estate: it will be mine," he gloated. "The princess is in debt for the refugees she has sponsored for emigration. She won't be able to pay the total even borrowing at horrendous interest. She will be trapped," he concluded.

Uncle looked at him in contempt. "What do you think Kinner Khan will do? Sit by and let them be put out on the street? Fool, you may have canceled your status as favorite, when all this is revealed."

"No, Amja, I'll not be revealed as the one who forecloses, another will bear the scorn and be living in a neutral city. The Khan can't touch him," Yuzbasha smirked in satisfaction.

The uncle was quick and ready with a reply. "So he will declare the port as Khazar territory and invade it."

"That is my hope, Uncle. I want it inside our empire."

"And what of the letters, deeds, and debts?" uncle retorted.

"Sent by ship to an agent in Constantinople to continue the foreclosure. Believe me, Sir, I have thought of every contingency. They'll have no escape from my vengeance. The Khan will be gathered to the ancestors and eventually the property will be mine."

"Over confidence loses the game, Yeyen, the only way a fool learns is through the fire. I'll have my money now before it passes into this folly. How much is the banker taking?" The binbasha's face was set.

"Ten percent for the transaction and a quarter of any gains that require a loan. The Greeks will not give me as much, But this man is unscrupulous. He would sell his mother if the price were right."

"Perhaps, but my experience is that traps for fools are easily made and hard to evade. Your luck will not hold."

"My fortune is made and my revenge is sweet and my luck will hold, Amja, with or without your good will. Nothing can stop me now." Yuzbasha's face held contempt and a proud assurance as his Uncle, the general, left abruptly. Yuzbasha remembered the oily sleekness, perfumed beard, and gleaming eye of his agent and banker, Ebenezer bey, He was the Jew, who would get a quarter interest in the estate and income from The Bend. Yuzbasha knew that every detail of the plan would be carried out as he ordered. It was a question of time and patience, until it fell into his lap. He must take residence near the estate and pretend concern as disasters befell the survivors; offering to buy but never providing the needed money. After all, one should gain by deception, what cannot be had by force. A true hero should look flawless, before the law, the governors, and the governed.

>- - - - - - - >

Oh, Judith dear,

You will never guess, no! Father told his secret. A marriage has been arranged. He has been in correspondence for a year about a young man who is advancing in governing circles and is a friend of the Basileus himself, yes. Imagine my shock, yes. For this all girls wait, no? Papa is a big tease, he says 'you will love it', no? But he won't tell me his name. He says a letter will come from the man himself, yes. A love letter from my groom to be. I am delirious with joy, yes.

You will be able to come, no? I feel you are mama and sister all in one, yes. I will not marry unless you can come here. You say prince Ilkin is better now, so I will expect you here. You can tell me about the little Tartar from the East who came to collect money in Getchet City for sick relatives. I'm glad Khan Kinner did not kill him. If Bata Khan is dead as is reported, then there will be a release of persons detained. They say the new Tartar Khan is trustworthy and interested in the protection of merchants and traders on caravan. More facts will be known later. The man is reported to have said that Kaya has recovered from a wound he got on the Volga River, and Fewsoon has delivered a healthy boy child in her mother's home. It is her mother who is wife to the new Khan. That will make her a princess, yes? Kaya deserves such a one, no? Tell Sherbet the good news and that I love her. You have a sister to share things with, like Olga and Sarayjuk. I have always envied them having a close friend so near. I have had only Stefen, who being a boy, doesn't understand much about girls, but I see he notices them now, yes.

While there on my visit, Gochen said a strange thing to me, no? It sounded like something Kaya would say, yes. I told him how I admired his loyalty and service to his master, the prince. He replied that 'great guilt produced great efforts to make recompense', yes. He said, 'I intended to do in an enemy and by mistake did in a friend'. Also that: 'The evil that we would do, always comes back on us,' I asked, but he would not explain. I said, 'For this we have confession permitted to the priest or a Christian friend 'He replied that Yesu had shown him a way to alleviate the damage he caused and it would take as long as God wished, for he had received grace and prosperity, even promotion, for his efforts. Then he excused himself and rode away on some errand. I am not surprised that he now commands the garrison and is his prince's agent for all activities.

Most of the life of Kaya and the prince I heard from Ozkurt and so I know quite a lot about their life with you. Now, I know even more. I love the two-year-old, Gray Cloud, but her color is so unlike her mother's, the beautiful Altom. But her spirit is more like her. I suppose that this is one of the joys and trials of motherhood, seeing the differences and finding similarities in the offspring, where you don't expect them. However, all the children of love are wonderful, regardless of differences, no? God has made us so, yes. He provides wonderful differences and challenges, so close to our hearts.

When I have my groom's name or other information on dates and places, I'll write you, yes. Kiss Sherbet and thank the giant for me. Kiss little Daniel for me and tell him that

'Me-yen' loves him. Tell your husband, the prince: I pray for him every day.
Love and hugs from your joyful sister,
Merien Papasian

>- - - - - - - >

Jonny's band's return was by feel rather than by sight. They literally felt their way up the steep cliff near the waterfall. Trying every crack and cranny, they made their way up to the garden door of the Hermit's room. Three sick men, one with fever and two with coughs, were left with the horses, beyond the ridge. Another pair were at the bottom of the climb, a third sat at the top and one outside the door. Only four would enter, one to stand in the door of the first room and secure the exit. Jonny would enter first with the *hanjir*, a short sharp dagger. The other two men would be route markers and guards to assure an easy escape.

The quickening light of moonrise guided the three, who passed into the office in slow motion, passing their hands before their faces and down to their knees in slow sinuous movements. With each step, so slow and careful, they stopped and listened to the night sounds in the sleeping building; their bare feet feeling the way. Each door was a crisis to be passed, opened with painfully slow motions. Every noise was followed by long pauses and listening. Unconsciously, the tension in the invaders mounted. The sounds of sleeping children filled their ears. They passed the doors leading to the dormitories.

They paused painfully at the first choice of stairs down or corridor. they left a guard and continued down the corridor. The pair came to the door at the end of the corridor. Within a faint sound could be heard. Someone talking? Slowly they tried the door flap. The leather fasteners were untied; there was no resistance. The stiff panel moved inward with only a slight sound. Across a long room a single candelabra illuminated the Tau cross casting a large shadow against the back wall. A human form was doubled over crouching before it, casting a long, low shadow on the floor.

As they entered, the bowed figure rose, straightened and turned to move toward the two. With the light behind, the man's shadow moved before him, filling their eyes with menacing largeness. Jonny paused, momentarily paralyzed with fright, pulled his hanjir and rushed forward voicing an involuntary cry of fear and victory. The victim raised both hands, but went down without a sound. Jonny felt the knife buck, once, twice. Now the sticky, warm blood touched his hand. It burned like fire up his arm. He cried out again in dread and superstitious fear. Wheeling around he fled precipitously.

Both assassins rushed down the corridor to their guard. In their haste they knocked him down the stairs. The guard came back up, crawling on all fours, cursing and calling. An opening door flap caught

Jonny full in the face. A frightened voice called out, "*Kim or'da*? Who's there?"

Behind the voice a buzz of noise rose. Cries, whines and the excited voices of children filled the corridor. The two men rushed stumbling over Jonny who was down on the floor. As he straightened up, the first of the dorms older boys dashed out and bumped him. Others followed shouting to each other as they grappled in the dark with moving shadows.

Jonny pushed on violently to the office and exit door into the moonlight as the corridor behind filled with the noise of activity. Outside there was a cry and crash when a raider slipped and fell descending the cliff. The children ran to the overlook and an older boy shot some arrows from the bow and arrow set on the office wall. Sertol, too, appeared with his father's war bow to send arrows after the departing sounds. They sank with a thrum into the night. Lights were appearing as they heard the drumming of horses' hooves fleeing to the distant ridges and valleys. Gradually the voices of authority brought order. Children were sent to the kitchen and gruel was served up before returning them to bed.

>- - - - - - - >

Yuzbasha stared hard at his ***gelen*** and she looked down unable to resist the force of his anger. He hissed the words each separated from the rest. "You'll nurse the prince during his wife's absence." Then, he relaxed a bit and spoke carefully. "The letter arrived and I had the luck of being there to make the offer. The date is not set yet, but we must be ready. I missed the visit of the Kertch Port bitch by a few days. I still have matters to settle with her. I'll clear her and all her people off the coast within a year. I'll swear a blood oath on it.

"However, you will look after the prince and give the medicine I've bought for him. Do it with a smile and leave off your sulky ways. If you do it right, you'll soon be the owner of one of the best farms of the frontier. I don't care if you don't like it. We can trade it for a palace in Getchet City, once we're established. We'll be friends of the future Khan of Khazaristan. We are so close. Our prince rises in esteem, while Ilkin becomes a more doubtful choice for Khan. I'm a hero in everyone's eyes. We have a whole lifetime to enjoy greatness." He straightened and watched the effect of his words. His hunter spirit showed in his narrowed eyes.

"I can't! They came to our wedding and brought presents for us. I'm not used to invalids," she protested. "Mother won't like me waiting on another man. People will talk," she bleated pitifully.

"If I black your eye they will talk more," he hissed again. "This is the only way to accomplish my task. There must not be two heirs, only one: ours. She will be gone about ten days. Ilkin is fragile, we will weaken him gradually. He will die when under her care again. There are many who dislike her origins and murmur against her. We have a perfect plan and powerful friends, nothing can stop us but your weakness. Put it down and accept greatness."

She nodded helplessly, She couldn't holdout against him. In truth she was afraid of him. She remembered how pleased she had been when her mother had revealed the name of the man she was to marry. She had such illusions and dreams of the hero, but they had been shattered. Fear came where love had been expected to grow. She found she did not want to bear him a child. She would rather die. She wondered if the medicine he had bought would cause pain if taken. She also wondered if it could be detected if administered to anyone.

How long would it take? It would be like playing Tanra to decide who would live and who die. What would happen to people who played this kind of game? She had her eyes closed when he struck her. Her cheek stung with the force of the blow.

"Jevap ver! Answer me! I'm waiting for your answer," he growled. "It had better be, ***evet***, yes," he required. She ran weeping to another part of the building. He let her go, his plans were well laid, and they could not fail.

>- - - - - - - >

Oh, Judy,

The truth is out at last. I have a letter from Petrus, my friend, the son of the governor of Pontus. You remember, no? He informs me of his coming to Kertch Port as agent for trade, a pro consul, representative for the empire, His father did the matchmaking and papa consented. We will be married this spring, yes. I can't stand the wait for his arrival! I'm in love, no? Wait till you see him, then you will know, yes.

Thank you for the details of Yuzbasha's wedding last month. Is different customs from Rome, no? I can't understand why Khan Kinner would make him a general, when he was absent from the fighting in Ukraine. He will not be fighting pirates on the Dneister or Bug Rivers. Kaya and Ozkurt would do a better job, no? I must not wish him bad things, but I'm glad he did not come during my stay at The Bend. I hope he is stationed far from our Black Sea coasts, yes. We agreed that you would set aside ten days for the visit before the wedding.

Yes, I know that you became pregnant when the prince was up and about. But you will not be so far along as to be a danger when you travel here, no? Besides, now that the prince is better, you can take time off, no?

We will find an agreeable date for both of us. I wish it were today, yes. I love you and pray Hesus for a safe, normal carriage and delivery, yes.

Your concerned friend,
Merien Papasian

>- - - - - - - >

"I don't like to complain Die-ya Chavush, but the girl the family got me is timid, yet stubborn, and not too bright. I mean to say not knowledgeable. She has no talent." Yuzbasha confronted his uncle.

"Not like the one you left in the big city, son," the uncle chided. "No, boy, Lahlee comes from a good military family and they have their influence where you need it. She's a country girl, but likes city life, I'm told. Your ***gelen*** will be teachable and a pretty bed partner.

"Your Amja, the general, paid for the whole affair for you. Surprised me, I didn't think he would part with such a sum. But I left the capital a month after you did, so I haven't talked to him yet. I just saw him at the wedding briefly."

Yuzbasha changed the subject quickly. "I'm accounted a friend of the prince, our sponsor," he bragged. "We see eye to eye on the subject of a more aggressive moving on the western frontier. The Huns continue to retreat. We can hurry them and gain a great name by our victories."

"The Huns withdraw after they have squeezed an area dry of all wealth and people, son. Don't think it's because of weakness. Prince Ilkin's policy is smart, even if we aren't part of his supporters. The policy won't change while he's alive." Both men nodded knowingly.

"By the way, you've heard now about the death of Miakim," the uncle offered. "They never caught the tall man, who threw the pot of flowers and broke a mirror at her house. I've always thought that if you had not been at the hotel that last night, you could have saved her life. The town was really broken up by her loss."

Yuzbasha's face went flat and glum. He found an excuse to leave.

> - - - - - - - >

They found the body of the hermit at dawn, the ancient wolf-headed knife in his heart and a smile of wonder on his face. Those who found him moved him before the altar under the T of the cross. Fewsoon and Kaya recognized the knife resting in the body before the altar under the cross.

"It is my *hanjir*, from the log in the woods, taken by the Tartars at the Ural tower," Fewsoon declared.

"It has killed too much. It must be put away where it will be used no more, lest it spread more evil," he said. Kaya took a small wooden chest from the Hermit's office, emptied it of its papers and placed the blooded knife on Fewsoon's silk scarf in the box and laid it before the alter cross. The room quieted and all knelt as Kaya spoke.

"It has drunk holy blood. It must now stay to remind all worshipers that violence and instruments of death cannot destroy that which God has made holy. Tanra has taken our teacher to Yesu's Garden. There we may hope to see him." Then Kaya began to sing his farewell:

KAYA'S LAMENT

1. I cry, when I see your place.
   I sigh, when I miss your face.
   I think of your loving care.
   I know you gave all to share.
   I wish, in this last goodbye,
   That you did not have to die.
   I hope we will meet again.
   I feel my heart is breaking.
   I can't go on.
   I can't forget you,
   And never will.
   You are with me still.
   God keep you in His care. Amen.

2. We know all will have to die;
For sin, foolishness and pride.
We fear, as we wait the day;
We work, stay busy and play.
We wish, we could find the road,
Be free, leave our heavy load.
But none came to show the way,
Till Yesu bought our pardon,
Opened the door,
To Yesu's garden.
We share a place;
We will see His face.
We trust His changeless love. Amen.

>- - - - - - - >

Ozkurt spoke to Kaya privately, after the service. "We may face these raiders again on the road south through the mountains. They are sworn and cannot return without vengeance. This matter is not ended yet."

Kaya looked at him solemnly. He sighed, replying, "The chain of blood continues without pause or hindrance. Who knows whom it will touch next?"

"We can't go directly to Erkan's yurt. They will expect us to go there to procure troops," Ozkurt stated. "I'm a hill man, we can evade them by going a slower, but safer way to E'peck Kent. It's beyond Chipchak country, but we'll be safe with Jomer and Ahjit bey, until our people pick off the Tartars."

Kaya agreed, "They may already be hunting them. We can't endanger the children by staying here. The head master is competent, the children well trained for guard duty and defense, Sertol alone could defend the hermitage with his father's war bow."

Ozkurt smiled grimly. "We'll run the gauntlet tonight. The hunter, Avja will lead the way out and return home afterwards."

NORTH GATE E'PECK KENT

PEOPLE, PLACES & PLOTS IN CHAPTER 14

Ah'jit and Shef'talee: continue to serve and receive a mixed reward.
Er'kan: angered by Tartar invasions and anxious for city armor.
Ertach: the yuzbasha, lieutenant, sent to collect Tartar heads.
Fewsoon: happy to be home, but aware of danger as they go.
Gatekeeper: faces a serious challenge to his authority and duty.
Jo'mer: disposes of his wealth and rewards his servants and heir.
Kansu: father of Ertach, and counselor of Khan Erkan.
Kaya: still unsettled and suspicious, yet anxious to see Jomer.
Merien: hears bad news from a friend and offers to help.
Optal and Pesh: are old and poor, but still greet and meet friends.
Ozkurt: caught up in the excitement, shares dangers in the city.
Yuzbasha: offers help to a neighbor and prepares for battle out west.

GLOSSARY HELPS

amja: paternal uncle; father's brother.
bash'un-na sah'luck: health to your head; expression of sympathy.
boo-rda ne yap iyor son uz: what are you doing here?
do'er: stop; halt.
E'peck Kent: Silk City.
ha'mom: public baths; Turkish baths.
is' a niz le: with your permission; permit me; excuse me.
ja'num: my soul; my dear; expression of affection.
koo'zay: north; cardinal direction.

14 ARRIVALS

THE ADVOCATE

In the yurt of Khan Erkan a solemn face was displayed on every occupant. The report of Tartar raiders deep in Chipchak country reminded everyone of the raid when the main village was plundered and the Khan's wife lost. The fact that it was more than ten years back did not relieve the tension. Erkan was old, bony and shrinking in strength and control. The eyes of his counselors were averted. Erkan flared out at his men as they considered the latest report.

"The north village must be fined for not advising us sooner of the passing of a Tartar band. The cold and storms not withstanding, we must have immediate notice of any trespassers. Defend them and you condemn us to raids again. Are we weak southern people that take to our beds on the days of frost and wind? Have we lost the heartiness of our ancestors and quake at cold? Even the reindeer people will despise us. The horse tribes will force us into the desert to raise sheep." Erkan's threat raised a roar of protest.

"Great Khan, hear me," protested one tracker, the Yuzbasha Ertach. "The prints seemed to be from Chipchak horses. Tracks and goods can be falsified and the invaders were leaving Chipchak gear at their camping spots. We know now, that they were planned plants to deceive us. We saw the single trail of a mountain man crossing the trail, but all were going south to the Hermitage. We thought they were inquirers to learn of God's will. We are at peace with the mountain people by your son's doing." All heads nodded in agreement, but Erkan's wrath cooled not one bit.

"But not one of you cast one eyeball over the horde nor the single traveler. Blind men beg on the silk road, that mercy may sustain them. If my men have become blind, their fate deserves to be the same. My son, God forgive him, makes peace with all who wish it. Peace is good with strong foes, but with miserable, weak people it is another matter.

How can we grow and get lands and goods if every sniveler is taken as secure? We should, at least, be entitled to tribute, goods and girls from these people."

"Lord, let off your village. They have trackers out and will surely contact the Tartars. Speculation is that they were following your son, the lady Fewsoon and child, and their hill-man friend, the hero Ozkurt now at the Hermitage. Both bands were moving at top speed. They were present and gone in a matter of hours during the storm, when your son tricked them at the river fork," the advocate for the Kuzay Village pleaded.

In spite of his anger the Khan's ugly face changed into a slight smile. "It was a neat trick. I, myself would not have fallen into it, but the caved bank with the horses prints in the new mud, going up the bowed river to the Hermitage looked convincing. They were backing out and taking the little fork to the ridges above the valley to the Hermitage. The back entrance was short and fast." He nodded his head in approval, but frowned again, recalling his grievance. "You finally got three of them; sick and dying of some pox or sweating sickness. Abandoned by their force to die. What did you learn of them? Well, Yuzbasha?"

"Two were dead and the last, his leg shattered by a fall, asked to be finished there. He felt compelled to tell us the number and destination of the force, for us to agree to an arrow to the heart. There are seven left. They run south to refuge in a city or to catch the heir on the road. He was half delirious with the pain, so I'm not sure of how much is true. I sent a squad ahead and came back to report."

The Khan accepted the report, but frowned his displeasure as he returned to his perennial grievance. "My great oaf of a son is only able to scrape from disaster to ruin, time and again. He will destroy the tribe by his wild ways, nor is his friend better." He fell into a familiar lamentation, which had grown more frequent with the passing years. "I had thought to change our luck, when I gave myself and the tribe to Yesu, Tanra's example and way for men. However, I find myself, after many losses, with nothing but lion-colored horses and two sons; neither fit to rule the tribe."

"One, with his head in the clouds, will follow the Hermit and teach useless things about numbers, countries, religions, languages and writing for clerks and merchants. The other fool travels, joins the merchant Jomer and neglects the affairs of the tribe. He wars far from home to no profit for the tribe, makes peace with those neighbors who would be easy to put down, and provokes the Tartars and Huns, who can do us real damage. I have but one heir, a grandson I have never seen. Why does Tanra pay me in this way? The Goth told me this when we talked of God, but I forgot: 'Your own plans and desires will not fructify, but Tanra will do the great, unexpected and profitable things for His purposes.' Was that it? Very confusing, why would anyone say that? All I want is for things to be normal, like other Khan's lives. Power, money, prolific animals, a huge tribe with lots of loot and conquests. Isn't that what every man wants for himself and his heirs?" He looked round as all of his men nodded their heads understandingly. They were accustomed to his outbursts.

One, Corporal now Counselor Kansu, spoke up. "What of the invitation of the merchant Jomer? It is said that he will divide his goods while he yet lives and invites you, your son, Kaya, and Lady Fewsoon. His chief men will no doubt be present to receive a part, but what is his purpose in inviting you? Will he enrich the tribe?"

"It is fitting that he should contribute to our strengthening and armament. We, who have suffered cold and heat, attack and loss through the action of numberless, nameless desperados and exiles. All this to protect the gains of fat sellers of distant goods." The Khan shook his head as he considered the injustices of life. "They are as low and despised as farmers," he stated with conviction. All listeners agreed.

"But they are rich and protected within the walls of their cities and caravansaries," Counselor Kansu added.

"We will go to his town and receive a part of the much, all those merchants owe us. My wandering, blockhead son will no doubt receive a generous portion to which the giving of the knife of Onder entitles him." The burn scars on the face of Erkan twisted in a grimace, as if the memory of Onder had touched a raw nerve. He stared into the distance as silence fell over the yurt. "I will accept Jomer's good invitation, go to the banquet, worship in the church there in that town. I have never visited it. We will hunt along the way for the Tartars; we might take a few heads. Those in the city will see the glory of Erkan, High Khan of all the Chipchak bands." The council nodded its approval. "Bring out the best armor and harness for our entrance will be impressive, but small lest we frighten our host. Prepare now. I would think alone."

He nodded silently as each man rose and spoke the words '*Is a niz le*', 'With your permission' and moved from the yurt. The proud old man sat with his memories.

Outside the yurt the *Koozay* village advocate stopped counselor Kansu, made a motion of silence and whispered. "Doesn't he realize the extent of his prosperity? The greatness of his sons?" The companion lifted his head in a negative nod.

"He has become greedy and querulous. It is hard to live with famous sons and be as if dead, before one is dead, knowing the tribe already obeys the heir in all vital matters. This will end badly I fear."

>- - - - - - - >

The small party of travelers entered the walled town huddled under cape and hood for warmth on their horses. It was not yet the time of caravans and most travelers were in winter quarters still. It had taken three weeks of travel to gain the security of the walled city.

The town of E'peck Kent was quiet in winter, and would wake only on market day and for special celebrations. Such an occasion had now arisen, for before the gate of Jomer the merchant, the curious and the idle congregated. They were shivering, but hopeful of a distribution of candies. Beside the wall near the door set in the gate of Jomer's compound, two men sat huddled. One, drooling beside a drum, was clutching a beggar's bowl in one hand, while with the other hand kept a brisk rhythm. He chanted a song while staring at the sky. His companion played the flute. The crowd milled about uninterested in the familiar sounds, but all the children joined in the song.

COME TO HINDUSTAN

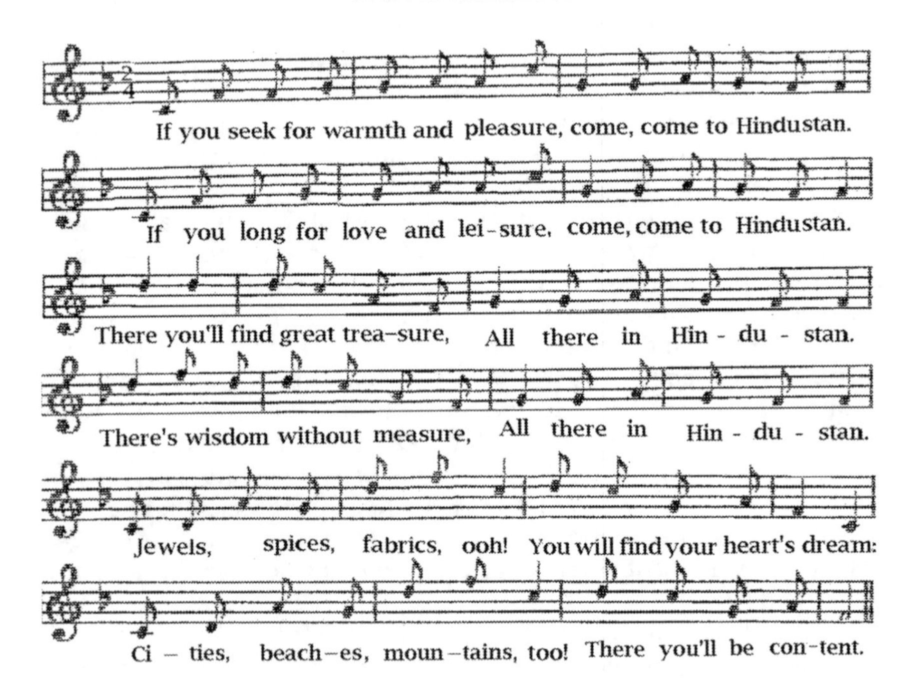

If you seek for warmth and pleasure,
Come, come to Hindustan.
If you long for love and leisure,
Come, come to Hindustan.

There you'll find great treasure,
All there in Hindustan.
There's wisdom without measure,
All there in Hindustan.

Jewels, spices, fabrics, ooh,
You will find your heart's dream.
Cities, beaches, mountains, too,
There you'll be content.

The music struck Kaya like a blow and he was off Altom and through the crowd to confront the old man, who with his white hair, still looked solid and strong.

"*Boor'da nay yahpee yore soon* ? What are you doing here?" he demanded. "Where is your bear?" He shook the man impatiently, "What are you up to now?" His face was thrust belligerently into the old man's face, shouting.

"Easy, Master, we come to greet you and wish you welcome. We have no bear and seek to gain a few coins from the distinguished guests," His voice was smooth and controlled. He didn't seem to be intimidated by Kaya's actions, although his hands trembled as he was hoisted to face the young warrior. Kaya shook him again, then returned him to his feet.

"You are harbingers of disaster and trouble. Every time you appear, my life becomes hard, bitter and full of changes," Kaya was now looking down, as the drooling drummer stared up, and started nodding his head and making babbling sounds. Kaya and Ozkurt gazed in astonishment at the changes in him.

"He recognizes you my Lord. See how pleased he is? This is a great wonder. Sometimes he fails to recognize me. He knows you, a generous friend from the past. See how glad he becomes?" The bear-master rubbed his hands to warm them.

"You've come far from the great Mother of Rivers, where you last appeared," Ozkurt said as he came up beside Kaya to stare at the uncouth drummer, Pesh, and Optal, who bowed in humble acknowledgement. Their faces all smiles.

"We've returned to our adopted home to pass our last days. We've a small room behind the bath house where we're permitted to stay in exchange for our work, but we must depend on others for our bread. Good sirs, may we now be generously helped toward that end by your own good fortune? Aren't you the heir of the rich merchant, Jomer? It's said he'll now distribute his goods and trade empire to you and other favorites. You can favor whom you will. Look kindly on us, friends from other, better days."

Kaya looked perplexed and uncertain for a moment, but turned to Fewsoon saying "We'll give them our travel food. We've arrived." He turned to the men, "We come from the Hermitage. I've no coins today to give, but the food we'll not need. Take it and welcome." Fewsoon placed the small bundle into their hands.

The others waiting, protested, "Have you nothing for us? We too are needy. See our clothes?" They crowded round, but Kaya pushed past into the door of the building, which had been opened by a servant. The servant sent out young Onder with candies, which the crowd pushed and shoved to get at, grabbing handfuls, and the boy threw the last in the basket into the air as he withdrew after the guests.

Inside the great hall, the merchant Jomer lay in state, covered with rich quilts and bedding. Ahjit, thin and pale, stood beside him near the charcoal burning brazier. He moved with a limp, as he walked to a low table where several pages of rice paper lay. Turning he said, "The list is complete, sir. You've been generous with all your servants, the tribe and the heir. The authorities of the town have been informed. The judge has witnessed copies of the original papers now."

>- - - - - - - >

Some days after Kaya's arrival, the Khan followed riding his great lion-horse beside his young lieutenant, Ertach, at the head of a column of armored Chipchak troops. The gains of years of trading had been put to good use in arming the tribe. Thirty troopers followed in pairs. They rode boldly up to the open city gate. The gatekeeper and some troops on duty came forward blocking the entrance with uplifted hand.

"*Do'er*, Halt, who are you? What is your business?" The worried keeper looked at the well armed line. He pulled briefly at his mustache, and cleared his throat motioning to his assistant to quietly rouse the garrison.

"I am Erkan, chief of the Chipchak, invited by Jomer, the merchant, to a feast. I come with but a small guard." The old man added proudly, "Our great hordes are numberless, but I'll leave half outside since you fear."

"I know your name, but not your face, great Khan," replied the keeper. "We can't let fifteen armed men into the town without authorization." He rubbed his head recalling. "Your son is Kaya the Conqueror, isn't he? The one who has fought the Huns and Tartars? He came in with his family and one man. You can do the same," he smiled weakly as the Khan's head rose in a negative gesture. "If you'll but wait a moment, I'll confer with the Captain for permission."

>- - - - - - - >

Jomer reclined in his bed, hollow-eyed and pale. He spoke in a voice clear and strong in spite of his physical appearance. Kaya and Ozkurt stood near his side, while Ahjit stood across from them. Fewsoon shared her baby with Sheftalee, now an older woman, near the door. Jomer spoke his prepared piece.

"I've called those dear to me for my farewell. I realize the thing below my stomach grows and brings times of pain and weakness. I've seen others die of this evil and, unfortunately, the prayers of the temple apostolos, his deacons and acolytes produce no change. I'd tear out the source of pain, but men don't live without bowels. I go to join my fathers and their dear ones. I've prayed Yesu that we might be together. My dear friend, the Hermit said, 'The end of a man's life is more important than the beginning, for each starts helplessly where Tanra has placed him, but each finishes where his own choices have put him. One has a measure of control and is completing what he started; the whole value of his life is revealed.'

I have sinned much, and also been forgiven much. I distribute my accumulated goods to you, the friends and family I've chosen."

He nodded to Ahjit who produced a sheet of Chinese rice paper with writing and gave them to a secretary. From them the scribe read the following statements:

"These are legal documents with the details of the legacy of Jomer.

1. My properties and moneys I leave to Kaya, my chosen heir. How quickly and willingly he learned the trade.
2. My cloths and fabrics I leave to Fewsoon, who knows quality and value.
3. My animals I leave to Ahjit, my faithful steward and caravan leader, his sons, though young, show excellence in working with animals.
4. To Erkan, chief of the Chipchaks, I leave thirty complete sets of armor and weapons for the greatness of his people.
5. For the Hermitage; I have dedicated a part of my investments and the money lender will send each season, enough money for goods and services to feed the orphaned and needy.
6. I leave a like amount to the church and hospital. Let them pray for the souls of the poor and that my soul may rest in Yesu's garden."

The secretary stopped and added. "It is signed before the local judge and city authorities. The document is legal and acceptable to the council." He looked at the man under the rich brocaded covers, bowed and waited.

"Let my heirs approach and acknowledge my generosity and their conformity," stated the dying man. Kaya and each of the persons named in the document came knelt and kissed the man's hand pressing it to his forehead. The pale face pouted and spoke. "Where is Erkan whom I honor? I make my friends great by my gifts."

Kaya smiled and replied. "Generosity is your name and your greatness, *Die'ya*, Uncle. The others have their own. My father will come to you according to his promise," Kaya laughed. "He wants the weapons and armor. Death couldn't keep him away."

>- - - - - - - >

"I wait for no Captain. I am a Khan and will enter with my troop," the scarred old man replied and proudly motioned the whole troop on. The great horse took two leaps forward with the troop following when an arrow took Erkan in the throat and few heard the strangled cry, 'Yesu,' as he pitched back on the horse's haunches.

There arose a spontaneous shriek of anger and disbelief by the troop of Chipchak warriors as they saw their ancient leader fall back on his horse. The prominent arrow told its tale of murder. The riding line of men that had already started toward the small entrance of the city whipped out sword or bow and arrows and struck any who barred their way or raised weapons against them. The small garrison of gatekeepers were swept away or fled.

Buzzing like hornets round a destroyed nest, the troop lingered by the North Gate ransacking all the goods and slashing the dead bodies. One of the younger men led the horse to which the body of Erkan still clung, blood bathing the hindquarters of his horse.

Several bowmen who were above on the wall had retreated after launching their arrows and from a nearby tower an urgent trumpet call was rousing the town. Armed men started to appear on the walls and tops of houses.

The troop's rage abating, some talked excitedly of putting the town to the sword, others of returning to the tribe with the body of the Khan or seeking Kaya who was said to be in the town. They had heard the words of the gatekeeper and the possibility of seeing Kaya intrigued them. Several of the tribesmen had journeyed to Jormer the merchant's center for trade, knowing that their Chipchak Yuzbasha, now called Ahjit, was the foreman and would welcome them. They decided to go to seek Kaya and Ahjit at the merchant's warehouses near the north-west wall. The lieutenant, after dispatching two men as messengers home, led the way. Women's screams and the shouting of men punctuated their advance across the town. They rode to the main east-west road. Passing the church on the west, took the next street north, leading to the merchant's stockade and inner gate. More trumpets sounded near the principal North-east gate tower.

>- - - - - - - >

Oh, Judy,

How tragic for you. How your dear husband will be missed, yes. Your newest surprise and family addition won't be able to receive the blessing of his father, no? I cry, so forgive the stains, yes? I'm so glad you had time after my wedding to be with him. It was a big sacrifice to come here, but I will always remember your part in the ceremony; standing in for my dear departed mama. You are so beautiful and papa said that you have made mama happy to see such a person sponsoring me, yes. I will always love those moments.

Words of comfort that should come so easily to our lips, because our heart is full, find trouble to be said, no? We stumble and blunder to speak them. I have never lost a husband, no. The thought and words stick and strike terror in my heart, yes. I know... but cannot know how you feel, no. But my heart cries with you, yes. I can say no more, yes, words fail me.

Great anger fills my heart, Yuzbasha again makes trouble. Why do his people think him so great? He dared tell Khan Kinner that the people will not accept a ... such a dirty word he use to say your children are only half Khazar, no? He claims that fear of him will cause a Hun withdrawal to their Rumanian lands and mountains. When did he fight? Your dear husband's agreement not to shame the Hun army was the reason for gain. I hate the Khazar hero, he is sham, yes! His wife cared for your husband while you came to wedding, but I agree with Sherbet, yes. She was not too careful about what he ate, no. He have up-set stomach before you return. You were wise not to let her care for your boy, yes. I, too, think of the trouble they have brought your family. He openly supports disgraced son they say here. Everyone has different opinion, no? Everyone talks about Khan Kinner's demand to return Kertch Port to Khazar control. No neutral port allowed. Takes commerce from Azov Port. Yuzbasha promotes aggressive policy and the khan listens now.

More of your people came through and Ebenezer, your agent says that they will be good settlers. However, the land ownership laws may change they say and taxes are increasing.

Oh, Judy, I start to tell you my sorrow and end telling you my fears, no? How terrible of me! How inconsiderate to let our fear rule our hearts when love and sympathy wish to rule our lives. Forgive me, I find more reasons to ask forgiveness now as I grow older. How we do need the grace and pardon offered by Hesus, yes.

Your constant friend,

Merien Papasian

PS: Please send me Altom's filly if they threaten to take her for the prince's debts. I will get together whatever I can to help you, yes. True friends must help meet true needs, no? MP

>- - - - - - - >

The sound of a trumpet in the distance filled the sickroom with an awareness of growing sounds and the shouting of men. The sound of running horses filled the room. Ahjit and Kaya ran out to the filling courtyard before the palace. The men of the Chipchak troop swelled the area with their presence. Whooping angrily they circled and led the horse with the body of their khan before Kaya. The young Ertach dismounted and kissed Kaya's hand, touched it to his forehead and while crying, embraced him. He found his voice at last.

"*Bash un ah sah luck*, God protect you. Your father is dead. We only wished to pass the gate with half a troop, and they refused permission. While we talked, a man from the wall shot deliberately. He

intended to kill the Khan. It was murder. We forced the gate and killed those who resisted, but the guilty man escaped. Now the entire city is aroused against us. What must we do?" Expectantly, he looked to Kaya for directions.

"Close the gate to the compound. Come, let Ahjit lead you to the armory. There are goods to take to the tribe, tribute from the good merchant Jomer whose goods your fathers guarded on the silk road. You'll need extra horses. They belong to Ahjit, our old Yuzbasha, you know the stories of his power. Go, bring back the tribe armed. I'll send the hero Ozkurt and my lady Fewsoon on my horse, Altom, with you. You'll close up the city so none enter or leave. We must obtain the punishment of the guilty ones. We'll negotiate a new treaty with the city. One that brings power and justice to the Chipchak people. You must exit through the merchant's gate. It's not guarded or used in winter. Hurry!"

Ahjit directed the tribesmen to the armory while calling the guards under his command to hold the inner gate.

Kaya returned to the door of Jomer's palace where Ozkurt stood with bow at ready watching the running men.

"I've named you regent of my child and heir to my people. For the love and companionship we have shared; fail not. Go supervise the retreat to the tribe. Let Fewsoon and others persuade them. You lead and return. I'll prepare the way here. We'll control the grass road from this city to the Urals. The silk will flow through our hands. Go, encourage lieutenant Ertach. He is your second." Each man paused with his hand on the other's shoulder and looked deep in the others eyes. "Stay well," "Go well," they said quietly.

Ozkurt ran to join the band preparing the escape. "We can't leave without food!" he shouted to Ahjit. Kaya entered the building.

"Fewsoon janum, my soul, you must go to the tribe and rally them to surround the city, get them to back Ozkurt and let them obey our laws. The ones you and I made up when we were children and the things we've talked of since. You must ride Altom so you both will be safe. We must leave the Khan's body here as evidence to persuade the city authorities that he was murdered. Then, they will have to find the murderer, make recompense; to surrender something, to save face and yield advantages to our people."

She nodded her head but looked at him with sad, soulful eyes. Her cheeks were pale where tears were beginning to course. She gulped and whispered. "I was going to tell you here in the city, another life has started in me. I long to call her Cheechek, if a girl. You'll not send me away? I'll be safe with you." He put his hand on each arm and leaned his head to talk in her ear, their cheeks touching.

"You're a jewel of a woman, all men love and value you. The child can be Cheechek or Jomer, if a boy. Ozkurt will protect the rights of the children. You must be his voice with the tribe. They honor, but don't know him. I must stay with Ahjit, but will be safe here. Money and secure routes are their main considerations. They're not a united people. Unless a madman is in control, we'll solve everything the first week of the siege." She sniffed and sighed her consent, turned to take the child, went to kiss the silent Jomer's forehead and hand. She went to the stables with Sheftalee and commanded the loading of her gear and some new cloth samples in small bales.

City men hammered the gate to the merchant's palace while the Chipchak troop, with extra armor loaded on the horses, decamped through the merchant's private gate. Ahjit sent his young sons, Chavush and Erkan, to protect his animals, while Fewsoon took the most precious bales of silk with her. She mounted behind her child who was sitting straddled holding Altom's mane. Kaya sent gold coins with Ozkurt for possible bribes on the road.

Meanwhile, the body of Erkan was taken to the hall of Jomer and cleaned by the servants. The clatter of the departing troop sounded in the courtyard and the thud of the gate closing signaled their safe departure.

The merchant's inner gate hammered and echoed with frustrated cries. Then a sudden cheer sounded and the blare of trumpets close at hand. The city guards had arrived in force before the inner gate.

THE ASSASSIN'S SHOT

PEOPLE, PLACES & PLOTS IN CHAPTER 15

Ahjit: finds himself and family held hostage.
City Captain: has a duty for the safety of the town and a rich reward.
Erkan: makes a dramatic entrance into the city to rest beside Jomer.
Jomer: not allowed to die in peace, his riches bring trouble on all.
Kaya: resolves to learn more and see the affair through to the end.
Lahlee: happy to be allowed to go to the capital by her husband.
Meryen: marriageable daughter of Ahjit bey, held hostage.
Optal: gives helps and hints to save his remaining human bear, Kaya.
Son'der: infant, baby of Sheftalee.
Ted'bir: enters the picture and tells an old story.
Uri: a drunk and hang-about, fond of wine and tricks.
Yuzbasha: gets his assignment as general on the Western frontier.

GLOSSARY HELPS

***Ba-bam':* my father; daddy; head of family.**
***git'sin-ler:* get out of here; get out; let them go.**
***jan'um:* my soul; beloved; dearest**
***or'du-gar:* army headquarters; military center.**
***soos:* hush; quiet; shut up.**
***sore hoe'sh:* drunk; intoxicated; stupefied.**

15 SPIDER'S-WEB

PATROLED VIGIL

"The Ordugar has moved to the Dniester River, they've called me to come. We force the river boundary this spring." Yuzbasha exclaimed to his wife, Lahlee, as he ran into the house. "The heir is in charge and I go as adjutant general. I leave The Bend today." His face was bright with excitement.

"I'll go stay with mother," she countered practically. "You won't want me around, underfoot, while you're out leading the action." She turned to continue the task he had interrupted.

"You don't seem too excited by the prospects," he complained.

"Nonsense," she countered, "when you return a hero, I'll be the first to greet you. I'll accompany your mother to the celebrations."

"We'll be rich and I'll be in charge of the Rumanian territories," he boasted. "All the lords of new settled lands will send their guards and dependants to fight."

She shook her head doubtfully, "I'm not sure about The Bend and the upper Don River. Commander Gochen is not your friend. He has been angry since Prince Ilkin died."

He looked at her critically and grabbed her face with a hand, "Remember we're in this together, you doctored the food. It's our secret. You'll profit by this as much as I."

She shook herself free and walked to a door. "I want no part of any of your schemes, scams, or dirty plans."

"I can find someone who will, when I return." He shouted. He knew she would tell their secrets if he threatened more; so, he left, sure that he deserved more than the simple daughter of a military family.

> - - - - - - - >

Ahjit and Kaya went to the inner gate guarded by Jomer's caravan guards. There the noise had assumed an organized pounding.

Ahjit consulted with the guards. "Have any city officials appeared yet? Do you recognize anyone we can deal with?" An old man on the wall popped his head up for a quick look and gave a toothless grin as he turned to Ahjit.

"The Captain of the guard has just ridden up. They know that the troop has escaped, and we are left weakened."

"Let them cool their heels and tempers a bit. Start talking: tell them of Jomer's invitation; of Kaya, the heir's interest in safe trade routes; of Erkan's death; the riot of the tribesmen; mention that we are preparing the bodies of the dead for mourning. Threaten them with sacrilege. Say the death feast is almost prepared, and they will be invited at midday. Tell them we will not fight if the Captain assures us of his protection. The man knows me. Tell him we will remember any favors." The old man's head popped back above the wall, and he started to shout at the crowd as if he had been wakened from sleep by noise at the door. Ahjit turned, with a smile, to Kaya who indicated the store-houses with an upward motion of the chin.

"Take some men and secure the goods. Leave them as guards. Make sure the cooks are forward in their food preparations. I will see to the funeral preparations." He turned toward the guards and the old man, "Ask for someone to go call the apostolos of the church for the funeral." He turned toward the palace. The pounding at the gate had stopped, but the old man was arguing still while the guards were slowly preparing to open it. Kaya ran into the palace.

"Forgive me foster father, that I must exhibit you with the dead. It is not lack of respect or love on my part, but a simple necessity." Jomer's voice and luster of eye had faded since the morning. His reply was weak.

"A good man is good company to keep, living or dead. Your father was a worthy leader. I regret his death." Kaya lifted him from the bed and walked to the hall.

"Worthy leaders are sometimes rotten fathers. You were more father to me than he was, and I thank Tanra for your interest in me." He deposited him on a table beside the corpse of his father. An accompanying servant brought the brocaded covers and arranged them while Kaya leaned close to hear the last feeble whispers.

"I have heard in the book, 'He has loved us with an everlasting love.' I have tried the heavenly way and it is good, so I love you, foster son." Kaya straightened, stood as if on guard as the city's captain and soldiers ran into the room. Behind them the sounds of shouting could be heard, angry voices, but no clash of weapons.

"Surrender your arms. We take you to the Council," the man shouted. Then suddenly, he realized that the figures in the center were on display and dead. He and his men stopped and looked at each other in embarrassment.

"I have no weapon, and I mourn the dead with respect as a son should." Kaya held out his hands, but did not move from his place. "You should see to the security of the goods for the council will not wish loss of valuables to the mob."

"*Soos*, shut up. I'm in charge now. Stay where you are." He motioned to two men, "You stay here with him." The captain turned and ran out. His voice could be heard outside shouting to his men, "Clear the grounds. Search all who leave through the gate." The two remaining men took position on each side of the two silent figures. Kaya started the eulogy to the dead. He sang it as a dirge.

1. Glorious in life, be tranquil in death.
   Praises and honors will follow your rest.
   Honest and truthful until your last breath,
   Help, gracious counsel and honor to guests.
   God's powerful guidance meets life's every test.

2. Faithful in life God guards you from wrong,
   Resisting selfishness, evil and hate;
   Like gold your merit and worth all along,
   Tested and weighed in the balance of fate.
   God's richest honors to you will belong.

JOMER'S DIRGE

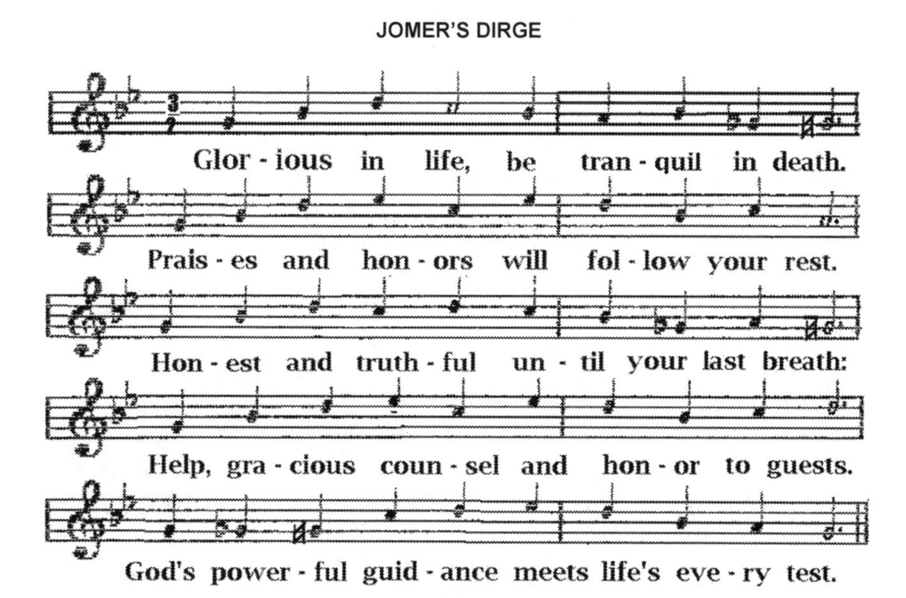

3. Godly and wise, rich, powerful, strong;
Generous, kind to the children of men.
They celebrate you with verses and song.
Goodness, simplicity, freedom from sin,
Christ's great redemption will right human wrong.

4. Brave men of light, God's Glory display.
Call every soul to repent and obey.
Sin, sorrow, bitterness fill up man's day,
Without God's power your joy will delay.
Death comes to everyone, find while you may.

> - - - - - - - >

The guards and prisoners stood waiting before the governor's house while council members came and went. Ahjit and Kaya stood with wrist and ankles bound in chains, awaiting their summons. The merchant's caravan saray guards had been left at their post under the captain's command and the servants continued to mourn the death of their master. None mourned Erkan, the tribal chief, but though some cursed him, no one moved his body. It was evidence of the murder.

The bear-master appeared from a wicker door in a mud wall beyond the edge of the building. He walked straight to Kaya and looked compassionately up into his face.

"Young master, I sometimes beg at the door of the church. The Apostolos is known to me. Would you like to send him a message? I will take it now."

Kaya, feeling his regard, replied urgently. "The funeral must be postponed. Conditions are too tense. The bodies can be preserved in a storage place. Everything must be done properly, when we are freed. Ask the apostolos to care for the details." The face of the bear-master became very grave and sad.

"I will obey and carry the message, but one might suggest that a quiet, rapid funeral would clear the air of recriminations and excuses. You both might be allowed to attend," he paused and shrugged. "I don't know for sure."

"I will give you a small gold piece for your trouble and for your friend," Kaya searched into his sash.

"You were always generous, even as a boy, but I will accept only silver. Remember my example, only silver not gold." He lowered his voice. "The gold is dangerous, I can say no more." He raised his voice as Kaya fumbled up a silver coin from his money belt. "Blessed be Tanra who spreads his gifts abroad. We will eat well tonight. The apostolos will have your message within the hour." He left, but carefully scanned the crowd around them as he went. Kaya stared at the ground pondering for a long time.

"I was a prisoner, free in the Ural tower with my foster mother; I am a free man chained in my own city. I had nothing to lose in the first case and everything in the present. Leaving mother, I left something important to me and now, I leave what is important to others. How true the hermit spoke, 'Everyman's life is unpredictable, full of surprise. Ours is a God of wonder.'" Kaya shook his head thoughtfully, "May I learn to be content in any situation."

"Your foster mother is alive? Vashtie your wet nurse? You saw her?" Ahjit's voice grew in excitement. "Why haven't you told me these things. You arrived here last week!"

"Forgive me caravan master, in the press of arrival and Jomer's illness I have not even thought of your love for her. You have a wife and family. One forgets you married late, in hope of finding her." Kaya abjectly took the hands of Ahjit between his own. Ahjit stared angrily at him.

"No love is ever forgotten or replaced by another. Each has its own character and qualities, like cities on a caravan route. As one travels one must be content where one is, though dreaming of other places." His face softened. "Tell me all you remember."

> - - - - - - - >

Taken into the reception of the municipal building, Kaya and Ahjit were surprised to find themselves alone with one man, the brutal bully Kaya remembered from his childhood encounter in the city *hamom*, sauna baths. Ahjit's dislike caused him to ignore the man, and he refused to speak. Kaya looked at him curiously. He had heard much of this man.

"You will never imagine the satisfaction I feel in seeing you here in my power." The large, powerfully built man leaned forward rubbing his hands together. "I have waited for years for this opportunity, for our lives have been linked since the year before your birth."

"I know you only as Tedbir, the Persian, rich and unscrupulous by reputation, involved in city government and dubious affairs of business and politics. You tried to extort protection money from my foster father." Kaya looked carefully at his adversary, he had expected the whole council. He was suspicious now, his opponent was amused.

"Yes, you have learned his defiance well. You know you will be fined for harboring and supplying the tribesmen. Since you are their new Khan, we will hold you hostage. The inheritance from Jomer can be put to court as illegal and not approved. No one will find documentation. I have it all."

"Why do you show such personal satisfaction with your threats and projected activities? What damage have we Chipchaks caused Tedbir, the Persian?" The big man laughed.

"Ask Gooch, the marauder. Son of an impoverished merchant, he learned the ways of Ahriman, the evil one, and prospered. He had spent months planning and recruiting men for an attack that would put him beyond need. Then, one stubborn merchant alerted the Chipchak guards who, under your Khan, destroyed his hopes of complete victory. Gooch planned a sweeping revenge. The merchant died in season, but the Khan never deigned to come to the cities. Tartar lords can be bribed into damaging attacks which, as rivals, they would normally carry out anyway for goods. Weak, venial city officials can be stimulated to extravagant demands on the tribe and invitations made to encourage visits to the town center, but all in vain. Today, after so many years, the offer of war goods and death of a friend brought him to my hands." The man leaned forward gloating, "And you as well."

"So, Gooch became Tedbir," suggested Kaya, "a rich official and gained all he would have gotten from a complete success originally. Why do you continue in your thirst for blood? Do you not forget nor forgive anything?" Kaya spoke, avid for the response.

"No man thwarts my will without damage. You cannot imagine how satisfying it is to possess complete power over enemies, to watch them moan for mercy." His eyes glowed with pleasure as some past event came to his mind.

"You put yourself in Tanra's place to play God, but not a God of good and mercy, but of evil."

"I become one with Ahriman the God of this world, ruling from of old, His will mine, and mine His. There is joy in the suffering and frustration of mere people. It slacks my thirst to rule." He turned to bellow at the door, "I thirst; bring wine." He looked back. "You will join me."

The tray was full with three beakers of beverage, and the servant bowed while offering Kaya and Ahjit beakers of gold. Tedbir gestured grandly, "Tarim wine from the gardens of the south." He took the silver beaker and drank a mouth full, rolling it round on his tongue. "Ah, here is the road to paradise." He raised his cup with both hands in a traditional toast, "To the silk roads and the eternal glory of E'peck Kent!" He swilled more from the cup, looking up.

"You've said you'll destroy us. I don't drink with enemies, but only with men friendly to our city and its prosperity." Kaya shrugged, "If it were a matter of money or mere properties, we might come to an agreement."

Ahjit nodded his support and added. "You have shown yourself more interested in wealth than revenge in the past. You have waited for years to pay the Khan who did you the most damage. You try to frighten us with your talk, but you are a business man first, interested in wealth. I know where the property papers are hidden. There is more wealth to Jomer's estate than meets the eye."

"You could have died quickly. Now you assure your slow, painful death, for I'm determined to learn your many secrets," Tedbir's lips twisted in a grimace, "I want Onder's knife, the jeweled knife of the heir, with the right to the inheritance."

"I know where the knife is hidden," Kaya said in a matter-of-fact tone. "I received the knife from Jomer's hand and later hid it for I was afraid I might lose it." He looked at Tedbir intently. "The inheritance is worth much more than two men's lives." Ahjit looked stricken by this revelation while Tedbir laughed.

"I offer you much more than two lives. Come to the door and look at the number of people at the bottom of the stairs." The two men obeyed and saw Ahjit's city wife, Sheftalee, their daughter, Meryen and two little children, Vashtie and baby Sonder. Several of the older servants from the palace were there. The old groom from the stables lay by the door with blood on his head. They looked up with dull, frightened eyes and the children whimpered. The women cried out, calling "*Ahjit janum*," and "*Babam*."

Ahjit cried out in consternation, fury rose in his face and he turned on the giant man who held the door. He threw his weight against him, trying to push him down the stairs. Tedbir pushed him aside and hit him in the head with a stout metal club attached to his wrist by a thong. Ahjit fell in the doorway at the top of the stairs. His forehead bled profusely. His wife and daughter ran up the stairs to attend him. He lay dazed, but angry, and pushed the family's ministering hands away. He tried to force himself up. "I should have killed you the day of the great battle. I should have sought you out."

"I have wondered if you might not have been there, you citified cur of a tribal dog. I could have settled score with you long ago, had I but known." He glowered as he stared and considered the facts just revealed. "The musicians! Damn those two incompetent bastards. They must have known it. They didn't tell me." He shrugged, "They'll pay for that dearly."

Tedbir looked again at the huddled group with contempt and sneered. "A touching scene you must admit." He sighed regretfully. "I was prepared for a long siege and an exciting time with you men and your helpers, but I suppose I must let myself be bought off. The amount will comfort my deep disappointment!" His eyes gleamed wolfishly. "Come, waste no time, tell me where it is hidden."

"First, let Ahjit go with his family. These people must be freed. They know nothing of these matters. You can release Ahjit and the estate people, they have no documents that can force the city's hand. Your business is with me alone. The knife of Onder can give you, rather than the city, power over the estates outside the walls. Jomer's wealth is scattered far, from the Yellow river to the Greek cities of the Black sea." Kaya's voice was firm.

"*Git sin ler*, Let them go! I can have them anytime, if you are false to me." Tedbir brought his face close to Kaya's, "Don't try to play games with me. Swear by your God to do as you say." He raised his voice. "Guards, let the people return to their places, but warn the gates they cannot pass. Unchain the caravan master."

"Yesu is my witness that I deal in the truth with you. I intend no deception." Now he studied Tedbir's face. "Is there any you swear by, any who support your integrity?

"Beside the dark Lord, perhaps by Manis the Persian, the leader of the sect of the Manichaeans. I like his teachings: The flesh is nothing; the spirit is all. Enlightenment leads to the empowering of the high ones. Ascetic or indulgent the contact with the spirit world is all important. You know that Manis was what you Christians call the Holy Spirit. Many of your people have left the churches to follow our teacher here in the heartlands."

"Mani was crucified by your king Bahram for good reasons, and he did not rise again as Yesu did. What regard did Manis have for truth who despised the words and acts of the body in preference to the imaginations of the mind and spirit? Would he approve the completion of a promise if the master spirits indicated otherwise?" Kaya shook his head.

"You have no choice, but my will. My vengeance is now complete. I'm willing to let you go free if you enrich me. I am willing to kill you slowly if you don't. It's very simple, 'Better a live dog than a dead lion'. Great wealth is useless to a dead man. My patience is ended. Decide now."

"We hid it when I was a boy. It's in plain sight in the office of Jomer. A great *kalkan*, a leather war shield is hung on the wall. There is a peep hole in the upper center where the eye of the jeweled handle shows through and holds up the shield. Only he and I knew its place. Unless he has moved it, it will be there."

"You're wise. I'm a determined man. I leave you the liberty of this room while I claim the prize." The man went down the stairs and from outside came the sound of a horse moving away briskly. A sudden silence filled the room.

Kaya stared at the door listening, and when no one entered, he walked to the table where the silver and gold drinking cups sat on the tray. He lifted the gold cup to his nose to sniff the contents. He growled. He sniffed the second gold cup as well, wrinkling his nose. He lifted the silver cup and after a long sniff, drank deeply of the contents with a smile. He hummed a bit of his old song 'God is sending summer.' He drained the cup and pausing to listen, poured one of the gold cups into the silver up to the point where Tedbir had left it. Walking to a window he dashed the remaining wine from the gold cup on the outside wall and watched the liquid stain run down. He placed the empty cup beside the two on the tray.

Slowly and purposefully, in spite of his chains, Kaya started taking everything off two walls and breaking or tearing it. He tested some of the copper and brass plates hung there for hardness and put two, a plate and a vase, in the corner. He piled some of the cloth and furniture before the same corner. He then tore his clothes, jacket sleeves and pant legs, shredding them. He was careful not to touch the tray. Finally, when half the room was a wreck, he sat on the floor in the debris of the readied corner and dropped his head on his chest and started to snore. Outside, the sound of a running horse drew near. Tedbir's voice roared. Men's feet ran up the stairs.

"Damn your smooth tongue. You lied." The men saw the room and gasped. "What has happened here?"

"The man's gone mad!"

"Just look at it!"

"He's drunk."

"Damn him." The four men stood in shocked astonishment. One man walked over and grabbed Kaya by his torn vest and lifted him up to face him. He shook the limp man vigorously and let him drop.

"*Sore hoe'sh*, drunk, phew, stinking drunk, he's out for the night." They all looked at the tray. "Only one cup is empty, The hero doesn't hold his liquor well." They laughed about their new found superiority. They shook their heads in agreement. "He can't take it!"

"Just look at the mess he made, must have gone mad."

"Good thing he was chained!" Tedbir glowered at the fallen Kaya and at his men.

"The mix must have been too strong." He picked up the empty gold cup, up ended it to watch the last drops seep out, then he grasped the full one." He extended it to one of the smallest of his men. "Here Uri, you try my wine. There is not much too strong for you."

Uri stuck out his chest, and grinned a wide snaggle-toothed grimace. He drained the cup in one long pull, and dragged his sleeve across his mouth with a sigh of satisfaction. He showed off his knowledge.

URI BRAVES THE BREW

"It's local wine from the south, but with a fruit-like addition. I could drink a dozen," he bragged. He looked at the silver cup hopefully. Tedbir took it up and held it up to his mouth.

"This one's mine, I didn't finish it earlier." He took a sip, then another one. He looked at Kaya in a cold calculating manner. "I wonder if Jomer changed the place. Or did he lie?" He walked to Kaya and bent over to shake him.

"I feel dizzy and sick," Uri's voice held a slow hypnotic quality. "The wine's bad. Is it poison?" Tedbir laughed loudly, turning back to the astonished soldiers.

"No, not poison, but yes, drugged. You will sleep it off, but first let me test it." He motioned to the other guards, "Hold him up lest he fall." He came to the group and slapped the man. "Uri, you were off duty the night a purse of money disappeared from this room. You and friends said you were gambling together. Did you get away and steal the money?" He put his face close to the slumped man, now suspended by the strength of the guards. He slapped again.

"Yes, I went out to piss and got in the side door. I had debts with the *hamom* master," his voice was weak.

"So my partner got my bag of gold, thanks to you." He slapped and shook the limp man, who did not respond. Tedbir backed up looking disgusted. He motioned the men outside. "Put him down on a barrel and pump him till he throws up. Then let him sleep. I'll block his pay till we're even." He motioned the men out.

"Now, I'll indulge my pleasure by killing Kaya. There are so many ways to die, and yet some are inadequate to the challenge of causing prolonged suffering and fear. Torture will not do for Kaya. He might cry out, inadvertently, but he would not cringe, whine or beg. I could do to him as his Yesu was done by, but there are no religious leaders present to condemn his faith. It would lack the garden arrest, trials and crucifixion drama. Perhaps something similar is possible. I will have to look for it. But it must be slow and observed by many. Let it be the consequences of refusing my will, so the weak may tremble and the strong worry lest they fail the tests. Perhaps a piece by piece cutting of the flesh or fingers and toes would prolong the misery. One part a week, so that the pain of anticipation will match the healing. It should give a world of pleasure to those of us who love such things. "May the spirits of the ancestors lead me in my choice. Ahriman, ruler of this world, must be my teacher. Kaya's death must provide a reproof to those who would impose moral values and deny me my will and pleasures."

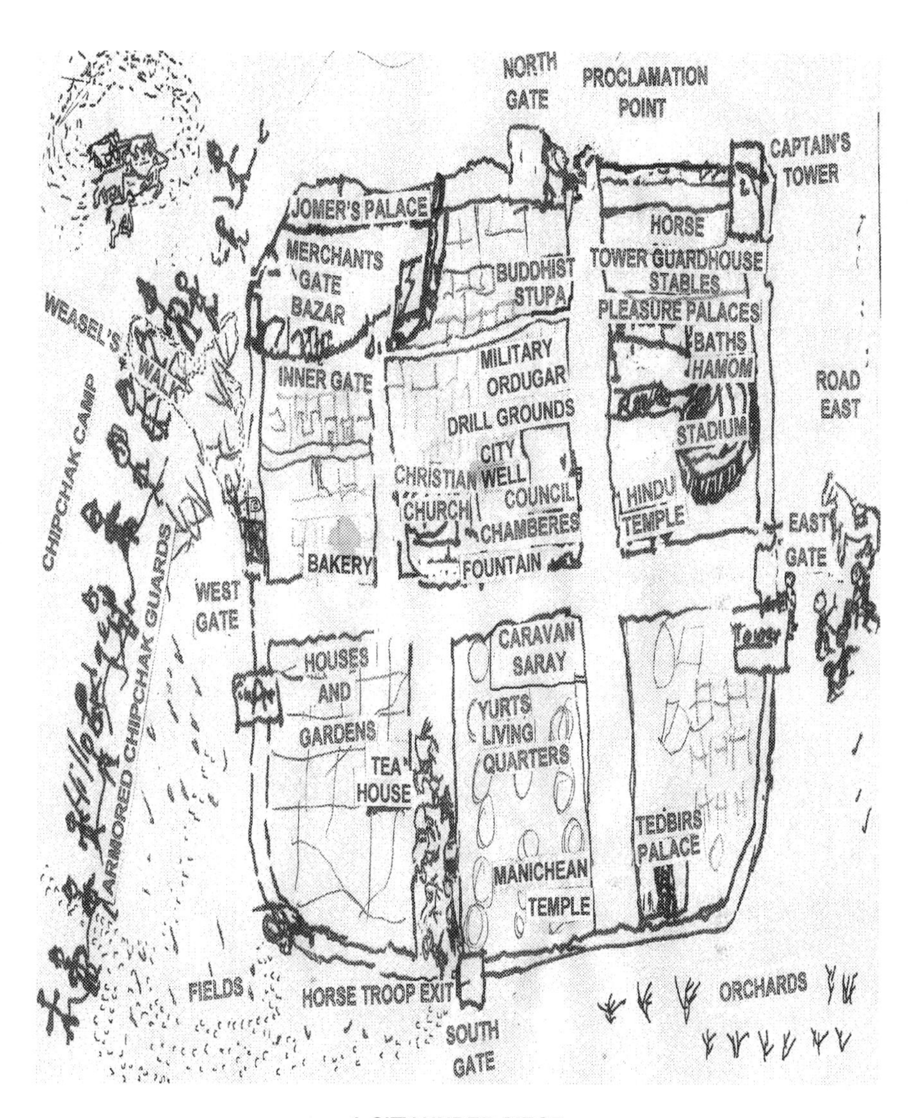

A CITY UNDER SIEGE

PEOPLE, PLACES & PLOTS IN CHAPTER 16

City Captain: probes the enemy force, and seeks his reward.
Councilor Peck: warns of impending doom and demands action.
Erly: second in command of the squad to reconnoiter the enemy.
Die'ya Chavush: the uncle knows the Hun army will not be asleep.
Er'tach: returns with terms of surrender: refugees may leave at night.
Orhan: ordered to scout the enemy camp with a squad of guards.
Kaya: finds no way out, but hopes that peace can still be made.
Op'tal: becomes a friend in need and plans to deliver Onder's knife.
Tedbir: plots his revenge with care and his escape as well.
Yuzbasha, the Khazar: feels that victory will be easy, but can't sleep.

GLOSSARY HELPS

bar'ish: peace; truce; time out.
bash un ooze'ah sah-luck: health to your head; be comforted; condolences for the grieving.
kah-ret'sin: curse it; damn it; blast it.
kent: city; large town.
soos: quiet; hush; don't talk.
shalvar: baggy trousers.
yor'gan: a very thick warm quilt, stuffed with down, cotton, or wool.
ye'yen: nephew or niece.

HEADS UP!

"We cross the Dniester River under the cover of darkness, Die'ya," Yuzbasha, now a general, shouted in his excitement. "We'll catch them all off guard, asleep!"

"Easy, Ye'yen, you'll wake them all," laughed his uncle Chavush.

"Here, at last, I have a chance to fight and confirm my being a hero.

Our prince will lead the attack. We'll devastate them: so small and unprepared." He chuckled with joy, rubbing his hands.

The uncle threw back his head with an upward, negative jerk. He said, "They know we're here. It's that reinforcements haven't arrived yet, but they will. Perhaps you should get some sleep before the attack."

"I can't sleep, Die'ya. She's always in my dreams talking to me. I don't dare let her get close. She tries to kiss me," he shuddered.

"Yes, we're all haunted by our loves and pursued by our mistakes. We go into battle by dawn. May the ancestors bless us with good fortune. We will awake and go forward, Ye'yen. We'll face our destiny like heroes."

>- - - - - - - >

Tedbir stood watching in disgust as they dragged the man Uri down the stairway. When they left he reached for the silver cup again.

He sat with his back to the wall contemplating the ruin. He spoke his thoughts in a slow, strange cadence.

"Why would Kaya react differently?" He suddenly looked at the cup he was sipping and flung it from him. It spun wildly and spilled its contents on the floor, and he floundered trying to get his balance and stand. A groan burst from his lips. The Han Chinese herbal drug had not failed. It held him in its grip.

"Jomer must have moved the knife. It was in place four years ago when I went on my journeys." Kaya rose carefully from his blocked corner, and walked slowly to stand before Tedbir. "Money is useful, but not as important as you make it out to be. I must know why you are so keen on revenge. You have already murdered two or more, plus those you killed in battle." He looked expectantly at the man as he sat on the divan beside him. Light was fading in the room.

"The excitement of the hunt is small compared to the exaltation of hunting a creature as intelligent as man. The surprise and agony of the realization of death. The despair as life slips away. A shared moment between victor and vanquished is the aim of sweet revenge." His voice was clear but slow. His eyes looked unfocused on Kaya's face.

"You make it sound like poetry. It doesn't disgust you? Tell me how it began." Kaya's face was grim.

"I murdered Onder a hundred times in my heart after our defeat. It mattered not that there were many dead, less to share the great riches we gained. We lost a part of what was mine; two men were responsible. To get information was my chief obstacle. Tribesmen are leery of casual visits, but I overcame all obstacles. I used the wandering musicians to penetrate the camp. Messengers came to Onder, and I knew when he would break cover and run. He had to have the great horse to gain mercy from Jomer. He was forced to bargain. The day before Onder's leaving I had hidden away in a cave that my men had enlarged before the attack on the merchant train. The rock and earth we had carried to the stream to scatter and wash away. Room for two, a seat to peer out through a chink hid by a thorn bush. From this point we had attacked the advance guard of the train. Now it became a hide away to spy from.

"I heard the quarrel about the woman between the tribesman and Onder. I heard the arrow strike and feared to lose my revenge to another. When I emerged from the cave a Hun was supporting Onder, but he feared to pull out the arrow lest he lose much blood. A furious woman came out of the woods. Then, as he rejected her, sobbing she struck him in the chest with a small copper knife. She fought with the Hun and biting his hand, escaped, but the man at that moment saw me and ran. I suppose the woman thought he pursued her, but he fled me. I dropped him with two Chipchak arrows gathered from the fight. Now I was frustrated. Another had taken my joy. Onder must be dying. A sound came from the stream behind and I entered the cave to sit and stare through the hole. I was desperate.

"Again I heard the sobbing of a woman and a groan from Onder. The sound from the stream drew near. Quiet exclamations and the sound of quiet talking came. Then, I heard Onder's voice. It spoke of rewards and gave messages. Then, I heard the sound of distant hooves. The sound of running as the Hun's donkey and horse were led off.

"I could wait no more or lose my revenge. I emerged as the two thieves hurriedly entered the stream passing behind the tunnel of willows. They were intent on escaping, and did not see me. I ran to the spot where Onder lay fainting. He opened his eyes in recognition as I pushed my hanjir into the hole where the copper knife had been removed, but I pointed my knife upward instead of down and cut the heart. The eyes dilated and his surprise showed. I felt thrill after thrill course through me. Another would be blamed for my murder. No one would search for me nor suspect. This made it doubly sweet. The sound of horses were outside the wood and I dashed to the stream, plunged my hand in the water and ran for the cave. As I entered the safety of the cave, I heard the sounds of an excited stallion and the sound of a hunting horn. My hanjir dripped water and I felt cold fear as the tribesmen raced shouting across the stream and back toward the east border looking for Huns. I realized later that I could have had the Khan as well had I waited in the clearing, but I was too shaken by emotion. In the night I followed the trail of the two beggars to my camp and paid them the price of the two animals. They never suspected how much I knew. I kept them on for petty spying. It delights me to torment them.

"I let an underling do my duty and kill the Khan. I admired Erkan as much as I hated him. He was impossible to get alone or out of his element. It didn't cost much to stir up trouble, but he didn't flinch. He went on raids or to the Hermitage, but nowhere else. Assassins couldn't get at him!" He shook his head as if in wonder and sighed. His chin dropped to his chest. He seemed to sleep. His breathing became regular and deep.

Kaya felt lightly about the man's body and removed his small ankh shaped hanjir and a big key to some great clumsy lock in the house. He rose slowly to his feet and stepped forward silently in the dark.

"Tedbir Bey," screamed a terrified voice from below and feet pounded the stairs. "The city is surrounded. The Chipchaks have arrived." Men with lanterns came charging up the stairs. "Their camp fires are on the north and west side. Sentries can be seen from the walls. We heard the drumming of the horses' hooves, more troops are arriving."

"Councilor Peck has come!" called another voice from below. An imperious voice demanded, "I must see Tedbir Bey at once. The safety of the city is imperiled."

Kaya fell silently to the floor as the light reached the upper room. He feigned sleep as the guards entered the room to wake the burley man on the divan. Tedbir woke slowly and seemed confused, but grabbing one of the men, he pulled himself up. Then he called out to his men to follow, as he staggered down the stairs, shaking his head.

"To the walls, everyone. Call every household to send their men to the walls." The befuddled roar of his voice sent men running in every direction. A trumpet's urgent blare cut through the night air like a knife, hawking again and again. Councilor Peck intervened.

"We have urgent business with the council now. We must meet whatever demands they make. Barbarous tribe's people can be calmed with gifts and promises. We will have to release the captives. Perhaps the Apostolos can be brought in to demonstrate our sincerity and mediate some truce." Peck's high, aristocratic voice was panicked, "He has influence with some of the northern tribes."

"Defense first. We'll talk later, when we have reconnoitered the situation. You go talk to our rich merchants. All tribesmen treat only for gold," Tedbir dismissed the councilor with contempt.

"You there, Optal. You stayed to complete my orders at the merchant's palace. When I found no knife, I said to kill the servants. Have the guards finished carrying out my command?" His voice was harsh and bullying.

"Yes, Master, they were searching out the men when I left. Pigeons were released well before sunset. They flew north. The house and grounds are being examined."

"*Kah hret sin*, damnation, can't anyone do things right? Get upstairs and guard the prisoner. I want him nailed to the city gate regardless of the cost. Your life if you lose him. Slow torture, and for your friend too."

"Yes, master." The meek voice held a faint trace of resentment with fear. Slowly, heavy steps came up the stairs and a lamp gleamed on the knife just drawn from his sash and held in the hand of the bear-master.

"Are you awake, young Kaya? Come, I know you didn't take the drug. You have nothing to fear from me." His voice was sad and deep. He reversed the knife with a flip of the wrist and held the blade toward himself, then he extended his arm and held it near Kaya's face. "It is Onder's knife. It belongs to the heir, not to thieves and murderers. You will need it when this madness is over. Come take it. Let it be amends for the past lack of honesty on our part: my partner too, we could have warned you. Our master's madness grows. We have watched it grow, but did nothing for fear. Many are paying in blood for our fear. May your Tanra forgive us."

Kaya took the knife slowly and reverently from the proffered hand.

"Where did you find it? Not on the wall. Surely Jomer had hid it again."

The old man jerked his head up. "It was inside the *yorgan*, quilt that covered him. He slept with it, to keep it safe for you. When the

Apostolos came to carry away the bodies, I found it. When my master knows the truth, I will die. He lusts for it."

"Greed trusts no man, nor God." Kaya ran his hand over the familiar bumps and knobs then held the knife to the light of the lantern to see the color of the jade. "You could have kept this, so your friend could have care and abundant food."

Again the man's head moved up slowly. "My friend died yesterday in the church hospice. He is already in the burial crypt. I pray to join him where he waits." He brushed a hand up over his face and sniffed.

"*Bash un ooze ah' sah'luck*," Kaya comforted. "Yesu has room for all who come to him. He protects his flock." Kaya's voice was gentle. "Death is a worthy fear and so is pain. Men will kill for this knife and what it promises, but the promises are false,"

Optal sighed sadly. "My master was a brave warrior and worthy, when poor and striving. Money, vice and unmastered emotions have made him a ruin." He held up both hands toward Kaya as if pushing him away in a gesture of rejection. He continued his reply, "Destiny has put it in your hands. You must play and dance the part." His teeth shone in the light. "I might be willing to provide some of the music. I have already adopted our oldest tune to suit the Apostolos and I hope you, too. I'll sing it for you if you like." The man smiled almost shyly.

Kaya was surprised. "I would be honored. Music is something we both love." Kaya smiled his reply. Optal began to sing:

COME TO YESU

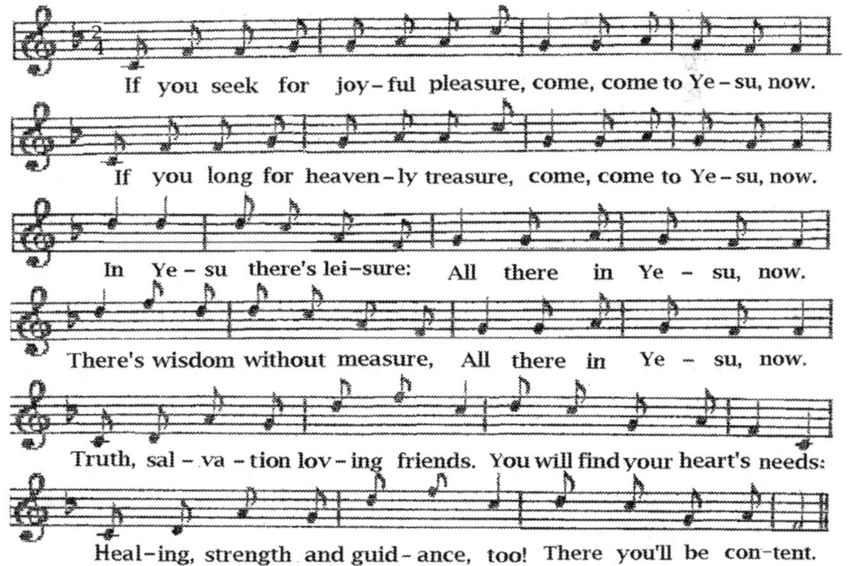

If you seek for joyful pleasure,
Come, come to Yesu now.
If you long for heavenly treasure,
Come, come to Yesu now.
In Yesu there's leisure,
All there in Yesu now.
There's wisdom without measure,
All there in Yesu now.
Truth, salvation, loving friends,
You will find your heart's needs:
Healing, strength and guidance too,
There you'll be content.

Kaya laughed softly, "It is beautiful. With a bear, you would be the star of any church festival."

"Those days are past, but I still know a trick or two to get the best out of any situation or animal, even if the Persian calls me Optal, a fool." His white hair shone in the light.

"Will you then, coax this bear and keep him in the rhythm?" The lantern shone on Kaya's teeth now.

"The secret is in the beat. You should feel it."

"I will try. With such masters as mine, how can I fail?" Kaya leaned smiling toward the man who replied.

"I have always loved my bears."

>- - - - - - - >

"*Barish*, peace!" The loud, deep voice of a herald shouted. The wall guard responded with the same word and torches were brought to see the messenger. The trumpet sounded at the main gate, an armored troop of twenty horsemen rode boldly up, displaying the Yak tail standard of the Chipchak horde. A wooden frame held twelve tails for the sacred number that is multiplied or divided by all digits from one to six excepting five, the number of one hand. It is a number of power. On the hill, other mounted warriors showed. Five of them held pikes with Tartar heads mounted on them, displaying the end result of the intensive hunt by the squad of men led by Ertach to end the incursion.

"Conditions of peace," the voice of Ertach stated. "To the merchant's guild and the City Council. To be made public for the benefit of all residents of E'peck Kent.

1. Surrender of the city gates by first light; with guarantees of safety and security for every house in the city. Those who keep the peace will lose nothing.
2. A small force of twenty men will be admitted at the North Gate to take possession of all the stacked weapons of the city guards. Other troops will not be permitted in the city.

3. A fine of 1001 gold pieces will be paid by the City Council and merchants guild, as blood money for the death of Erkan, the Khan of the Chipchak people.
4. The force of twenty will be the honor guard at the morning funeral service in representation of the tribe. Kaya, the new Khan, must be freed and present to participate.
5. The goods of Jomer, the merchant, will be divided in conformity with his will and the owner of the knife of Onder recognized as heir, without any changes by local authorities.
6. Those who wish to abandon the city may leave by families, and in small parties, from the East Gate with one mule-load of portable valuables. They will enjoy guarantees of safety through the gate and through the army from this present time. However, no escort will be provided against dangers of the road. All, who depart, leave at their own risk. Their city properties, however, are secure till their return.
7. Persons responsible for the death of the Khan, will be yoked or executed by first light. Their bodies or heads will adorn the gate posts. Five assassins, sent from the Tartar nation, have already paid for their audacity with their lives. We plant one head at each gate to remind you that we destroy our enemies.

"Hear and live, people of E'peck Kent! The road to the east is open now, 'Go or stay; but do not stray.' Those leaving the road will be killed. We return at first light. Let the gates be open and adorned. The weapons must be stacked here at the north gate. Live in safety with peace and honor, people of E'peck Kent."

The troop wheeled, armor glinting dully under the moonlight, and rode into the night.

>------->

Tedbir stood at the tower wall with the burley captain, as the troop rode off. He looked at his companion. "Do any of the men know that you killed the Khan?" The man looked glumly at his questioner.

"You came here to the guard house to ask me to do it. Nothing can be kept secret here. They were betting beforehand if I would finish it in one shot. I did, and they saw it. Money exchanged hands. No one will forget."

"You must encourage the council to resist the tribe's demands or your head will adorn a pike on the tower corner," Tedbir smiled, teasing the Captain in a friendly way. It was received sourly.

"Yours, too, you offered the gold, gave me half which I can produce to prove it. You are the one to persuade them," the captain's voice rose and he was shaking and red faced. "Don't think I'll let you out of this."

"*Soos*, hush, don't think I'll leave you. First we must know the exact strength of the enemy. Send the weasel over the wall and a reconnaissance in force," Tedbir suggested smoothly.

"I'll do more than that, but you had better produce the other half of the promised money or your head will be hung first. I want it by the end of my watch tonight"

"You will have more than I promised. I have just thought of a second way to help you, but I must ponder it for a bit. You are the right size. In the dark no one would know. But the face, that would be the problem, unless..." The man Tedbir began to chuckle, and some of the guards turned to look through the dim moonlight at the source of the sound, with a shudder.

>- - - - - - - >

"We are ordered to conduct the raid from the South Gate. It is further from the enemy camp, but will give us a bit of shelter from the campfires' light, and permit a flank penetration. A squad of ten is all they can spare. Two others are being sent out through the East gate to move round to the north. They will go out with those who leave the city under guarantee. They'll backtrack to spy on them." Orhan, the Onbasha, looked at his men carefully. "Our job is to get information not stay and become heroes by fighting battles," one of the men laughed, but was stared down.

"Dead heroes are of little importance in a trapped city," Erly the second spoke, "Just don't stay to count the horde, and we'll get you back. If they invite you to dinner, it may be you." The men chuckled nervously, looking at each other inquisitively. One older man made a motion with his head. "Time for a drink around. Have the keeper put it on my account. I've found a worn bridle strap, and I'll get another as a replacement at home. I'll be back before moon set."

>- - - - - - - >

From the top of the tower wall Kaya could see a fair distance. Just beyond the hills, were the light of fires, many fires. They covered all the north and west of the city. In the distance the pounding of horse's hooves could be heard. A great horde of warriors were gathering—horsemen, armed and ready to fight to release their hero leader. Shouts in the camps came from time to time, exultant war cries and the smell of cooking, roasting meat, came to his nose, appetizingly. His stomach growled hungrily. He licked his lips, but his escort had other matters on their minds. He was fitted with a yoke made of a young cedar log long enough to span the gate and rest on the buttress. The chains were reinforced with the rawhide thongs. Optal looked at him with pity as he spoke.

"They intend to hang you over the gate -- leave you here to die, young master, but we will trust and wait. I will take the message with the knife as you ordered. I will wait until they are occupied. Have you the gold coin you offered me earlier?" Kaya smiled at him.

"It was profitable when you took silver for gold. This, no doubt, will also profit us. There is a coin sewn in the hem of my '*shalvar*' one on each ankle; take them." Optal knelt before Kaya to rip out the coins and hide them.

"What was the name of the young lord with you?"

"Ozkurt, he has not seen Onder's knife, but knows of it. Fewsoon will recognize it." The man nodded, but stayed at his feet for a moment more.

"Yesu, your God will help me. I trust him." He stood and moved casually to stand near the tower stairs.

It was past the hour of vespers, Kaya looked west and started to sing softly:

1. Evening ends the day with splendor;
   You have kept us, guided and fed us.
   For this bounty, Dear Lord, we thank You.
   For the goodness of creation,
   Lord, receive our grateful praise.

Chorus:

Oh, Dear Yesu, Lord and Savior,
Come and help me by your favor.
May my life obey your will.

2. In the dusk the moon shines brightly;
   For its beauty, Dear Lord, we thank you.
   Work is finished, dear ones will gather.
   Night is coming with it's dangers;
   Keep us till the morning light.

Chorus:

LAST VESPERS

He wondered if he would see morning light. He wondered what the ending of his life would mean to his family and his tribe. He was the child of promise. He was a hero returned home. Was this his only welcome: to come and die? He wondered at God's purpose.

PEOPLE, PLACES & PLOTS IN CHAPTER 17

City Captain: archer who demands 'pay now or lose all.'
Er'tach: becomes keeper of the city's East Gate for refugees.
Er'ly: hears men dying behind his reconnaissance squads.
Or'han: charges into the enemy camp in pursuit of gold.
Kaya; is left with no choice, but must let others chose for him.
Tedbir: eliminating everything in his way, as he plots his escape.
Optal: sure that no man is a fool, if he chooses to do the right.
Weasel: an infiltrator and informer, arrives with one word.

GLOSSARY HELPS

ark'a-dash: **friend; one who guards one's back.**
bowsh: **nothing; meaningless; empty.**
bow'sh ver: **it's nothing; empty talk; meaningless.**
do'er: stop; **stay where you are; don't move.**
dose'tum: **my buddy; intimate friend.**
ev'et: **yes; of course; I approve.**
gel-den: **you came here; you came; you're here.**
heliography: **messages sent by mirrored reflections of sun light.**
hi'yer old-mahz: **it can't be; impossible: don't let it be.**
jan-o-var': **monster; evil creature.**
kim'oh: **a challenge, Who's this? Identify yourself!.**
sev'ge-lim: **beloved; my lover; dearest love.**
soos: **quiet; don't talk; hush.**
ya-sock: **forbidden; prohibited; not allowed.**
yew'rue: **walk out; move it; get going.**
yuz'basha-yum: **I am a lieutenant.**

17 CONSECRATION

HUNG HIGH

Just out of arrow range of the East Gate, a young Chipchak lieutenant, Ertach, sat his horse and with six men, checked all travelers. One loaded animal with household valuables for each traveler was permitted. Only birding bows were allowed and small knives. The press of frightened people was such that the lieutenant was forced to space the travelers and to prevent bunching on the road. All were treated with aloof, cold courtesy.

Inside the gate, city officials were involved in the collection of a hastily imposed travel tax of one gold coin per adult male. The indignation and anger was general and some cried while others cursed. In the confusion no one noticed two well clad men in merchant dress who meekly paid the fee and left on beautiful, spirited mounts.

"We are merchants, Yuzbasha. We have our depot here and we leave it to your care," they smiled easily.

"It looks like you're in the wrong profession, your father was a fool not to put you in the army." Ertach's voice was cold. "Do you have weapons?"

"A small knife and bird bow each. My brother has the sugar sickness and I am lame. We are farmer's sons."

"We will look at your baggage. What is the price of silk this season?" The lieutenant motioned two families to pass without delay and sent one of his men to feel the loads on the men's mules. The man drew the birding bows easily and examined the knob point arrows.

"We buy at a minimum and sell as the price will bear." One of the merchants quipped. The Chipchaks looked at them angrily. Ertach's face hardened.

"A copper coin, a measure for the common household stuff," the other merchant hastened to add, giving a look of reproach to this brother, who shrugged.

"Stay with the people, and you will be safe through the army. Remember it's '*ya sack,*' forbidden, to leave the road. Your life depends on it." Ertach dismissed them with a jerk of his head. As they left, he lifted the lantern in his hand in signal to some one up the hill.

About an hour beyond the city the two men moved to one side and behind a tree, started to remove the saddle of their mounts and from a hidden place five war arrows each were drawn out. A split metal tube was pressed around the hub of the bows increasing their power and range. Mounting again they moved north. They left the mules not far from the road. The moonlight was dim but they knew the country. All was quiet - too quiet.

"*Do'er,* halt," came the call from the top of a slope, but they immediately fled in the opposite direction. The armor piercing arrows came from before them and cut them down. Their stripped bodies were taken back to the highway and left just off the road as a warning.

>- - - - - - - >

The troop of horse met within the South Gate. The Onbasha, corporal Orhan, had seven troopers present. Three had joined the growing exodus and escaped with their families. The few remaining talked in worried tones with the gate keepers.

"Let's get on with it. The moon's almost down. We're cutting it too close," Erly's voice was worried.

Orhan cleared his throat and raised his voice. "It's late now. The camp will be dozing. We have to get in fast and out again. We ride straight to the south flank up the hill and test their reaction and survey their force. A gold coin to the one who gets there first!" Orhan grinned at them encouragingly. He nodded to the keepers and the gate swung wide as the horses thundered through.

They ran west parallel to the wall for the first hundred meters. Then, gradually, they veered further south heading toward the southernmost campfires, which were glowing low in the sleeping camp. It was a long run, which would test the mettle of the horses.

There was no reaction from the tribe. They seemed to have the plain alone. They were spreading now as the individual differences in the horses' stamina came into play. Orhan and Erly led the charge. One thought he heard a couple of horses from the West Gate side.

There on the flanking hilltop they saw the figure of the camp guard silhouetted against the glow of the campfires behind him. It was useless to evade him so they directed their run directly at him. Blood would flow. Then, behind them came the scream of wounded horses and men. Yet, the thunder of hooves was of the same intensity even as animals dropped. Looking back, six figures on horse back followed their charge, the sounds of the wounded grew distant and fell behind. Two more horses closed from the west.

The riders' attention divided, they found they were upon the solitary guard whose height, Erly realized, was as great as his own, mounted on his horse! He shot his arrows at close range and the arrows snapped and ricocheted from armor, but some penetrated and the giant figure leaned away from them and fell flat. The screams of animals and men had followed them to the hilltop. There were still six figures following them, but more were dying on the trail behind them.

Erly wheeled south down the hill, but Orhan continued over and down the hill, to win the gold. Four of the riders continued down the hill behind the leader. Only two followed Erly. He felt the air of an arrow on his cheek and was tempted to try evasive tactics, but at this speed and darkness one could just as well weave into a miss as wait for a hit. The sounds of more hits and a fall came from beyond the hill. Then came silence except for the panting of his horse and the accompanying drumming of a running horse overtaking him. He remembered the stories of the lion horses of the Chipchaks. Far away he could see the gate, it was open. Then, in the increasing dark his wheezing horse made a misstep and darkness came up to meet him.

>- - - - - - - >

At that moment a rope dropped over the west wall and the figure of a tiny man seemed to ooze over and down. Ferret like, he would pause, move, pause and look around slowly with sharp, beady eyes. The rope was invisible in the dim light. Weasel touched down gently and disappeared in the brush at the foot of the wall. Slowly, he made his way toward the hill, avoiding the light, yet moving toward it, in round about detours and curves. It took a long time, in his deliberate, indirect way, to get to the low spot between two hills, each with a giant guard plainly visible on the summit.

Cautiously he raised his head, shielded by a bush, to the direct view of the horde and the fires. He gasped at the sight that met his eyes. He was so surprised that the gasp was loudly audible and an answering whistle indicated that it had been heard. 'Pip, pip, pip, pip,' the whistle moved rapidly toward him. A second whistle came from the opposite hilltop. It was folly to stay or to move: either would lead to his discovery. He moved fast, in a direct line down the hill and straight back toward the city wall. The whistles stayed on his trail, running behind, 'pip, pip.' Now, the running hooves of two horses were heard before him to the right, then two more to the left. Each pair came from the direction of a city gate. He would be cut off, if he delayed or paused for breath.

In the fading moonlight he saw the form of his city companion, motioning him, waiting at the end of the rope to draw him up. He was so close to the wall, but so were the riders. The sound of an arrow passed just over his head. He crouched lower and ran harder. Another hit the wall before him. He leaped for the rope and held. The whistle peeped below him. He felt the slash of a sword cut his leg, a pain in his middle as an arrow passed through, but he had no breath to cry out. Still, he held, his strong friend had him to the top in an instant, and then both fell on the walk behind the parapet with arrows in them. His friend moved painfully, "Well, what did you learn?" The ferret's eyes bulged. He opened his mouth trying to breathe, but only blood froth bubbled up and trickled out.

"*Bow'sh*, nothing ..." was the only word he was able to whisper, then, he lay dead in the moonlight. The whistles had stopped and so had the running horses, but in the distant camp childish voices were spontaneously giving the war cry.

>- - - - - - - >

The two authorities whispered as Kaya lay, where he had fallen on the verge of the tower. His arms were out stretched on the yoke of wood. His face was swollen from beatings. Several of Tedbir's men stood near to continue this work if ordered.

"Men's bodies look much alike. It is the face that must be marred to prevent identity," Tedbir whispered. "The tribe has not seen Kaya for four years. Few will know him intimately. You will escape as a merchant. Council will be told that you have died as punishment, yoked for killing the Khan. They will be busy surrendering the arms and will not be curious about the display outside."

On the tower the Captain glowered as Tedbir explained the plan. Then, he growled. "The Chipchak horde has demanded the presence of the new chief for the funeral. How will you dare to kill him? The council will demand his person as guarantee to spare the city. Our reconnaissance has been foiled. We will surrender." Tedbir shook his head violently.

"Kaya knows too much. I must kill him and leave the city to its fate, but this ruse will give us the hours we need to reach safety. They will think you dead and Kaya locked away. We will be away and safe." He turned to the tower group.

"Optal, fool, come here. Did you find my key in the room?" The bear-master walked stolidly forward.

"I discovered no key, but this was found." He held a small ankh shaped knife, a tau cross with a metal loop above the juncture. The sheath about three inches long lay in his hand. There was a pearl, held by four tiny hooded gold snakes, forming the top of the juncture of loop and blade. A ruby adorned the sheath's side just below the arms. A finger size loop of silk-sheathing covered the metal loop above the pearl. Tedbir's teeth gleamed as he took the weapon.

"Come, Captain. We have business in my room. The fool did not find the key, but we will." To the men about Kaya he made a motion toward the gate. "Hang him there now."

They swung him up and out over the North Gate. The moon touched the horizon. The Captain and Tedbir, after a gloating moment of satisfaction, turned their backs to seek the awaiting treasure.

Kaya's body hung without support over the wall the log simply rested in two opposite depressions. He prayed,

"Yesu receive my life. I gave it long ago and now again. Keep the tribe in your care. Though few understand your ways, let their greatness last a thousand years. Your road is a rocky trail, but the end is forgiveness, comfort and grace." Weariness and numbing weight filled his body and mind. Time skittered by. Light hid away and the silent darkness reigned absolute. Psalm 88, the ending, crept like fog into his mind, forming words; 'You have taken my companions and loved ones from me; the darkness is my closest friend.' And it was so.

>- - - - - - - >

"Well, where is the key to this hoard of yours?" The captain snarled his complaint staring at the large metal box. "You owe me the entire chest, for if the truth were known, there is not a man in town but would kill you."

"*Bow'sh ver*, empty talk, who would love a tribal Khan more than their richest merchant?" Tedbir laughed confidently. "Any member of the council does have some enemies, but not everybody. How would he be elected?"

"None here would love a traitor and spy for the Persian kingdom. Do you think I have no eye for the arrival and sending of dispatches, no matter how cleverly hidden. I see that the Silk Road going to your Sanassid home territory is promoted and lists sent, smugglers' hiding places revealed, so taxes may be secure, while caravans using the steppe road to the north are regularly attacked and disrupted. Your bandits there receive prompt information of numbers, dates and valuables for each caravan that goes to the Mother of Rivers or the Far West. Your master pays to destroy that which will not enrich him. You pay us to do your dirty work."

"*Arkadash*, Friend, I know you for your ability and keenness. I had little hope of carrying out my years of service without notice by a few observant men. I have a fund on hand for such as will keep prudently silent."

"You promise much, but are slow. Our time slips past, our risk increases. First light is upon us."

"You are right. We will leave the chest for the one who finds the key. We must go without it. But I will give you this special treasure, dedicated to Kali the Goddess of Hind. Hold out your hand." Tedbir held up the ankh, now secured by the loop to his middle finger. He pressed the ruby and the triangular blade slipped out of the sheath, the runnels dripped a dark liquid toward the point. With a quick tap of his finger on the pearl top the small point was driven into the Captain's outstretched hand.

"*Jan'o var*, monster," screamed the captain and pinched the wound causing a black drop of blood to appear. He brushed the drop away and put his mouth to suck the wound as he drew his sword. The sword fell from his hand and he staggered, shuddering forward to the floor where he lay convulsing.

Tedbir smiled, "You will satisfy the Chipchak need for revenge."

>- - - - - - - >

"*Binbasha*, General, hear me," Optal stood before the Chipchak officer. He held up the gold coin.

"*Yuz'basha-yum*, I'm a lieutenant. I accept no bribes. Keep your money and state your business."

"I have a message from Kaya, the heir, to the hero Ozkurt. I hold the knife of Onder as proof that I come from Kaya with his message," he held up the sheathed knife.

"I cannot leave. At first light we will take all the money collected at this gate from the greedy officials and they will still pay the 1001 gold pieces from city treasure." He examined the knife curiously. "I will send you with a man to Ozkurt. You will be blindfolded, but if you remove it, you will see death."

"I have already seen death. I would see life now." He removed his turban and handed it to Ertach.

>- - - - - - - >

"*Yew'rue*, move on, let me pass!" In vain Tedbir pressed against the mass of people. They, too, had let time pass in the arrangement of their affairs and the packing of goods. Now, time drove them all. Animals and people pressed at the door of the gate. Almost free of the mob, Tedbir looked up at the road ahead. There he saw Optal, talking with an officer who held Onder's knife.

"*Hi'yer, old mahz*, No, it can't be. The fool is a liar and cheat." Tedbir roared his protest and struggled to clear the way. He unsheathed his 'gift of Kali' and prepared to sprint to the men. At that moment, a pack mule smashed into the giant Persian's side. He stared helplessly at the small knife with cobra venom, now planted in his chest. He cried out in horror, then fell before the crowd.

Ertach took Optal's turban and bound his eyes with it. They helped Optal mount a horse before a tribesman. He handed the tribesman the knife and motioned them away.

>- - - - - - - >

Dear one,

I understand your sorrow at the prospect of losing The Bend Estate on the Don River, yes. How could Prince Ilkin have so many debts, no? You say Yuzbasha, or should I now call him the Binbasha, will buy it? No, I hope not!

I have taken a loan from Ebenezer Bey for money to help you pay for the last refugees that have been sent up to the Ukraine, yes. What will they do in the future, if there is no source of help, no? Ebenezer bey, your banker, appears not to worry. He says that 'Heaven will not abandon one who spends to help the Lord's people do the Lord's work.'

He says: 'she will not lose her estate. I have inside information and am sure the prince's debts are paid off,' yes. He thinks: 'all the account papers have been sent away and all will be well for the present time.' I guess rich banker effendi can be confident, no?

Dear Petrus has taken a personal interest in this and is such a source of joy and encouragement, yes. I should like to start our family now, no? But we must wait God's time, yes.

A letter from Olga and Sarayjik says that General Evran is angry with the Khazars, yes. They have broken Prince Ilkin's agreement to wait for withdrawals before taking possession of land. He says: 'they have crossed one river too many.' The letter says that he is the keeper of the back door and none may enter without his permission. They say that all Hun Generals are more careful, since General Koosta's disgrace, no?

This is the news from our little port.

With love always,

Merien Papasian

PS News today from the capital reports a big battle and defeat of the Khazars passing the Dniester River, yes. A Hun ambush killed the newly recognized heir of Khan Kinner and his general. Khazar troops are in retreat to Bug River and beyond. The slaughter is great, no? Make many new widows, yes. The reports sent by heliography are usually true. You may have already heard, no? I don't know how this will affect you. I pray for God's good will. Love, MP

HAUNTING LOVE

>- - - - - - - >

Something vibrates his stiffness, and sore muscles groan their protest. A hot burning fills his arms and neck. Kaya's head feels divided into many small parts, each about to explode into yet smaller aching fragments. Two holes of agony sear where his eyes should have been. He can't breathe! Even a tiny pant of breath is sweet, but exhausting.

Again, the bump, magnified a thousand times, a breath fills his ear with the pain of sudden sound. "*Soos*, quiet, we will have you down in a moment. Patience!" The words hiss gratingly. There is a drop and a thump that brings a scream to his throat, but there is no strength for it to be born. Above, from the blackness, comes a challenge.

"*Kim oh*, who's there?" A long silence, broken by a breath of cold air, answers the inquiry. All is blackness, even the tribal campfires give no light. The sentry stomps his feet in the chill, and hurries back to the guardroom fire, unwilling to keep a vigil with death at the gate. It will soon be time to stack arms in the courtyard.

The small movements begin again. His chill flesh contacts bits of warm flesh, cold metal and leather. A movement up, first on one side and then on the other, then swaying. "He'll fall!" Agony and fear penetrate his mind. He's not dreaming, nor is he dead. He tries to rally his senses. He feels a lifting motion, then, a fall through the air, and a dull thump on body and face. Rocks and grassy weeds sting his skin. He is lifted again. The numbness is unfortunately passing, and new complaints are heard from every part of the body and head.

Another thump and he is dragged out away from the gate. His feet send the agony of crawling ants up to his brain. A stone strikes his foot and sends sharp protests through his nerves.

He strives to breathe, but it won't come. He is being pushed and pulled along a road. His feet don't co-operate with the motions.

Thoughts suddenly surge into his mind.

'I'm alive! I was to be sacrificed to Ahriman, but I live.' Joy surges through him. 'Why? For what has Yesu saved me?' Gratitude fills him.

There are some whispered consultations which he can't possibly decipher, though it concerns his well being. Then, he establishes an identity, 'Ozkurt is here. They must be ready to attack the city.'

He stretches his mouth. It's stiff and the tongue too large. 'Try again.' Nothing came that time. He mumbles and groans, his lips are parched. He can't swallow. He tries again and whispers.

"Ozkurt, *dose'tum*, my buddy. *Geldin*, you came." His voice sounds strange, not Kaya's voice at all.

"*Ev'et*, yes, we came." Ozkurt's voice doesn't sound right either. It has a nice wet sound that comforts Kaya's dryness. Someone puts something to Kaya's lips. It is paradise. It sends a thrill all over his body. It runs out and in and he coughs and tries to control the direction of the liquid. Life still holds the ordinary delights, magnified.

Words come and he understands, though they are not spoken to him. Others are here.

"We must get a chisel and hammer to get his chains off him. Better hold him up till then." Reason tries to take control of the aching mass of body, and succeeds for the moment. Kaya tries to focus and look in grateful joy in Ozkurt's face. He sees a dark blur beside him, another before him. He tries again.

"Ahjit bey? How did you get outside?" Confusion overwhelms him again. He shudders, "You were to go back to the palace and bury Jomer and Erkan."

"The Apostolos came and took them to the church for burial today. Jomer has a secret passage beneath the wall, used it when the city tried to interfere with his trade and break him. I, alone, know its entrances. We came after sending the messages by pigeon." Ahjit's voice sounds distant, the meaning garbled. Kaya tries to hold the thoughts.

"Pigeons, to whom?" He staggers again, but others hold his weight by the cross beam.

"Kutch, your brother is in charge at the Hermitage. He is their director now. He will send word to all the tribes in our brotherhood to come. The city will meet our terms now."

"You got here for a dawn attack. How have you managed all this? How did you get troops so quickly?"

"Could I live with Kaya for four years of travel without learning how to stretch numbers and confuse enemies?" Ozkurt was deliriously happy. "We used the Khan's troops for fighting and display; Ahjit's sons and extra horses running in big circles for sound and dust; the empty armor to make sentries round the many fires we set. We had four men on each gate to stop any reconnaissance. We opened a gate to permit deserters to exit. Fear bled the city of men. The rest gathered wood, cooked and made noise. When they put you out on the city gate, we had but to wait till the moon set, to lift you off and set you free." Ozkurt laughed uproariously and pounded Kaya on the back. Kaya fell against Ahjit, who steadied him. Ozkurt continued to talk excitedly.

"You would have made me your heir, but I left a small cousin in the hills when she was but twelve. She will be waiting for my return, now, grown and ready to marry. I have no desire for tribal politics, or consoling the widow of a great man." While he spoke, Fewsoon rode up on Altom. She dismounted and came to hang on Kaya's neck and cry. Altom whinnied and nuzzled his swollen face. Kaya lost his voice again.

Fewsoon sighed, "*Janum benim, sevgilim*, my soul, my love." He stumbled in his chains and yoke, but everyone continued to hold him up, taking the weight of the yoke on their own backs, walking beside him. Fewsoon continues to cry, and hang on his neck. Kaya spoke in a whisper to all his friends.

“I have learned something valuable: Ahjit, Chavush and I have each been yoked in unjust punishment. We join Yesu in a fellowship of suffering. Now, we know that even that fate can be faced, if we trust Tanra and have friends who love us. Accepting the worst that can happen: we know that there is resurrection-grace to pass even that ordeal. Yesu’s presence and garden wait beyond all human hate and harm.”

>- - - - - - - >

HOME COMING